C000146029

Love to Hate You

Hope Valley

A Single Mother Small-Town Romance

Jessica Prince

Copyright © 2020 by Jessica Prince
Updated 2023
www.authorjessicaprince.com

published by Jessica Prince Books LLC

All rights reserved.
No part of this book may be reproduced in any form or by any electronic or
mechanical means, including information storage and retrieval systems,
without written permission from the author, except for the use of brief
quotations in a book review.

Discover Other Books by Jessica

WHITECAP SERIES

Crossing the Line

My Perfect Enemy

WHISKEY DOLLS SERIES

Bombshell

Knockout

Stunner

Seductress

Temptress

HOPE VALLEY SERIES:

Out of My League

Come Back Home Again

The Best of Me

Wrong Side of the Tracks

Stay With Me

Out of the Darkness

The Second Time Around

Waiting for Forever

Love to Hate You

Playing for Keeps

When You Least Expect It

Never for Him

REDEMPTION SERIES

Bad Alibi

Crazy Beautiful

Bittersweet

Guilty Pleasure

Wallflower

Blurred Line

Slow Burn

Favorite Mistake

THE PICKING UP THE PIECES SERIES:

Picking up the Pieces

Rising from the Ashes

Pushing the Boundaries

Worth the Wait

THE COLORS NOVELS:

Scattered Colors

Shrinking Violet

Love Hate Relationship

Wildflower

THE LOCKLAINE BOYS (a LOVE HATE RELATIONSHIP spinoff):

Fire & Ice

Opposites Attract

Almost Perfect

THE PEMBROOKE SERIES (a WILDFLOWER spinoff):

Sweet Sunshine

Coming Full Circle

A Broken Soul

CIVIL CORRUPTION SERIES

Corrupt

Defile

Consume

Ravage

GIRL TALK SERIES:

Seducing Lola

Tempting Sophia

Enticing Daphne

Charming Fiona

STANDALONE TITLES:

One Knight Stand

Chance Encounters

Nightmares from Within

DEADLY LOVE SERIES:

Destructive

Addictive

PROLOGUE

HAYDEN

S tanding in the middle of the expensive, luxurious boutique in downtown Richmond, surrounded by lace and silk and satin in every color, I felt completely and utterly ridiculous. I couldn't believe it had come to this, but desperate times called for desperate measures, and I was nothing if not painfully desperate.

"Hi. Can I help you?"

I looked up from the garment rack, the hangers holding tiny scraps of material that would barely cover my hand let alone other parts of my body. The sales clerk was a tall, svelte, modelesque blonde dressed in all black—from her sky-high heels and tight pencil skirt to her sheer silk blouse and the lacy bra beneath.

I'd never felt so frumpy in my life. I was suddenly blindingly aware that my body wasn't what it used to be back before pregnancy and childbirth changed it. I hadn't been one of those women who barely gained weight and only looked pregnant when they turned to the side. Everything from my toes to my nostrils had swelled. I'd gained more than fifty pounds while I was pregnant, and I had the stretch-marks on my stomach and breasts—even my hips—to prove it.

I lost a lot of the baby weight, but not all, and I was no longer the slim, straight size four I'd once been. My body had permanently changed. I now had an hourglass figure. My hips were wider, my butt and chest bigger. There was no longer a gap between my thighs, and the skin around my middle was looser than it had once been.

I hadn't thought I looked bad at all, just . . . more womanly. I thought Alex would like the changes to my body, especially considering those changes came from bringing our daughter into the world. But as time passed, his interest in me seemed to be dwindling.

I could feel the distance growing between us with every passing day, and I knew I was partly to blame for it. Ivy was four now, but I'd wanted her for so long that, once she arrived, she'd become all I could see.

I'd dreamed my whole life of being a mother, and after years of trying and failing on our own *and* with medical assistance, one heartbreaking miscarriage after another, we'd finally gotten our miracle baby. Nothing mattered to me but her wellbeing, and as the years passed, I started to neglect other aspects of my life. Especially my husband.

But that was all going to change.

When I woke up this morning, I'd rolled over to find Alex's side of the bed already empty and the sheets cold. That was becoming our norm. He got up early, did his thing, and left for work without so much as a note or text.

Used to be, when things were good between us, he couldn't bring himself to leave for the day without waking me up for a goodbye kiss. Nine times out of ten, that led to hard, fast, dirty sex that left us both breathless and smiling before he inevitably forced himself to break away from me so he could head to work.

I couldn't remember the last time we'd had a day start off like that, and this morning I woke up missing it terribly. I also woke up with a fire in my belly, determined to get us back to where we used to be.

Hence the babysitter for my daughter and the high-end lingerie store for me.

I'd gotten up and actually took the time to put some care into my appearance. None of my clothes from before Ivy really fit anymore, and Alex was always making off-handed comments about me waiting until I was back to my pre-baby weight before buying anything new, so I had extremely limited wardrobe choices, but did my best. And I *thought* I'd made it work . . . until Runway Barbie showed up.

Now I was uncomfortably aware that my jeans looked—and felt—glued to my skin, and that I was currently holding them closed with a ponytail holder since I could no longer get the button anywhere near the stupid buttonhole.

"Oh, uh . . . I'm looking for something," I started lamely. "A surprise for my husband."

The woman's smile was warm and inviting. "Ah, very nice. I think I can help you find just the thing." She bounced from rack to rack, flipping through and pulling off hangers faster than I could process what was happening, all without once asking for my size.

Before I knew what was happening, I was herded toward the fitting rooms at the back of the shop. "I've grabbed some things I think would really do the trick and look fantastic on you," she said breezily as she hung my—her—selections along one of the walls. "Let me know if you need a different size in anything."

The deep red velvet dressing room curtain was slapped shut before I could manage to form a single word.

"What just happened?" I whispered to myself, slowly turning to take in the confines of the small room.

I slowly dragged the hangers back and forth, pleasantly surprised that the sales clerk had picked several pieces that were really pretty.

Stripping out of my ill-fitting clothes, I pulled one of the nighties off its hanger and tried it on. The soft silk was cool against my skin and slipped into place perfectly, proving that the clerk *really* knew her stuff.

I turned to look at myself in the long, gilded mirror. The nightie was held in place by two thin spaghetti straps. The neckline plunged into a deep V that showed a good amount of cleavage, but the A-line actually did an incredible job of keeping my breasts in place, making them look nice and perky. The hemline didn't even reach mid-thigh, revealing a *lot* of leg, and when I turned around to check out the back, sure enough, there was more than a hint of cheek peeking out.

The light, dusky blue of the silk actually looked really nice against my pale complexion, and the peach-colored lace around the hem and bustline complemented my light red hair.

All in all, I thought I looked pretty damn good, but as I stood staring at my reflection, the determination from earlier started to flicker. I felt myself losing steam. A pep-talk was seriously needed, so I pulled my phone from my purse and hit the number on speed dial as I paced my small confines.

The phone rang and rang before voicemail finally kicked in. "Hey, honey," I spoke. "So, I know this is the third message I've left you today, but I could really use my BFF right now. Or, you know . . . whenever you're available." I blew out a sigh and looked back at myself in the mirror. "I'm currently standing in the dressing room of a lingerie store, wearing nothing but a skimpy nightie. I need you to tell me if I'm making a mistake, babe. Call me back."

My shoulders sank as I disconnected and tossed the phone back into my purse. "Well," I said to my reflection, "looks like you're in this on your own. Might as well suck it up."

I spent the next few minutes trying on the rest of the sales clerk's selections. By the time I walked out of the store half an hour later, I had four new nighties, three bra and panty sets that were a whole hell of a lot better than the stuff I'd been wearing, a new robe, and a teddy I was sure I'd never have the guts to wear but had talked myself into getting anyway. Just in case.

It wasn't often I had some free time to myself. I decided to take advantage of the beautiful day and, having a babysitter for another two hours, headed to a little bistro a couple blocks down for lunch.

As I made the short walk at a leisurely pace, I thought over my plan again. Alex's hours had been erratic over the past few months, making it so he usually didn't get home until well after the sun had gone down and I'd already put Ivy to bed. Usually I hated his late hours and going to bed alone, but I intended to make it work for me tonight.

The plan was, after getting Ivy down, I'd change into one of my newest purchases and wait in bed for my husband to come home so he could unwrap his new gift.

I was feeling good about things, hopeful even, that this would be the start of getting us back to where we once were. Pushing through the door of the bistro, I had a smile on my face and a bit of a swing in my hips as I pictured Alex's reaction.

My good mood remained in place as the hostess grabbed a menu and led the way to my table. As I followed, my attention drifted, taking in the other diners who were enjoying their meals. I came to stop in the middle of the dining area when I spotted a familiar curtain of dark brown hair at a table near the back.

Krista hadn't been answering my calls, so it felt somewhat serendipitous that I'd happen to run into my best friend on the day I needed her most. This was the perfect opportunity to show her what I'd bought. I started toward her but jerked to a halt two steps later when I spotted her lunch companion.

The arm I'd been lifting to wave slowly lowered to my side and the smile fell from my lips when I saw him lean in close and press his lips to hers in a kiss that was so *not* suitable for public.

Realization slammed into me like a wrecking ball. Everything started to make perfect sense. The pieces snapped together like a jigsaw puzzle, revealing a picture I'd been too blind to see before now. Alex's increasingly late hours, his interest in me waning until almost completely gone, the unexpected business trips out of town . . . and the fact that

Krista had been avoiding me more and more over the last few months.

"Ma'am?" the hostess asked. "Are you okay?"

I absolutely wasn't.

Because I had just realized my husband and best friend were having an affair.

ONE
HAYDEN

I never thought I'd be in this position: a thirty-three-year-old, freshly-divorced, single mother whose husband had spent the better part of a year banging her best friend behind her back.

In the past few months, I'd taken hit after hit from those two assholes, starting with the fact it hadn't been just sex: they'd been in an actual relationship. Then there was the hit that came when the man I'd been married to, the man I'd loved with my whole heart, basically laid the demise of our relationship at my feet. *I* let myself go. *I* cared about our daughter more than him. *I* stopped making an effort to look good for him. Basically, it was my fault he no longer found me sexually attractive and had tripped, landing dick-first into another woman. I sustained another hit when he informed me he wasn't in love with me anymore; he loved Krista and wanted to build a life with her.

But the absolute worst, the hit that burned like lashes across my skin, had come when he confessed that she was pregnant and they intended to marry soon after our divorce was finalized.

Hearing that she'd so easily given him something I'd struggled tirelessly for years to give him, enduring one heartbreak after another before it finally happened, had been devastating.

But that was the past. The life I thought I was destined to live until my last breath was over. The house we'd started our family in was now empty, waiting for its new owners to move in. My girl and I were about to start on a new adventure, but before we could set off, my ex and his new fiancée were enjoying one of their scheduled overnight visits with my baby.

I spent the evening in our little hotel room, trying to distract myself from imagining them playing the perfect little family by slathering on a face mask, giving myself a pedicure, and binging on episodes of *The Office* and *Schitt's Creek*. Unfortunately, none of that worked, and before long my mind started to wander down some not-so-cheery paths.

What few friends I had before everything went down decided to hitch their wagon to Krista, so there was no one I could call to vent to. I hadn't had a job since before Ivy was born, so there were no co-workers I could confide in. I was well and truly alone, and the knowledge of that was suffocating. It didn't take long to get sick of my own company, and screaming into my pillow had gotten old *really* fast. So when the walls felt like they were closing in on me, I grabbed my purse and room key and booked it out of there, heading for the pub a few blocks down from my temporary home.

The air smelled of hops and spice and polished wood when I stepped into the bar. Alex would never set foot in a place like this, and for that reason I immediately found the place charming.

It was nothing like the stuffy wine or tapas bars and five-star restaurants I'd been forced to suffer through with his insufferable colleagues or asshole clients. It was a place where you kicked back with some greasy, carb-loaded bar food and a couple of beers, the latter of which I was in desperate need.

I made my way to the bar. Spotting a stool near the curve on the far end, I hooked my purse and jacket on the back, hefted myself up, leaned my elbows onto the scarred wood top, and looked toward the bartender.

He glanced down the length of the bar and caught my eye when I waved to him, tipping his chin, indicating he'd be with me in just a second.

"Bet it wouldn't take me more than three tries to guess your drink."

At the deep, husky voice, I swiveled in my seat to face the man on the barstool beside mine and nearly fell out of my seat at the first glimpse of him. His light brown hair was long on top and cut close on the sides. It looked like the only styling he did was to drag a hand through it to brush it back off his forehead. Stunning grassy green eyes smiled down at me from beneath a thick fan of dark lashes. Those eyes and the man's sharp cheekbones might have made him look almost too pretty, but his bristly square jaw and Roman nose gave him a rugged appeal. His full, plump lips were turned up in a tiny grin that showed off a perfectly straight smile.

He had the shoulders of a professional linebacker, with thick, rounded biceps that strained the sleeves of his gray Henley. This dude was either one with the gym or had the kind of job that required *serious* manual labor, but either way, *holy God*, did he have a body. I wasn't sure I'd ever seen such a good-looking man in real life. On TV and in movies, sure. But *never* up close and personal in real life. He couldn't possibly be talking to me.

I glanced over my shoulder, wondering if there was some tall goddess of a woman behind me, but there wasn't.

Turning back to him, my lips quirked up in a puzzled smile. "I'm sorry?"

"Your drink," he stated, his grin curving even higher. "I said I bet it would only take three tries to guess what you're gonna order."

What was happening? "You want to bet that you can get my drink order right?"

"Yep. It's kind of a talent of mine."

I felt my own smile grow as well as I asked, "All right. Say I take this bet. What do you get if you win?"

He looked up thoughtfully. "How about your name?"

"Seems like a lot of trouble to go through for a name when you could just ask." Was I flirting? Holy *shit*! I was totally flirting!

Turning on his stool to face me full on, he rested an elbow on the bar top and leaned just the slightest bit closer, "Well, there's also the added perk that I'll get it right and you'll be so impressed you won't tell me to leave you the hell alone."

I narrowed my eyelids and hummed contemplatively. Just then, the bartender stopped in front of me and asked, "What can I get you?"

I arched my brow at the sexy stranger. "I don't know, what do you think?"

He lowered his brows and gave me an intense top-to-toe,

like he was focusing hard to come up with an answer. "Dirty martini?" I scrunched my face up in disgust. "All right, maybe not," he said with a warm chuckle. "How about . . . red wine—no, scratch that. Make it white wine."

"Nope," I said on a giggle. "Last chance."

"I got it," he exclaimed, giving the bar a victorious slap. "Cosmo."

"Wow," I dragged out, making my eyes go big.

"That's it, isn't it? I got it."

I shook my head. "No. I'm actually surprised by just how *bad* you are at this game." Turning back to the bartender, I said, "American IPA. Whatever you've got on tap is fine. Thanks."

The bartender moved down to pour me a beer, and I turned to the stranger sitting beside me.

"Christ. That loss hurts," he grunted, fighting back a grin. "Never would've thought a woman as gorgeous as you would order a beer."

The divorce settlement as well as my cut from the sale of the house had left me with a lot more money than I'd been expecting, so one of the first things I'd done—kind of as a *fuck you* to Alex—was go out and buy a whole new wardrobe. It was amazing how clothes that actually fit could change a woman's battered outlook on her figure.

When I'd decided on this outing, I hadn't put much effort into my look, choosing a pair of skinny jeans that hugged me in a good way, and that I could actually button up, and an off-the-shoulder sweater. I'd slid on a pair of zip-up, high-heeled ankle boots and headed out the door with no makeup and hair hanging loose and wild. Hearing him call me gorgeous when I hadn't really taken any care with my appearance was a major confidence boost—something I hadn't had in a really long time.

I picked up my beer as soon as it was placed in front of me, bringing it to my lips. "I'm Hayden, by the way," I told him before taking a drink.

He hit me with the full impact of a megawatt smile that made the space between my legs pulse and quiver. "Micah. Nice to meet you."

"You too. And that stool's all yours as long as you want it."

———

Sometime into my second beer, Micah had suggested we move away from the bar and grab a table, something I was more than happy to do. Instead of sitting across from me, he'd taken the chair right beside mine, scooting it even closer so our knees brushed together with even a slight movement.

A couple hours later I was working my way through beer number four. My cheeks were hot, and not just from the alcohol. My head felt nice and floaty and there was a really pleasant warmth blooming beneath my skin.

At some point during our chatting, Micah had positioned himself so one of his arms was resting on the table beside mine, and every now and then he'd slowly drag his fingers across the back of my hand as he spoke, the touch barely there, as though he didn't even realize he was doing it. If he wasn't doing that, he was reaching out to brush my hair away from my face. Sometimes he'd tuck a lock behind my ear, dragging the pads of his fingers along the column of my neck gently before pulling back. Other times he'd simply reach out to caress the strands.

"Fuckin' gorgeous hair, sweetheart," he'd rumbled at one point. "And so damn soft."

I'd nearly melted into a puddle right there in my seat.

As it was, those small touches had me riled up in a way I hadn't experienced in a *very* long time. I'd been in a constant state of arousal for a while now. My nipples were so tight they ached and my panties got wetter every time he laughed or smiled at me. Hell, just the scent of his aftershave, something clean and musky, was making me lightheaded.

"So tell me something about yourself," he insisted.

"There's really not much to tell. I'm just a normal, boring chick," I answered evasively, as I'd been doing every time he asked me about myself. I was in this bar in the first place because I needed an escape from the shitstorm that had become my life. I'd been in search of a reprieve from the dark, and I'd gotten just that in a very big and unexpected way with a sexy stranger. No way in hell was I putting a damper on any of that by talking about my ex-asshole.

"Somehow I doubt that very much, Red. You gotta give me something."

I played off the fact that nickname sent a pleasurable tingle up my spine and arched a single brow as I sipped my beer. "Red?"

He grabbed another piece of my hair and gave it a playful tug. "Seems fitting. Now answer *one* question for me. You live around here?"

"No." The answer fell off my tongue without any thought. It wasn't *technically* a lie. Ivy and I would be moving in a matter of days, and it wasn't like I was ever going to see this guy again. Evasion was the name of the game. "Just here for a few days for . . . work." I lifted my beer and gulped. "You?"

"Grew up here but moved away after college. Just came back for the weekend 'cause my little sis is having a baby and the devil woman decided the shower was gonna be co-ed."

"Ah, gotcha. So, family obligation brought you back."

"Partly. Mostly it was the threat of death from my old man if I made my sister cry by not showing up."

My head fell back on a long laugh. When my hilarity tapered off, I caught Micah staring at me, his green eyes flashing with heat that made my heart beat faster. I cleared my throat and teased, "So, if you're supposed to be here for a baby shower, what are you doing in a bar?"

"Met up with some old buddies for a drink. We were just finishing up when I saw you walk in." He leaned closer, lowering his voice as his fingers took another trip along the back of my hand. "Decided the smartest thing I could do was stick around after that."

I was suddenly feeling lightheaded in a way that had nothing to do with the beer. The green of his eyes flashed again and his nostrils flared as he watched my lips part and my tongue peek out to swipe across the bottom one.

I'd never in my life been in a situation where I craved a man I didn't know to the point it made me squirm. I wanted Micah in a way I hadn't experienced in way too damn long. I'd never pictured myself as the kind of woman who could pull off a one-night stand, but the thought of missing out on this chance left a sour taste in my mouth, and the more time we spent together the more I turned that idea over in my head until it seemed like the most brilliant idea *ever*.

It wasn't until my body's unexpected reaction to him that I realized I hadn't had sex in nearly a year. Once that little discovery pushed itself to the forefront of my mind, it was like a fire had been lit in my blood. Having sex with Micah was all I could think about.

I felt like I was someone else as I leaned forward and placed my palm on his thick, solid thigh, and I hardly recognized the throaty voice that came from my mouth as I said, "I have a room a few blocks away if you want to come back with me."

I didn't get that flash again, but that bright, vibrant green suddenly turned dark as he rasped, "Fuck yeah, Red. Let's get out of here."

TWO

HAYDEN

What the hell was I doing?

You're having fun, and hopefully *getting an orgasm at the same time,* the voice inside my head declared. I imagined her as the devil on one shoulder and waited for the angel that was supposed to be on the other to speak up, but apparently, she'd taken a vacation.

I could feel Micah right behind me, the heat of his big, strong body pressing against my back as I swiped my keycard over the scanner. He reached around me the instant the lock beeped and the light turned green, twisting the handle and throwing the door to my hotel room open.

Nerves fluttered in my belly like leaves caught in a harsh wind as he used his weight to guide me into the room and closed the door behind us. At the sound of the lock clicking firmly into place I experienced a brief second of *I'm not sure I can do this,* but that fear faded as soon as he brushed my hair aside and started trailing his lips up and down my neck. My nipples tightened and my breasts grew heavy. My head fell back against his shoulder on a sigh while my lips parted to let out a low moan.

Every inch of my body felt like an exposed nerve as he snaked an arm around the front of me.

"Christ, you smell good," he rumbled against my skin, sucking on the cord of my neck as he slipped his fingers into the loose neckline of my sweater and cupped my breast in his large hand. "Feel really fuckin' good too."

God, so did he. "Micah," I said on a throaty whisper, twisting my neck so I could gain access to his lips. He didn't make me wait. He fused his mouth to mine as soon as it was within reach, kissing me like he'd been starved for it. His tongue thrust in, stroking against mine as he spun me around and dug his fingers into my hair, gripping it and bending my head so he could get better access.

The kiss went from sizzling to downright electric in a blink. Lifting up on my toes, I fed deeper, tasting every inch of his mouth, getting off on the hoppy, tangy flavor left behind from the beer he'd been drinking.

I was so consumed with his taste, with the way he was running his hands over me like he couldn't feel or explore enough, that I hadn't realized he'd moved us until my back slammed into the wall.

For some strange reason, the impact made me burn even hotter. I moaned into his mouth and wound my arms around his neck, scratching my nails along his scalp as the kiss turned molten.

One of his arms came around me, his hand slipping down to palm my ass and give it a harsh squeeze that nearly bordered on painful. It was so strange, but instead of being turned off at the near-brutality of the touch, it sent fire blazing though my veins. I craved *more*.

My mouth disengaged from his and my head dropped back on a groan at the feel of his fingers digging into my flesh through my jeans.

"You like that?" he asked, before pulling the lobe of my ear between his teeth and nipping.

"*God,* yes," I answered as my body shuddered.

"You like it a little rough, Red?"

I never had before, or at least I didn't think I had. But for some reason, the thought of Micah being a little rough with me made my clit tingle.

"Yeah," I sighed before going back in, drawing his bottom lip into my mouth and giving it a little bite.

I swallowed his growl hungrily as he fisted my hair tighter, forcing my head back. His tongue flicked across my pulse, and there was no holding back my needy whimper.

When he pulled away his pupils were blown, his eyes looked nearly black with desire. "Fuck me," he rasped. "You wet for me, baby?"

Fighting his grip on my hair and growing wetter at the slight sting in my scalp, I leaned into him and dragged my tongue across the seam of his lips, feeling like a completely different woman as I replied in a husky whisper, "Why don't you find out?"

He didn't have to be told twice. His hand at my ass moved fast as lightning, unbuttoning my jeans and shoving past the waistband. His fingers dove past my panties, pushing straight between my thighs to graze the most sensitive part of me. He let out a long groan as I sucked in a gasp at the feel of him beginning to toy with me.

"Jesus, you're soaked. So slick." He hummed appreciatively. His middle finger found my clit and pressed down. "You need more?"

"*Yes*," I hissed, circling my hips to get just that. *More*. "Please, Mi—" My words cut off on a sharp inhale when he drove two fingers deep inside me. "Oh, God," I panted, rocking harder against his hand. "Yeah, Micah. Just like that."

A cry of protest spilled past my lips when he pulled his hand away and took a step back, but before I could voice my displeasure, he reached behind his head and grabbed the collar of his shirt, pulling it off to reveal the slab of chiseled marble that made up his phenomenal chest and stomach.

"Holy shit," I murmured on an exhale, all the air expelling from my lungs as I reached forward and dragged my nails down his sculpted pecs and defined abs. "You're incredible."

A low, rolling sound, like a combination of a purr and thunder, vibrated from his chest at my touch. I was so lost in my exploration of his physique that I was taken by surprise when he reached for the hem of my sweater and whipped it over my head. That sound came from him once again, and after brushing the hair from my eyes, I saw him staring at me like I was an ice cream cone on the hottest day ever recorded. I was suddenly glad I'd thrown out all my old underwear after the divorce and went on a spree, buying all new frilly, sexy bras and panties. As of that very moment, I considered it the best money I'd ever spent.

"Jesus, fuck," he grated. "Your body's a goddamn work of art."

He was back on me in a heartbeat, popping the clasp on my bra and tossing it across the room. He palmed my heavy breasts, thumbing my painfully stiff nipples before bending down so he could suck the aching peak into his mouth . . . *hard*. The sting quickly gave way to pleasure that soaked my panties through. It had never happened before, but if he kept going, there was a very good chance I could come just from this.

"God, *Micah*," I panted, grabbing his hair and holding him close as he switched to the other breast. I rocked my hips against him, feeling the outline of his erection behind his jeans. It was hard as steel, bigger than anything I'd felt before, and I wanted it more than I wanted donuts to contain no calories. "Need more."

He shuffled me away from the wall toward the bed. A whoosh of air left my lungs when he pushed me back onto the mattress and made quick work of my boots and jeans, leaving me completely naked.

I had a fleeting moment of panic at the thought of this man, with his perfect body and flawless, masculine face, seeing my less than perfect body, but before self-doubt could begin eating away at me and ruin the moment, he rasped out a string of curses. "Jesus," he grunted, almost as if he was speaking to himself. "Goddamn perfection."

What the what!

"Micah," I gritted, the desperation to get off making my whole body so tight I thought I might shatter. "Clothes. Off."

He shot me a smirk that was downright decadent in all its cockiness, making him so damn hot I had to clench my thighs in search of relief.

The clink of his belt being undone filled the room, making my breathing accelerate. I pushed up on my elbows, my gaze riveted as he unzipped his fly and started pushing his jeans and boxer briefs down his thick thighs. Saliva pooled in my mouth the instant he revealed his long, thick, *painfully* hard cock.

I didn't shy away from giving blowjobs, but they weren't exactly my favorite thing. However, as I stared at Micah's solid erection, I wanted my mouth on this man more than my next breath. It was pointed right at me, the purple head leaking with arousal.

Without thought, I sat up and reached for his straining length. Fisting the base, I bent my neck and licked the tip, his taste exploding on my tongue.

"*Uhn!*" he grunted, fisting my hair to stop me before I could suck him into my mouth. "Fuckin' hell, Red. I'd love to have your mouth on me, but I'm already feeling crazy. Need to fuck you. *Now,*" he finished on a growl.

"Hurry," I whimpered.

At my command, he bent at the waist, reaching into the pocket of his discarded jeans for his wallet. He pulled out a condom and tossed the leather billfold to the floor before ripping it open with his teeth and sliding it down his shaft.

"You want it rough?" he grated, stroking himself in a tight fist.

"Yes," I breathed, licking my lips as I watched him jack himself. "*God* yes."

He moved so fast the room blurred before my eyes, grabbing hold of my hips and flipping me to my stomach like I weighed next to nothing. Before I could catch my breath, he jerked me up to my knees and gave my ass a slap that made me yelp.

I shot up on my hands, looking back over my shoulder in

shock as the burn on my skin slowly began to fade into something *way* better. Did I . . . *like* that?

As if reading me better than I could read myself, he did it again, striking me on my other cheek. "Damn," he sighed, almost reverently. "Your ass has been driving me crazy all night but seein' it red with my handprints . . ." he trailed off, letting out another rumbly purr. "Gonna take everything I have not to come as soon as I feel you wrapped around me."

His dirty talk was making me come out of my skin. "Micah, please," I rasped. "Fuck me."

He didn't need to be asked twice. Grabbing my hips in a viselike grip, he lined himself up with my entrance and drove in to the hilt with one hard thrust. I cried out at the sensation of being stretched so full at the same time he grated out a string of curses.

"So tight," he hissed, pulling out slowly and powering back inside. "Jesus, like a glove."

It had been a *really* long time, but I wasn't about to tell him that. Not that I could form words just then—I was already dangerously close to falling over the edge. "Oh, *yes*," I cried, throwing my hair back as he started fucking me at a relentless pace.

His hips slammed into my ass with every thrust, his cock rubbing a place inside of me that no man had ever found before. Pressure began to build low in my belly as I started driving myself back into him in time with each snap of his powerful hips. "Micah," I groaned, digging my nails into the bedspread. "So good."

"Fuck me. You're *wild*."

I was. I'd never felt so wild in all my life.

"More," I demanded. "Harder."

He gave me what I wanted by adding a slap to my ass after every plunge of his cock. With each strike and thrust, I felt my walls begin to quiver and grip tighter. "Fuck yeah. She likes that," he said in an approving tone as I arched my spine, tipping my ass up so I could take him even deeper inside me. "Wild woman."

"I'm close," I said, my voice husky with lust.

"I know, baby." He gritted. "Can feel you squeezing the life outta me. Need you to come."

It was building so fast and so strong it overwhelmed all my senses. I couldn't think or see anything outside of what my body was feeling. My impending release was growing so intense I almost feared it.

"Too much," I whimpered as my elbows gave out, unable to hold me up for another second.

"I got you, Hayden," he said, coaxing me closer and closer to the edge. "Let go, wild woman."

Before I could do as he commanded and let go, one of his hands released my hip and circled my waist. At the same time he pinched my clit he landed a smack on my ass so hard the sound cracked through the room, all while driving deep and grinding himself into me.

I went off like a rocket, screaming as I came so hard stars burst behind my eyelids. Every bit of air expelled from my lungs as my release dragged out so long I thought I might pass out.

Seconds later, Micah buried himself balls deep and let out an animalistic roar as he spent himself into the condom. Shivers wracked my body with each twitch of his cock as his climax slowly left him. Once it did, we both collapsed onto the mattress in a tangled, sweaty, panting pile of limbs.

"Holy shit," I rasped, my throat hoarse from my orgasm.
"Fuck, that was . . ."

"Holy shit."

Neither of us could find the words to properly describe what had just happened. *Never* in my life had I experienced sex like that. It was so good it shook me—literally and metaphorically.

Seeing as this was my first experience with a one-night stand, I didn't really know what was supposed to happen next. I assumed that once we were done we were . . . well, *done*. The longer we lay there in silence, the more anxious I became.

Expecting him to get up soon and beat feet out of there, I started to scoot to the edge of the mattress so I could get up and get dressed.

I barely got an inch away when his arm banded around my waist and jerked me back against him. "Where're you goin'?" he murmured against my ear, burying his face in my hair.

"I was going to get dressed."

His arm around me tightened. "Nuh uh, Red. Clothes will just defeat the purpose. I'm nowhere *near* done with you yet."

Inconceivably, he was ready again in no time.

Hours later, with the room completely dark, I was roused from a deep sleep as he brushed my hair back from my forehead and leaned down to place a kiss on the corner of my mouth. "Thanks for giving me a fuckin' incredible night, Red."

This was it. We were finally done and he was leaving . . . and surprisingly enough, I was okay with that. Actually, more than okay. The sex had been out of this world. The chemistry and attraction was staggering to the point it had left me feeling somewhat unsettled. I'd just gotten divorced after having my heart stomped on and my world ripped from beneath my feet. The last thing I needed was a man I could easily become obsessed with. And I had a feeling a man like Micah could *easily* become an obsession.

I let out a sleepy hum and burrowed deeper into my pillow, more exhausted that I could remember being in a long time. "Pleasure's all mine, stud," I muttered as my eyelids drifted back down. "And thanks back. That was incredible."

With that said, I was asleep before the door closed behind him.

THREE

MICAH

"Welcome back, brother." My partner Leo came up behind me, clapping me on the shoulder as he moved past to his desk. "How was the shower?" he asked with a condescending smirk.

"Fuck off," I grunted as he took a seat across from me. "Whoever's idea it was to start co-ed baby showers can rot in hell. Madeline melted candy bars into diapers so it would look like chunky shit, for Christ's sake. Then everyone was expected to sniff *and taste* it to identify what it was. Not sure I'll ever be able to eat another candy bar."

Leo's head fell back as he laughed uproariously. "Damn, he chuckled. "That had to have been a special kind of hell for you. Stuck playin' baby games and shit instead of out chasing tail."

While that bastard got off on my misery, my mind flashed back to a particular part of the weekend that had been pretty fucking spectacular.

This wasn't the first time images of that night had popped into my head. Far from it, actually. I'd jerked off more in the past couple days than I probably had in years. Every time I thought back to that night I got hard as stone, unable to get it under control and left with no choice but to fuck my fist until I came with the image of Hayden on the backs of my eyelids.

I hadn't been able to stop thinking about that night, and it was really screwing with my head. I'd never had a woman invade my thoughts the way she had, but it had just been so damn good. The best I'd ever had. I wanted a repeat. Then another. And another. That was uncommon for me. The feeling . . . the *need* was so goddamn strong it was unnerving.

Not only was it a pain in the ass, it was also a bad time for my head to be fucked up, considering everything that was going on.

For the past five months, Leo and I had been investigating the murder of a fellow officer. At first we'd gotten a whole lot of nothing. Each lead we ran down took us to a dead end. Then we hit pay dirt when a woman tied to ex-drug kingpin and current resident of the state penitentiary, Malachi Black, came forward with information on the shooting of Officer Darrin Callo.

It was worse than anything we could have expected. Not only was a cop dead, but it looked like there were other cops involved. We were now investigating our own, which meant we didn't know who the hell we could trust.

Unable to bring in other officers to assist in the investigation, we'd connected with Lincoln Sheppard, a former Marine who ran a private investigation and security firm based here in Hope Valley. The man and his team had a gift for uncovering dirt, as well as a litany of other skills most civilians wouldn't be able to wrap their heads around.

With everything we were doing needing to be covert and completely under the radar, I couldn't risk my head not being in the game.

"You make it sound like all I care about is getting laid."

"Maybe not the *only* thing," he said. "But I'd be willing to bet it's up there in the top two."

I leaned back, kicked my boots up on my desk, and smirked. "Don't hate me just 'cause you got yourself tied down and have to live vicariously through my incredible bachelorhood."

He chuckled, giving his head a shake. "Keep telling yourself that, man. One of these days you're gonna meet a woman you can't get out of your head, and you'll be fucked. And I'll be the first to tell you I told you so."

Red hair and eyes the color of sapphires came to mind . . . glorious curves and flushed, creamy skin. And *fuck me*, I was getting hard again.

Gritting my teeth against my body's uncontrollable reaction, I tried to shake off what my partner had just said, only it was harder to do this time. "Not a chance in hell."

My cell went off just then. One ring, then the call dropped. It was a signal from my informant to call her back. It was a code we'd come up with for when I was at the station and unable to talk.

Knowing exactly what that ring meant, Leo pushed to his feet, asking, "Feel like a coffee run?"

"Cup of joe sounds good."

We exited the bullpen and headed out of the department. As soon as we were far enough away, I pulled the phone from my pocket and hit speed dial.

"What do you have for me," I asked the instant the call connected.

My CI's voice came through the line a moment later. "Not a lot. But, Micah . . . I think we may have a problem."

Fucking shit. "Are you safe?" I growled through the line, feeling the hairs on the back of my neck stand on end.

"Yeah. I mean, I think so . . . for now. I just . . ." She trailed off, her voice tiny and indecisive, so unlike the woman Leo and I had come to know.

Charlotte Belmont was a fighter, stronger than anyone I'd ever met. She'd lived a life I wouldn't have wished on my worst enemy, and yet, despite all the nightmares she'd endured, she never once just gave in. She was tough as nails, refusing to roll over and accept the shit hand she'd been dealt. And now, she'd purposefully put herself in a dangerous situation in the hopes of *finally* being able to pull herself out of the muck once and for all.

"Charlie," I said on a low, gruff clip. "What the fuck is going on? Is it Cormack? Is he getting suspicious?"

Leo's back went straight at the mention of Darrin Callo's partner on the force. When Darrin was killed, Leo and I had discovered he'd been looking into some of the unsolved drug cases. The man aspired to be a detective and was taking the initiative to get there.

A while back, Malachi Black, had run his meth operation from a hidden location up in the mountains. He'd been a thorn in the side of every cop in three counties, keeping his hands just clean enough that none of us could touch him. Everyone knew what he was doing, but there was no way for us to prove it or tie him to the drugs leaking into Hope Valley and the surrounding towns. We hit gold when he bought out a local strip club and started moving his shit through there. We worked with a couple of the dancers who weren't big fans of Black's new "private dance" policy and didn't like being forced into dealing, and with their help, we shut that bastard down.

Now he was rotting in prison, but the streets hadn't gotten clean. His product was still being moved, and we didn't have the first clue how that was.

We'd suspected Callo's death had something to do with the cases he'd been looking into, but we weren't able to piece together how. Until Charlie came into play. She'd been living on the streets when she met Black and made the mistake of thinking he could be her savior. She'd been an unwilling participant in his business, knowing the ins and outs better than most of the other players. As soon as he went down, his partner stepped into his place, and to hear Charlie tell it, he was even worse than Black.

It hadn't made sense how, for years, Black had been able to allude cops from three different cities. Until Charlie filled us in on who his partner was.

Officer Greg Cormack had been with the department going on fifteen years, starting as a rookie, and hadn't once been promoted to a higher rank in all that time. He'd been just quiet and unassuming enough that no one really paid much attention to him. People had questioned why he hadn't moved up the ranks, but other than that, no one thought much of it. As it turned out, he was too busy with his illegal side hustle to work his way up in the department.

He'd been the key reason it had taken us so long to take Black down. He'd also been the one who told Black when we were about to raid his strip club, making it so the man could abduct two women before going on the run. It was a goddamn miracle neither of them had been hurt.

Now, with Black gone, Cormack was filling his shoes while growing the drug business. Problem was, he played his shit much closer to the vest, not nearly as trusting with his crew as Black had been, so his was the only name Charlie had been able to give us so far.

Neither Leo nor I liked her putting herself in this position, but after Callo's death, she'd been adamant that she help us take down the person who'd killed an innocent husband and father. There had been absolutely no talking her out of it, and Leo and I both had tried . . . hard and often.

"No. At least I don't think so. I'm not sure if he suspects I'm working with the cops, but something's got him seriously tweaked. He's closing ranks. I'm still in the inner circle, but I'm not sure how much longer that'll last. Think he's feeling the noose tighten."

I cut a look to Leo and gave my head an angry shake. "For Christ's sake, Charlie, pull back. Let us get you out of there."

"Not yet," she demanded. "I can do this, Micah. I'm seeing this through to the end. That woman goes to sleep each night without her husband beside her," she bit out, speaking of Darrin's widow, Sidney Callo. "And his two babies probably won't even remember their dad when they're grown up. These asshole's need to pay for that, if nothing else."

I stopped in the middle of the sidewalk, with Leo at my side, scanning the crowd to make sure there were no eavesdroppers. Squeezing my eyes closed, I pinched the bridge of my nose and let out a beleaguered sigh. In the months we'd been working with Charlie, I'd developed a tight-knit relationship with the prickly woman. She wasn't a typical CI. She'd become like a sister to me, and the more tangled up she'd got in this mess, the more I stressed. "They're going down, Charlie. You have my word on that. But it's not gonna help anyone if you get hurt or dead in the process. I get you have some demons of your own, but this isn't how you work them out of your system, sweetheart."

"This has nothing to do with me," she clipped, that hardness I was so used to coming back into her voice, only now it was directed at me. "I'm not trying to rewrite my past or whatever bullshit you think this is. It's about right and wrong, plain and simple. I'm in a position to help, so I'm going to *help*."

"Goddamn it," I gritted.

"Deal with it, Langford. And keep an eye on Cormack. I'll call if I hear anything, and you do the same."

Before I could get another word out, she disconnected, leaving me standing there pissed and worried out of my mind.

"Fuckin' Christ," I grunted, stuffing the phone back into my pocket. I started toward Muffin Top, careful to make my strides easy and calm despite the tempest swirling inside of me.

"What've you got?" Leo asked under his breath.

"A headache and a whole lot of nothin' else, that's what," I seethed. "She says Cormack's freaked, closing ranks, but not sure what's got him that way."

Leo's brows sank into an unhappy V. "And let me guess. She's not pullin' back."

"You know that woman as well as I do. What do you think?"

"Fuck," he hissed under his breath. He was close with her too, and the level of responsibility we felt for her welllbeing wasn't something either of us took lightly.

"Exactly. So now we gotta watch him, see if he suspects anything's happening, *and* keep an eye on her to make sure she doesn't get dead."

"God deliver me from hardheaded women," he sighed just as we reached his woman's shop.

The smell of sugar and coffee filled the air but did little to touch the anxiety churning in my gut. "Don't let Dani hear you say that. She'll cut me off simply out of association with you, and if I lose out on her coffee or pastries there's a good chance my head will explode."

Trying my best to shake off the discomfort clinging to my shoulders, I pasted on my charming smile, like it was just any other day, and pulled the door open. I needed coffee now more than ever. Along with a shot of bourbon.

FOUR

HAYDEN

"So, baby girl, what do you think?" I asked, looking back at Ivy through my rearview mirror.

"It's so pretty!" she squealed excitedly.

She wasn't wrong about that. I hadn't been here often—less than a handful in the past decade since my husband hadn't been a big fan of my eccentric great-aunt Sylvia—but I was no stranger to this small town. Even then, I never got over how beautiful Hope Valley was. Each visit had been like seeing it for the first time, and as I drove through the main drag just then, it was no different.

After lecturing me for what felt like an eternity about loosening my grip on my husband so that he slipped through my fingers—their words—my parents had insisted Ivy and I move in with them when everything in my life had fallen to shit. That was completely out of the question. I loved them, but our relationship had been frayed for as long as I could remember. Though we'd lived in the same city, we didn't see each other on a regular basis. In fact, I'd gone out of my way *not* to attend family dinners and the like. They were impossible to please. Nothing I did was ever good enough. Even my accomplishments were ridiculed. I'd get an entire list outlining how I could have done better.

They didn't like the way I did my hair or makeup. They didn't like my clothes. They didn't like the name I'd picked for my daughter or the house we lived in or the car I drove. Everything I did or had could have been better, better, *better*.

The rest of my family was exactly the same, cut from the same cloth as my parents, and I couldn't imagine ever leaning on any of them, let alone during such a hard time in my life. I understood that blood was thicker than water, but sometimes you had to cut out those people who made you feel bad about yourself . . . even if they were your family.

There was only one relative I'd ever felt a real connection to. Even though I hadn't seen Aunt Sylvia in years, we were still close. We'd kept in contact with emails and phone calls. We'd bonded over being the two black sheep in our family, and that bond had stayed strong, keeping us connected no matter how long it had been since we were face-to-face.

When I called to tell her my world had basically imploded, she told me emphatically she'd been thinking of slowing down but didn't have anyone she trusted to take over the reins of her flower shop. She went on about the timing being kismet and all but demanded I move to her "little slice of paradise."

Hope Valley was a little less than an hour from Richmond, making it easily drivable, so Alex hadn't given me grief when I told him I had a job opportunity there. I assumed it also helped ease things with his pregnant fiancée that the woman he'd thrown over and the kid they had together were no longer going to be living in the same city.

But I tried really hard not to dwell on that.

Another thing I'd worked hard not to think about was my night with a certain stranger I'd picked up in a bar. I had started to wonder if I made the whole thing up. He'd been too damn good to be true, it *had* to have been my imagination. But even days later, I'd move or shift in a certain way and feel a twinge that reminded me that night had been very, *very* real.

Those twinges were gone now, but the memories certainly weren't, no matter how many times I told myself to stop thinking about it. I was never going to see Micah again, after all. I just prayed he hadn't ruined me for all other men.

Ivy stared out the window in wonder as we passed through the town, pointing out everything that caught her eye, which was a lot. She was particularly taken with the clock tower in the center of the town square, and rattled on and on about it until the moment we pulled up in front of Sylvia's house, an adorable bungalow overrun by so many shrubs and plants that her front yard looked like a jungle.

Her love for all things green had carried over from her flower shop. There was a trellis covered in wisteria at the side of the house, a line of rose bushes to the left of the porch. Azaleas, butterfly bushes, hydrangeas, elephant ears, and so much more. The backyard looked much the same. Her property was, hands down, my favorite place on earth. It was like stepping into a whole new world. I'd spent hours and hours in her yard, weeding and turning soil or curling up on one of the cozy chairs or loungers she had scattered throughout.

"Mommy," Ivy said on a wondrous breath, "it's like a secret garden." I threw the car in park and glanced over my shoulder, seeing my girl's face and hands pressed against the window. "Do we get to stay here?"

"Yeah, love bug. This is our new home. You like it?"

Ivy sucked in a huge, dramatic breath before declaring in a voice so loud it nearly burst my eardrums, "*I love it so much!*"

"Then let's go check it out."

I killed the engine and pushed the car door open just as Sylvia appeared, like a brightly colored beacon amidst all the greenery.

"Yoohoo!" she called, waving an arm in the air, making her dazzling, brightly colored caftan sway in the breeze. "There they are! Welcome home, my lovelies!" She reached the edge of her walkway just as I pulled Ivy from the car.

For a woman in her early eighties, she was so full of life it practically radiated from her pores. I'd gotten my strawberry blonde hair from her, and she was obviously keeping up with regular salon visits to keep her once-natural color intact. Making my way toward her, my vision blurred as my eyes welled. The sense of relief and familiarity that washed over me was almost overwhelming.

"It's so good to see you." My voice radiated with emotion as I whispered into her ear, inhaling her familiar scent. She'd been using Chantilly dusting powder for as long as I could remember. I associated that fragrance with so many happy memories, and smelling it now made me smile.

"Oh, my precious girl." She pulled back. Her fingers, slightly gnarled with age, pressed against my cheeks as she took my face in her hands. I looked down at her, seeing the many years she'd lived—enthusiastically sucking every drop of life from them—written on the soft, papery skin of her face beneath the impeccably applied makeup she wore every single day, no matter what. She'd taught me that beautiful undergarments made a woman feel sexy, even if no one was going to see them, and that there was never an excuse for a woman to go out in public without lipstick. She was of the mindset that it made you feel good to look good. "I'm so happy you're here."

Stepping back, she looked to my daughter, her eyes lighting up as she threw her arms out at her sides. "Come give your Auntie Sylvia a hug, darlin' girl."

Ivy clung to my leg, her little arms like a vise as she looked up at me, her blue eyes wide and inquisitive. I nodded reassuringly and gave her a little squeeze. "It's okay. You've met Aunt Sylvia before. You were just really little, so you don't remember." Leaning down, I whispered conspiratorially, "She's my most favorite aunt in the whole wide world."

That did it. Letting me go, she ran the distance between me and Sylvia and wrapped her arms as far around her middle as they'd go. "Hi, Auntie Siva! I'm Ivy!"

My great-aunt smiled down at her, running her fingers through my girl's pale red curls. "I know, darlin' girl. I actually planted some ivy near the back porch just for you the day you were born. Would you like to see it?"

Ivy gasped and shouted, "Yeah!" She latched onto one of Sylvia's hands and looked back at me. "Come on, Mommy."

"You two go explore. I'm gonna start unloading the car."

Sylvia gave me a wink, knowing I needed Ivy occupied while I tried to get our stuff into the house. My girl would insist on helping, which would take twice as long. "Come on, precious. There's a lot to explore. Better get started before we lose the sun."

I watched as my aunt guided my daughter around the side of the house and out of sight. Then I went about unloading our lives from my four-door sedan.

————

I felt like I was running on empty as I made my way down the stairs to the kitchen in the back of the house. Sylvia was sitting at the small dinette table tucked into the bay window. The top was covered in a bright mosaic she'd made years ago, using broken stoneware and vases. The whole house was full of vibrant colors and crazy patterns—from the big, over-stuffed velvet couch in burnt orange, with its eclectic collection of throw pillows, to the squishy lounge chair in peacock blue, to the rugs and the paint on the walls. It looked like a rainbow had exploded, or the sixties had a massive acid trip and puked all over the place. I absolutely loved it. It was funky, just like her—and like how I used to be before I'd tamped that part of me down for Alex.

I'd spent years living in a monochromatic show house where everything from the dinnerware to the light fixtures matched. It hadn't been me, not in the slightest. But I tried to appease myself by claiming that I'd been happy so I didn't care that Alex had shot down every one of my design ideas.

I would never make that mistake again. From here on out, I was living my life on *my* terms. My house would look how I wanted it to look. I'd dress how I wanted to dress. I would be exactly who *I* wanted to be. Never again would I let someone mold me into their version of Hayden.

"Is she down?" Sylvia asked, closing her sudoku book as I pulled out the chair across from her and took a seat.

"Yeah, finally."

She reached for the drink shaker beside her and poured the concoction into an empty glass she had waiting, then slid it in my direction. I lifted it up and took a sip, already knowing what it was. My great-aunt drank a Tom Collins every single night before bed. The sweet, lemony flavor burst on my tongue, followed by a slight burn the gin left behind as I swallowed and let out a heavy sigh.

"She really loved the teal walls and the butterfly canopy over the scrolled iron headboard. It took forever for her excitement to wear off so I could get her to sleep."

Sylvia smiled. "I'd like to say I did that just for her, but that room's looked like that for as long as I can remember."

I giggled and sucked back more of my drink. "I don't doubt that for a second."

My aunt studied me as she sipped her cocktail. "You know, you're more than welcome to make this place your own, sweets. I told you, this is yours now. Feel free to change whatever you want."

In the hours Ivy and I had been here, Sylvia had already made me feel more at home in this house than I ever had in the home I'd shared with Alex. I'd expected Ivy and I would get the guest rooms upstairs, but after hauling everything in and starting to unpack, Sylvia told me the master bedroom was all mine. She'd already had someone come and move her into the carriage house she'd converted to a small apartment years ago at the back of the property. She used to rent the space out, but it had been empty for a while.

"Really, Sylvia, I can't thank you enough for taking us in, but you moving into the carriage house really wasn't necessary. I'd have been more than happy making one of the guestrooms my own."

She waved me off like I was being ridiculous. "Nonsense. It was the most logical choice. I've been struggling with those stairs for quite some time now, and this house is too damn big for me. I'm sick and tired of having to clean it. Honestly, sweets, you're doin' me a favor. I'm not as young as I used to be. My soul might feel like a fresh-faced twenty-something, but my bones refuse to get onboard."

She liked to talk as though she was feeling run down, but there wasn't a doubt in my mind the woman could run circles around me. "Haven't you heard? Eighty-three is the new thirty."

She scoffed, lifting one of her perfectly penciled brows. "Tell that to my hips and knees. I was doing yoga in the garden the other day and nearly got stuck in downward-facing dog."

I laughed for a good long while at the vivid image she'd painted. Once it tapered off, I looked across the table to find her studying me, her eyes shrewd. "What?"

"Nothing. Just glad you're still able to laugh like that after everything."

I swallowed, my throat suddenly feeling thick. "Laugh like what?"

"With abandon, my darlin' girl. A woman gets knocked down the way you did, she could lose that. Puts my heart at ease that you've managed to hold on to it with all the ups and downs of late."

God, I loved my aunt. Not for the first time I thought of how much my family was missing by regarding Sylvia as nothing more than a nutty hippy spinster. Was she a little nutty? Absolutely. However, she was more bohemian than hippy. And she wasn't a spinster. Far from it, actually. My aunt had her "lovers" tucked away for whenever the need arose, but she lived her life on her own terms and never felt the need for a man to be a permanent fixture. It was an arrangement that worked well for all parties involved.

And she was so incredibly wise, always had been. Our flesh and blood were missing out on the wisdom she could impart.

I loved that she had faith in me, but I wasn't sure if I deserved all of it. I watched my finger as I traced the rim of my glass, mumbling, "Yeah, well, it's all because of Ivy. I might be rocking in a corner somewhere if she wasn't around for me to take care of."

"What a load of hogwash," she chided before taking another dainty sip. "You got knocked down by that human piece of garbage you called a husband. Then that waste of oxygen he's shacking up with kicked you while you were down. As if that wasn't bad enough, those vultures we're related to came to pick over your carcass as you lay bleeding. And here you are, sitting right before my very eyes and *laughing*. That precious girl up there might partly be the reason why, but the rest, my lovely Hayden, is sheer resilience and a spine of steel. And *no one* can take that away from you. Hear me?"

"I hear you," I said softly, a smile pulling at my lips.

"Good." She knocked on the table decisively. "It's a good thing you're here. Not just because the mountain air will work wonders to soothe the soul and calm the mind, but because there's somethin' in the water here that makes the men folk all *kinds* of fine, believe you me. If I were forty years younger. *Phew*." She waved a hand in front of her face, making me laugh again.

"Believe me, Sylvia, the last thing I'm in the market for is a man." *Tell that to your vagina that's still thinking about Micah the sex god*, the little devil on my shoulder said. "But it'll be nice to have some eye candy."

"If it's eye candy you want, then you've come to the right place. Why, just next door there's a man who could make your spine melt and your mouth water. Bonus, the *fine* young man wears a badge. Them boys in uniform are really somethin'."

I already knew all about melting spines and watering mouths, and I seriously doubted Sylvia's next-door neighbor could compete.

We spent the next few minutes catching up and finishing our cocktails. Sylvia left a short while later, taking the cobblestone path out back to her apartment, and I moved through the house, shutting off the lights and locking up before climbing the stairs to my new room.

It amazed me how, as soon as I laid my head on the pillow, I felt like I was exactly where I was meant to be.

It was on that thought I fell into a deep, peaceful sleep.

FIVE
HAYDEN

I'd officially been in Hope Valley for a week and a half, and with each passing day, I grew happier that I'd taken Sylvia up on her offer. I felt a peace in this small town that I hadn't known I was missing until I experienced it.

I'd worried about putting Ivy in daycare while I worked the shop since she had stayed home with me every day since she was born, but the moment she caught sight of the coloring station, she was in heaven. She loved the place and was already making friends with the other kids.

Aside from adding a few personal touches, I hadn't changed much of Sylvia's—my—house. To me, it was perfect just the way it was, from the chunky crocheted afghans to the macramé wall décor.

Every evening after work, Sylvia took Ivy and me through yoga poses to help us relax and unwind from the day—my girl was surprisingly good at yoga—then I'd make dinner for all of us. I'd forgotten how nice it was to eat a meal as a family, sitting around the table and listening to Ivy as she regaled us with exciting tales of the life of a preschooler.

Once I put her down for bed, Sylvia and I would share a cocktail, sometimes at the kitchen table, but more often in the back garden where I found it the most tranquil. She told me stories about the people she knew in town, going on about kidnappings and drug dealers and such. Most of what she said sounded too farfetched to believe. Hope Valley was a quiet, idyllic little town you'd expect to see in a Thomas Kincaid painting. I couldn't imagine it being a hotbed of criminal activity.

Still, as she ordered, I made sure to lock all the doors and windows, even when Ivy and I were home. Although I hadn't met our new neighbor yet, it was comforting to know there was a police officer living right next door.

I was finding my footing at Sylvia's shop, Divine Flora. She was slowly starting to shift the responsibilities of running the place to me while teaching me everything she knew. I'd always been good with plants and flowers, but she was teaching me how to make eye-catching arrangements as well as the fanciful little fairy gardens I'd fallen in love with at first sight. It was only a matter of time before she'd be able to come and go as she pleased.

I was in the zone, clipping the stems of flowers I thought would look pretty together and stuffing them into a really cool art-deco vase when I heard the bell over the door ring. Looking up from my work, I watched as two women walked inside, heading straight for the counter where Sylvia was working.

One was a short, curvy woman with huge doe eyes and an incredible head of long, thick hair. I wasn't sure if it was dark blonde or a super light brown, but whatever the case, it was gorgeous. She was also sporting a noticeable baby bump.

The other woman was equally curvy, only taller, and she also had incredible hair that was a red several shades darker than my own.

"Hayden," Sylvia called from across the shop. I looked her way to see her waving me over. "Come over here for a second, darlin'. There's some people I want you to meet."

"Be right there." Tucking the stem of the orchid in place, I took a step back and tilted my head to get a good look at what I'd just created. It wasn't bad if I said so myself. Wiping my hands on the front of my tie-dye apron, I headed toward the trio.

"Hayden, this here is Eden and Nona. Ladies"—she waved her hand toward me—"this is my great-niece, Hayden Young. She just moved to town and is helpin' me out with the shop until I can convince her to step fully into my shoes so I can retire once and for all."

"Hey. Nice to meet you," I greeted with a congenial grin.

"Right back at you, doll," the redhead returned. "So, where'd you move here from?"

"Oh, just Richmond. So not too far away."

"What brings you to Hope Valley?" Eden asked.

"Oh, uh . . . Well—"

"It's a tale old as time," Sylvia cut in. "Cheating bastard of a husband sleeps with wife's best friend, blah, blah, blah. You know how the story goes." She waved her hand as though the bomb she'd just dropped was no biggie.

"I'm so sorry," Eden said, those big eyes filling with sincere sympathy.

"Oh, babe. Been down that road," Nona commiserated. "Only, my ex didn't bang a friend. He banged the town skank. But that's a story for another time."

As strange as this whole conversation was, I kind of wanted to hear the vivacious woman's story.

"Well, that's over and done," Sylvia declared with finality. "What matters is that she and her daughter are here now, they're doing just fine, and I'm havin' a cookout next weekend to celebrate their arrival, so be sure to spread the word, ladies."

"Ooh!" Eden cried, clapping her hands. "Are you going to make that hummus with the lemon juice and chives again? That stuff is amazing and one of the only things I'm able to keep down. This little bean isn't letting me enjoy much of anything these days," she said, giving her belly a rub.

"I can certainly add it to the menu."

I looked to my aunt in shock. "When did you plan a cookout?"

"Just now," she answered with a shrug of her shoulder. "One thing you'll learn from me, sweets; the best parties you'll ever attend are the ones that form outta thin air."

"Seriously, Sylvia, you don't need to do that."

"Shush, dearie. It's already done." She looked back to Eden and Nona. "You'll pass word along, yeah? Any and all are welcome. I only require each guest to bring a dish."

"We're on it," Nona assured her before turning to me. "Your aunt throws the *best* parties. Last time, she started an impromptu yoga class. There had to have been like, forty people in her back yard, following along."

"Oh. And remember the one where she accidentally set out her *special* brownies instead of the regular ones? There were at least ten people walking around high as kites before she realized and stashed the rest away."

Both women laughed as I rolled my lips between my

teeth to hide my smile. Yoga and pot brownies . . . That was so Sylvia.

Apparently Nona ran the one and only salon in town—and it was the best salon in the state to hear my aunt tell it—and had a standing order once a week for an arrangement she kept at the front desk. Before they left they insisted on exchanging numbers so they could let me know when the next girls' night was happening.

I wasn't used to women being so upfront and friendly. The few friends I had back in Richmond—including Krista—had spent most of their time bad-mouthing the others when they weren't around. I wasn't naïve enough to think they hadn't said nasty things about me when I wasn't there, and I was sure they were having a field day now that Krista had stepped into my former life with no problem at all. But what little I knew of these two Hope Valley women, I liked. Sylvia was a fantastic judge of character, so if she said they were good people, they were good people. And I liked the idea of a girls' night, especially if it was with women who weren't backstabbing gossips who'd known my husband was screwing around and had kept it from me the entire time.

"Well," my aunt said on a sigh as the door closed behind Nona and Eden, "I'd say that went over just fine, wouldn't you? Those ladies are good eggs. You'll fit right in."

I looked at her and cocked a brow. "So, in the span of a few minutes, you've already scheduled a party *and* worked your magic to find me new friends?"

"Sounds about right."

"You're a little crazy," I said on a giggle. "You know that, right."

"Of course I do," she declared, shooting me a sly wink. "And isn't it so much fun?"

It absolutely was.

———

After two weeks in our new home, everything had been going great . . . with one glaring exception. It was Friday afternoon, and Alex was scheduled to arrive at any second to pick Ivy up for his weekend visit.

This would be my first full weekend in Hope Valley without my baby girl, and I'd been a walking bundle of anxiety all day long, dreading the moment I had to hand her over.

The doorbell rang, followed less than a second later by Ivy's high-pitched shriek. "Daddy's here!" she screamed as her little feet pattered down the hall. "Mommy! Daddy's here! Daddy's here!"

I managed to paste a smile on my face even though my heart was shriveling like old fruit. "You think so, love bug?"

She started hopping in place. Since it was just the two of us most of the time now, I'd stopped dressing her like all the other kids in our circle of friends back in Richmond and let her pick her own clothes. Today she was wearing a pair of tiny pink Converse sneakers, black jeans with bright pink, yellow, and purple daisies embroidered around the cuffs that went all the way up to her knees, and a matching pink shirt. Her long, curly red hair was hanging loose and wild down to the small of her back. She looked absolutely adorable, and it was taking everything I had not to burst into tears.

"Yeah, Mommy. I *know* it's him! It's gots to be."

"Well then why don't we open the door and see?"

"Okay, yeah! Do it now!"

I gave her one last grin before turning to the door and schooling my features in preparation for facing my ex-husband. Taking a fortifying breath, I twisted the knob and pulled the door open.

Alex looked the same as he always did, and I couldn't help but wonder when seeing him would finally stop feeling like a punch to the stomach. His dirty-blond hair was parted at the side like he always wore it, brushed up and back from his forehead. He was still in his suit from work, but the tie and jacket had been discarded, the top button at his collar undone, and the sleeves cuffed. I used to love it when he came home looking like that, still sexy in his suit but a little mussed in a way that made him even hotter. Now I was comparing everything about him to Micah, a man I was never going to see again.

"Hey there, my little monkey." He squatted low and opened his arms, picking Ivy up and tossing her in the air until she squealed.

"Hi, Daddy," she said once he settled her onto his hip. "Can we gets ice cream for supper?" she asked with her adorable little toddler voice that turned all her Rs into Ws.

"Not for supper. But maybe dessert," he added at the end when she began to pout, making her smile big once again.

"Yay!"

While he gave her a tickle, I let my eyes drift, unable to watch the interchange between them without hurting. My gaze cast to the sleek red Mercedes parked at the curb, then to the brunette sitting in the passenger seat, wearing huge sunglasses like they could actually hide her identity.

I had to bite the corner of my cheek to keep from making a nasty comment about him bringing his former mistress to my house.

Once they were done playing around, he finally turned his attention to me. "Hey, Hayden," he said with a shadow of a smile as his eyes swept over me. "You look good." I was still in the same clothes I'd worn to Divine Flora: a pair of skinny jeans that were frayed at the ankles and had artful rips in the knees and thighs, and a V-neck camo tee in pale pinks and grays that I had knotted at my waist. It was one of the outfits I'd bought when I purged my closet of all the clothes from my former life.

I'd kicked off the super cute gray wedges I'd worn with the ensemble when I got home earlier, but fortunately the at-home pedicure I'd given myself a few nights back had held up, and my dark purple toe nails still looked good.

I thought I looked good, and I'd felt good all day long, but the last thing I was going to do was thank him for the compliment, especially when he'd brought *her* to my home.

I bent down and grabbed Ivy's pink unicorn duffle bag from the upholstered bench just inside the door and passed it to him. "Everything she needs for the weekend's in there, so you're all set."

He took the bag, but instead of saying his goodbyes like I'd expected, he placed Ivy on her feet and said, "Hey, monkey, why don't you let Krista get you all buckled up in your booster, huh? I need to talk to your mommy for a second."

My jaw ticked and my hands clenched at the thought of that woman coming anywhere near my child. However, as much as I hated her—and I hated her *so damn much*—she was going to be my daughter's stepmom, so I had to shove my animosity aside in order to make the best of the situation for Ivy's sake.

I bent down and pulled her into a tight hug, then peppered her face with kisses. "I'm gonna miss you like crazy, love bug. Be good, okay? I'll see you in a couple days."

"I'll be super good, Mommy. And love you too!"

I got one last squeeze before she took off toward the car, smiling and waving at the woman who'd just stepped out of the passenger side and was in the process of opening the back door.

Alex cleared his throat, drawing my focus back to him as he reached around to rub the back of his neck in discomfort. "Look, I'm sorry about her being here. I didn't plan on bringing her to pick up Ivy. She just kind of insisted—"

I held my hand up and shook my head. "Stop, Alex. I really don't care why she's with you. All I'll say is if this is going to be a recurring thing, you need to make sure she knows to stay in the car. I don't want her stepping foot on my property. You got it?"

"Yeah. Of course." He let out another sigh as he looked past my shoulder into the house. "So, this is where you live now, huh? It seems . . . colorful."

"We aren't doing this," I broke in before he could say anything else. "We're not gonna stand on my doorstep and make small talk like everything's peachy."

"Hady Cakes," he said in that soft voice he used to use every time he epically fucked up and wanted me to forgive him without an actual apology. "It doesn't have to be like this. We can still be civil—"

"First, don't call me Hady Cakes. You lost the right to

use that name the very first time you shoved your dick in my best friend. Second, *this*"—I waved my hand between us—"is exactly how *you* wanted it to be, so don't give me that soft voice and those puppy dog eyes."

"Sweetheart, I still care about you. Divorce doesn't change that."

"It absolutely does," I stated emphatically. "Because I can say with complete and absolute certainty that I don't give a single shit about you anymore. If it weren't for our daughter, I'd be more than happy to never see you again."

He actually had the nerve to flinch like what I'd just said hurt him. "Hayden—" he started again, only this time we were interrupted by Krista.

"Alex, honey? It's getting late and it's a long drive. We should get back on the road."

I looked back to the man I'd vowed to spend the rest of my life with and arched a single brow. "Looks like the boss is calling, Alex. Better get a move on."

"Hayden, we really need to—"

"Alex!" Krista called again, this time louder and with a hint of frustration.

"Call if there's an emergency, or if Ivy just wants to talk to me. Other than that, there's nothing else for us to say to each other."

With another sigh, Alex turned and started down the cobble path through the front garden that led to the street. I waited in my open doorway as the car started moving, raising my arm and returning Ivy's wave until they were gone. Then I went inside, grabbed my shoes and purse, and booked it to the nearest store. I was going to need *all* their wine if I intended to get through this weekend.

Six
Micah

I hadn't slept more than two hours a night for the past three nights. The dull thud behind my temples had become a pulsing behind my eyeballs, and the florescent lights of the grocery store weren't helping.

Between the Darrin Callo case, our other cases, keeping an eye on that asshole Cormack, and trying to make sure Charlie didn't get herself killed, Leo and I were stretched so goddamn thin I could barely see straight.

As soon as I got off work, I headed for the grocery store. I moved through the aisles with single-minded determination toward the refrigerated section. I hadn't had dinner—hell, I wasn't sure I'd put more than coffee in my stomach all day— but I was at the point that I didn't give a shit. I hit the beer cooler and grabbed a six-pack, letting out a sigh of relief. I planned to drink the whole thing, pass out, and, God willing, sleep for at least twelve hours.

Slapping the fridge door closed, I spun on my boot and started toward the front of the store when I spotted a head of wild, wavy, light red hair perusing the wine selection a few yards away.

"What the fuck?"

She stretched an arm to grab a bottle on one of the higher shelves, pulling my focus to her stunning curves and a lush, round ass. An ass I recognized. One that had been burned on my brain.

"What the *fuck*?" I repeated louder.

She turned just then and did a stutter step on her sexy-as-fuck wedges, nearly dropping the wine bottle as soon as she saw me. Her familiar gem-blue eyes went wide with shock. "*Micah?*"

"*Hayden?* What the fuck are you doin' here?" The edges of my vision started to close in. "Jesus Christ, did you *follow* me here?"

Her chin jerked back in shock. "Excuse me?"

"Don't think that was a hard question to comprehend, Red. What are you doing here?" I repeated, asking the question slowly.

The shock melted from her features and twisted into a furious scowl that I might have found adorable if I wasn't currently worrying that the best sex of my life had been with a raving lunatic with stalker tendencies.

"What's it look like?" she asked in a snotty voice while lifting the bottle of red in her hand. "I'm buying wine."

"Not what I mean, and you know it. What are you doin' in my town? How the hell did you even find me?"

"Are you serious? I didn't *find* you! This is purely coincidental. How would I even go about doing that when all I knew was your first name?"

I threw my arms out at my sides, exhaustion and stress

making me a tad bit irrational as I declared, "I don't know! I don't know how the hell stalkers think. Maybe you went through my wallet that night. Who the hell knows?"

"Oh my God!" she cried indignantly. "I'm not stalking you, asshole. I live here."

"Bullshit," I clipped, noticing from the corner of my eye that we'd gained the attention of the people around us with our loud argument. "*I* live here," I stressed. "Lived here for years. I know every resident of this town, and you are . . . not . . . one of them."

She crossed her arms over her chest and glared furiously. An expression so unlike all the ones I'd seen from her that night. "Well, apparently not *all* of them."

I mimicked her stance, narrowing my eyes in a glare. "Yeah? Since when?"

"That's none of your business," she returned snidely before letting out a dramatic groan and lifting her hand to rake her fingers through all that long thick hair. In spite of being in the middle of a yelling match, watching all that silky red fall made my dick begin to thicken. "Should've known he was a jackass," she grumbled to herself. "Jesus, I can really pick 'em."

"What the hell's that supposed to mean?"

Her face scrunched up in rage. "Again, that's none of your damn business. I'm so done with this," she clipped. She whipped around and started to storm off before changing course and stomping back up to me, shoving a finger in my face. "And you know what? You need to get over yourself. You weren't even that good!" she exclaimed loudly.

I let out a caustic laugh. "Sure, Red. Keep tellin' yourself that. I had the scratch marks all over my back for days to prove otherwise."

"Gah!" she shouted. "You're such a prick!"

"A prick who rocked your world!"

"That night was the biggest mistake *ever*!"

My mouth curled into a smug grin. "Yeah? Bet if I offered you'd jump at the chance for a repeat."

She threw daggers with her eyes. "Not on your life, asshole. I don't sleep with men I hate."

"Wanna put money on that, stalker? Hate sex is the best kind there is. Give me a few minutes and I'll prove it to you."

"Lick rust, Micah." With that, she spun on her heel and stormed down the aisle, her round ass and curvy hips swaying enticingly as she disappeared around the corner, leaving me pissed and turned on at the same damn time.

How the hell was that even possible?

———

Hayden

I let out a deep, cleansing breath as I followed Sylvia into the next position, but no matter what I did, I couldn't stop stewing over my encounter with that arrogant, narcissistic bastard from the night before.

"You know, yoga's supposed to help calm you. You're as tangled up as that piece of gum you had to get outta Ivy's hair last week. You wanna tell me what's going on? Is it 'cause Ivy's gone this weekend?"

"No. I mean, yes—well, kind of . . . It's not *entirely* that,"

I admitted, letting out a deep sigh. "Of course I hate not having her with me. I don't think that feeling will ever go away."

"I wouldn't imagine so. But if that's not the crux of your issues this morning, what is?"

Pursing my lips, I blew out a long, slow exhale as I adjusted on my mat to face Sylvia. She did the same, criss-crossing her legs and pulling her heels in much closer than I could pull mine. From so many years of yoga, my eighty-three-year-old great-aunt was about a million times more flexible than I was.

"I met this guy in a bar back in Richmond one night a few weeks back . . ."

Her blue eyes began to dance in the sunlight beaming down on us. "Ooh, this sounds promising."

I let out a laugh and shook my head. "Only you would think of admitting to a one-night stand as 'promising.'"

She scoffed in affront and exclaimed, "Well, of course I would. I see no harm whatsoever in a woman knowing her desires and doin' something about seein' they're fulfilled. I'll never wrap my head around these people who think it's wrong for a woman to go in search of great sex while a man gets a pat on the back for the same damn thing. Speaking of, how was it?"

"It was . . . incredible," I confessed, my shoulders slumping in defeat. "Hands down, the best I've ever had. Like, nothing before that even compared. And I had all these really great memories of that night that I thought I'd be able to look back on whenever I wanted."

She lifted an inquisitive brow. "I don't understand. Why do you sound so broken up about that?"

"Because I am. In a cruel twist of fate—since that bitch hasn't already gotten enough punches in—I discovered he lives here when I ran into him at the market last night."

"Well, that's a good thing, right? It means you can have as many repeats as you'd like."

"No! That's just it. It's a bad thing. As it turns out, the guy's a massive dick. I mean, he actually accused me of *stalking* him. He thought I was in Hope Valley because I'd followed him or something."

"The hell he did," she snapped in outrage. And an outraged Sylvia was nothing you *ever* wanted to mess with.

"He absolutely did. We got into this big shouting match right there in the middle of the aisle with all these people I don't even know watching like we were putting on a show or something."

"That's small-town livin' for you, sweets. Everybody knows everybody else's business. Don't worry, you'll eventually get used to it."

I collapsed back onto mat with a pained groan, staring up at the gorgeous blue sky and puffy white clouds. "This is just sad. I'm a thirty-three-year-old divorcee whose husband couldn't keep his dick in his pants and threw me over for the other woman. Then the best sex of my life turned out to be the biggest asshole I've ever met. Maybe I'm cursed or something."

"Oh nonsense. There's no such thing as curses."

I turned my head and looked up at her, lifting a hand to block the sun. "Yeah? Then what do you think the problem is?"

"You're simply crap at picking good men, that's all," Sylvia stated almost amiably before sucking in a gasp like she'd just had a lightbulb moment. "Oh! You know what? You should *really* meet my neighbor," she insisted, like I wasn't in the middle of a crisis.

"Sylvia," I groaned, "another guy is so not the answer."

"But I think this one may just be. He's a great man." She waggled her brows. "And I get a sense he's quite accomplished *in the sack*."

"And how would you have a 'sense' about something like that?"

"You get to be my age, you just know about these things."

I looked back to the sky and let loose a laugh. It had started off slow and quiet but built in speed and sound until tears welled in my eyes and spilled down my temples into my hair. *Man*, did it feel good to laugh like that after the shitty twenty-four hours I'd had.

"You're gonna be just fine, darlin' girl," Sylvia said, giving my knee a pat. "Now, if you don't mind, I'm gonna finish my vinyasa. And I could really use a glass of iced tea."

My laughter trickled off into giggles as I pushed up from my mat and started toward my back door. "On it. Be right back."

I skip-walked down the cobblestones, feeling lighter than I thought possible a few minutes ago. The second I pushed the back door open, I heard my cellphone go off. Moving to the counter, I pulled it from its charger and swiped to answer, holding it between my shoulder and ear as I moved around the kitchen. "Hello?"

"Hey, babe. It's Nona. From the flower shop the other day?"

"Oh, yeah, I remember. How's it going?" I asked as I

grabbed a couple glasses from the cabinet then headed for the fridge to get the pitcher of iced tea.

"Everything's good. I'm calling because there's gonna be a live band playing at The Tap Room tonight, and I wanted to see if you'd be interested in going."

"What's The Tap Room?" I asked as I poured the tea and moved to put the pitcher back into the fridge.

"It's the best bar in town. You're gonna love it, trust me. Say you'll come. I know it's really last minute, but it'll be a lot of fun. And Eden and I can introduce you to the rest of our friends. You'll fit right in."

Fitting in with a new crowd in my new town sounded nice, especially considering I didn't have a single friend in the world to speak of. Who was I to turn down a shot at making some new ones?

"You know what? That sounds great. What time should I meet you guys?"

"The band goes on at eight. How's that sound?"

The corners of my lips began to tilt upward and excitement bloomed in my belly. "Sounds awesome. I'll see you there."

"See you then, doll."

I hung up and set my phone down so I could grab the glasses of iced tea.

"Sure did take you longer than I expected," Sylvia said as I made my way to her through the garden.

"Sorry. Nona called while I was in there. She invited me to a ladies' night tonight."

Sylvia took one of the glasses from my hand and sipped while lifting a dainty brow. "Is that so? Well it looks like this day's takin' a turn for the better after all, huh?"

I sure as hell hoped so.

"Now help an old lady off the ground, would you? I still have a few miles in these hips of mine. Be a damn shame to break one now." She shot me a wink as I grabbed her hands and pulled her to standing. "Know some gentleman who'd be *real* disappointed if I was put out of commission."

God, my aunt was nuts. And I absolutely loved it.

SEVEN

HAYDEN

I wasn't sure what to expect from a bar in a small mountain town, but I was pleasantly surprised to find The Tap Room was huge and cool as hell.

The first thing I noticed when I stepped through the doors was that the place was packed to the gills. The second thing was the scent of beer in the air. The moment that malty, almost sweet smell hit my senses, it was like déjà vu. For a split second, I was transported back to that pub in Richmond.

At the reminder of that night, my breasts grew heavy and a shiver trailed up my spine.

Maybe tonight we could find a man to replace all those memories of Micah, the devil on my shoulder queried before I smacked her off. That was a mistake I had no intention of repeating. Especially in the place where I lived. If there was anything I'd learned from that one and only encounter, it was that I really wasn't the kind of woman who could pull off a one-night stand.

The nights were getting chilly with fall touching down,

so I'd decided on a pair of thick black leggings and a red and black checkered button-down that I tied in a knot right above my belly button, showing the barest hint of skin in the front, but the tail in the back came down low enough to partially cover my butt, making me feel a bit less exposed. My calf-high, lace-up booties with thick three-inch heels were cute, but in a cool as hell, edgy kind of way.

I'd given my locks a break from the flatiron and curling iron lately and discovered I loved the natural wave in my hair. It was wild, and it was another part of me my daughter had inherited, so I'd let it air dry tonight, hanging halfway down my back in wild, thick waves. I'd done my makeup a bit on the smokier side for more of a night time look without going too over the top, and to top off the whole ensemble, taking it from casual to casual with a touch of spice, I had gold bangles on my wrists and long, wide chandelier earrings dripping almost all the way to my shoulders.

All in all, I thought I looked pretty good, so I felt good as I stopped a few feet inside the bar and scanned the area for Nona and Eden.

I spotted their familiar faces a few seconds later, waving at me from a cluster of tables right at the edge of the dance floor, facing the stage.

With a big smile, I made my way to them, noticing the group they were with was much bigger than I'd expected.

"Hey!" Eden cooed, shuffling around the tables, belly first, in order to get to me and pull me into a hug. "So glad you could make it. When Nona said she'd called you I got really excited."

"I'm excited to," I replied, returning her embrace. "I appreciate you guys inviting me."

"Of course," Nona said, taking Eden's place and giving me a quick squeeze. "Let's get the introductions out of the way really fast, then we'll get you a drink." She shifted us so we were facing the group with her arm slung casually over my shoulders. "Ladies, this is Hayden, the newest resident of Hope Valley. She's in need of a new crew, so I invited her to partake in ladies night. She's Sylvia's great-niece. Hayden, you know Eden already. This here is Tessa, Gypsy, Tempie, Sage, Roxanne, Dani and Rory. Rory owns this place, but she took the night off so she could hang without a bar between us. And that's McKenna," she said, pointing to the last woman. "She owns a burlesque club just outside of town called Whiskey Dolls. That'll be where we do our next ladies' night. We try to alternate."

I was overwhelmed and wasn't sure I was going to be able to keep everything straight when the woman who'd been introduced as Rory spoke. "Don't worry about not getting all that on the first night. It can be a little much."

She looked like a rock and roll hippy with a colorful scarf wound through the beltloops of her jeans and another one tied into a headband, tangling with her long, sleek black hair. She was wearing scuffed cowboy boots and a form-fitting tee that stated, *"The only way to tap it is hard and fast."* Her smile seemed genuine, as did the looks I was getting from the rest of the ladies, but I wasn't ready to lower my guard just yet. Once burned, twice shy, and all that.

"I hope you're right," I said on a laugh as I grabbed an empty chair and sat down. "And I apologize in advance if I screw up any of your names."

"Don't sweat it," the blonde I thought might be Gypsy said. "Our group grows in number every year. You'll get who's who squared away soon enough. By the way, I totally dig your style. It's very . . ."

"Mountain bling," a woman with long mahogany hair almost as wild as mine chimed in. I recalled that Nona had introduced her as Sage. And I dug *her* look. It screamed biker babe through and through. Ivy would have flipped.

"Yeah, that's the perfect way to describe it. Mountain bling," Gypsy agreed. "It's working for you in a serious way, hon."

My cheeks started to heat as my smile grew even bigger. "Um . . . thanks." I looked down at my top, giving one of the ends of the knot a little tug. "I tossed pretty much everything in my closet right before I moved here and bought all new clothes."

That garnered looks of appreciation and curiosity from the women in our group. I let out a grateful sigh when a waitress stopped by, and I quickly ordered a Blue Moon.

"So, what prompted the move to Hope Valley and a brand new wardrobe?" the older woman with bright, fire engine-red hair, asked. I believed she was Roxanne. If I had to guess, she was somewhere in her mid-fifties. She was sporting blue eyeshadow and an extreme amount of cleavage in her skin-tight shirt, and somehow, she made the crazy look work. She was sitting beside Sage, and had the same biker babe vibe, but in a well-seasoned way.

I snatched up the beer the waitress had just set down and took a hearty gulp. "Well, um . . . I kind of needed a change . . . after I caught my husband having an affair."

"Oh honey," the brunette by the name of Tessa said, her gaze turning sympathetic. "I think you're gonna need something stronger than beer tonight."

"With my best friend," I quickly added. The group went silent, some of the women slow blinking in shock.

Gypsy was the first to shake herself out of her stupor. "*Definitely* something stronger than beer," she said, turning in her chair and waiving down our waitress. "Tonight calls for shots."

"*Shots!*" the rest of the women—excluding Eden, of course—shouted in unison. And I suddenly got the impression that the night was about to ramp up in a serious way.

———

"What a heinous bitch," Sage snapped as soon as I finished regaling the group with the story of my marriage's demise. "I mean, there's a special place in hell for women like her."

"Amen to that," Tempie declared. "Karma always comes around in the end though, so she'll get hers one of these days."

"To karma!" Nona prompted, lifting her glass high.

"To karma!" we all repeated, clinking our glasses together before sucking back more booze.

The night seemed to move at warp speed after that. Three Blue Moons and two shots of whiskey later, I was feeling nice and floaty. The band had been *amazing*, so good that some of us had danced for an entire set before the burn in my thighs forced me to take a break. The Makin Hardware Store Guys—terrible name, but the men could *rock*—were currently on a break, so we were back at our tables, drinking, chatting, and laughing so much and so hard my abs were getting a serious workout.

These women were absolutely *nothing* like my so-called

friends back in Richmond, and it had taken no time at all to loosen up. Hours later, I felt like I'd been a part of this group for years.

"Wait, wait, wait." I waved my hands to stop McKenna, mid-sentence. We were sitting near the end of our cluster of tables and leaned in close so we could hear each other over the din of music and other conversations happening all around us. "So, your club used to be a strip club until it went under because some bad dude was selling drugs and happy endings out of the back rooms? That's when you and your man bought it and changed it up?"

"Yup." She lifted her cocktail glass toward her lips to suck back more of her mojito but missed the straw the first two tries. Needless to say, we were all a bit tipsy.

"And you and Gypsy were dancers there when it was a strip club?"

"Yeah. But Gypsy wasn't just a dancer. She was the headliner. You should've seen her! That girl can *move*."

I leaned back in my chair. "That's . . . so . . . *cool*!"

McKenna's chin jerked back, like she hadn't been expecting that kind of reaction from me. "Really?"

"*Hell* yeah! You know, I took one of those pole classes at a gym back in the city thinking it would be really easy and fun, but I'll tell you what . . . that shit is *hard*! It takes some serious skill to do what you guys did. *And* in full hair and makeup like that? While looking sexy?" I blew out a raspberry and shook my head. "Me and the rest of the women in that class were flopping all over the place like fish out of water. There was nothing sexy about it."

"You know, Whiskey Dolls still has some poles for a few of the numbers the girls do. If you want, I could teach you."

My eyes bulged out as I shot forward and grabbed her hands in mine. "Really?"

"Yeah, totally! It'll be fun."

I let out a squeal that drew the other women's attention. "What's going on down there?" Dani, the sweet, beautiful owner of Muffin Top—the best coffee and pastry shop in the whole US of A, according to my new friends —asked.

"Mac's gonna teach me to pole dance," I answered, doing a little hip roll in my chair.

"Oh Lord." Roxanne rolled her eyes. "With her face, those legs, that ass, and all that hair, you teach that girl to work a pole, the single men in this town are likely to spontaneously combust."

A giggle bubbled up and burst past my lips before I could stop it. After years of being made to feel like I wasn't good enough, compliments like that made my chin lift a little higher.

"Ooh! We should totally set Hayden up with someone!" Nona insisted. "Hope Valley is the *perfect* place to find a hot, single man."

"No, no," I cut in. "Really, that's not necessary. I'm not looking for a relationship at the moment."

My words fell on deaf ears. "My vote's Dalton," Sage announced. "He's fine as hell. He's got that sexy country boy vibe, and his deep voice is like velvet." She shivered playfully. "But if any of you tell Xander I said that, I'll deny it to the grave."

"What about West?" Gypsy asked. "He's got that boy next door thing going for him."

"If the boy next door knew how to rip your panties off

with his teeth," Rory added, earning a high five from Gypsy and a laugh from the rest of us.

"Really, guys. The last thing I want right now is a relationship. I want to get Ivy settled and make sure she's handling these changes okay."

Eden leaned across the table and placed her hand on top of mine. "No one says you can't do both. You can do that *and* have a little fun for yourself. You're a hot, young woman. You deserve some fun."

"Hey, you know who'd be good for her?" Dani asked, pulling everyone's attention away from me.

I used that to my advantage and stood from my chair, moving toward the bar to order another drink instead of waiting for the waitress to come around and have to listen to my new friends pick out a guy for me.

Standing at the bar, I rested my elbows on the top and waited for the bartender to free up so I could wave him down and place my order.

"Hi, there."

I turned and looked to my right to the man who'd just come up to the bar beside me. "Hi."

"You're new here, aren't you? I've never seen you before."

"Man, is this town *that* small?" I asked on a giggle, making the man smile. He had a nice smile with straight white teeth. He was also good-looking. Not on Micah's level, but more on par with Alex.

He shook his head good naturedly. "Sorry, that probably sounded pretty weird, huh?"

"Nah. It wasn't that bad. And yes, I'm new. Moved here about two weeks ago."

"Well, welcome to Hope Valley. Hope you've been enjoying it so far. I'm Greg."

I turned more toward him and gave his hand a shake, the warm fuzziness I was already feeling thanks to my tipsy state making this handsome guy's attention feel pretty damn nice. "Hayden. And I am, thanks. This place is really great."

He took a step closer, making his interest known. There was no spark of attraction on my part, but there was no harm in a little innocent flirting, right? It was fun. "So, Hayden, I've got two questions for you. First, what is it you do here in Hope Valley?"

"I'm working over at Divine Flora. What's the second question?"

"The second question is . . ." He took another step toward me, closing more of the distance. "Can I buy you a drink?"

I opened my mouth to reply. The plan was to politely decline, however, before I had a chance to do that, a deep, husky voice spoke from behind me. A voice I recognized, and one that caused arousal to flood through my body. "That's not gonna happen."

Well shit.

EIGHT

MICAH

I t was well after ten by the time we finished our clandestine debrief with Linc and the small team he'd put together to assist with the Callo investigation. The central topic—as well as the biggest concern—discussed in that meeting was one Ms. Charlie Belmont.

She'd managed to give us the names of two more players in the operation, one a low-level street dealer we already had our eye on and the other an officer with the Hidalgo sheriff's department a couple towns over.

It went without saying that Leo and I were unhappy she wouldn't see reason and get clear, but what surprised us both was the level of pissed-the-hell-off Linc's guy Dalton exhibited when we told him that, once again, she'd shot down our request to let us get her out safely.

"You either get her to accept she's no longer a player in this game, or I'll go in there and drag her off the board my goddamn self," he'd snarled, drilling his finger into the top of the conference room table.

We'd shut the meeting down after that, knowing we

weren't going to get anything more accomplished other than giving each and every one of us a raging migraine. We waited to get the all-clear from Xander, who was monitoring the cameras at the alley behind the building to make sure no one was watching before pushing through the heavy steel door and stepping into the night.

"Don't know about you, but I need a fuckin' drink," I gritted out, rubbing my temples as we moved through the alley toward the main drag of town.

"Dani and the rest of her posse are at The Tap Room," Leo said. "I say we head that way and throw a few back. At least, once we're done, I can drag my woman's ass home and into bed."

"Sounds good to me." I needed a bourbon and a soft, warm woman to help shake off the ugliness I felt clinging to my skin like mist on a gray, rainy day.

We made the short trek to the bar and saw it was packed for the night thanks to the band I could see playing on the stage through the windows.

I pulled the heavy glass door open and stepped inside, out of the autumn chill that was starting to take over our valley. Moving toward the bar, I did a scan, in search of a couple empty stools, but what I saw instead brought me up short.

"What's the deal?" Leo asked when I stopped moving. He looked in the direction I was staring and let out a low whistle.

I knew the exact reason behind that whistle. It was the same reason all the blood in my body was currently rushing straight to my dick. Leo might have been in a blissfully happy, committed relationship, but the man wasn't blind or dead. Hayden was standing at the bar, bent forward to rest her elbows on top. Her ass was on display for every needle-dicked piece of shit in her general vicinity, and there were more than just a few taking the chance to ogle her. At the number of eyes on her perfect ass, that irrational sense of anger I'd felt at Fresh Foods the night before, causing me to act like a dick for no good reason, came rushing to the surface.

"You gotta be fuckin' kidding me," I clipped under my breath, glaring at the woman who had the attention of half the men in this goddamn bar, myself included.

I could feel Leo turn his attention to me, but I couldn't pull mine off the woman who'd been fucking with my head for weeks. "What's the problem? Figured you'd already be movin' in on a woman like that. You don't act fast, no doubt another man in here's gonna beat you to it."

"Already had a woman like that," I grunted. "In fact, I had that *exact* woman."

"What? When—wait." He started laughing at my expense. "No, fuckin' way. That's her, isn't it? The woman from the weekend you did your sister's baby shower in the city? The one you had a showdown with in the middle of the refrigerated section?"

"Sometimes I hate small towns," I grunted to myself. I finally tore my gaze off Hayden's ass to shoot my partner a murderous glare. "Glad you find this funny, jackass. Remind me to never confide in you about another damn thing."

"Are you kidding? This is great. It's been *weeks* you've been strung up on this chick. And Christ, man, I can see why. She's—oh shit." His humor instantly fled. "We got a problem."

I shifted my focus back toward the bar and felt my blood turn to ice. "*Fuck*," I hissed as soon as I spotted Cormack. The bastard was making his move right then, and he was making it on Hayden. "This can't be happening, right now. Of all the shitty luck—"

"Not sure how the hell you're gonna stop that, but you better think of something. Last thing we need is that asswipe turning his attention on your girl."

"She's not my girl," I clipped, but even as I said the words, a voice inside my head was screaming for me to make him bleed if he so much as laid a hand on her.

She giggled at something he said and tossed that thick mane of hair back off her shoulder. A sick feeling hit the pit of my stomach like a sledgehammer when he smiled at her. He shifted closer, she turned toward him, and they shook hands.

I wasn't aware I was moving until I nearly took down a waitress carrying a loaded tray. I issued a distracted apology and kept moving, closing in. I was just within earshot when I heard her honey-coated voice ask, "What's the second question?"

That prick actually had the balls to move closer to her. "The second question is, can I buy you a drink?"

"That's not gonna happen."

Hayden whipped around, her jaw hanging open in shocked anger, but I was too busy trying to melt the skin from Greg Cormack's face with my eyes to acknowledge her wrath. He'd invaded her space. He'd smiled at her. He'd *touched* her. His hands were covered in Darrin Callo's blood, and God only knew who else's, and this fuck actually had the nerve to *touch* Red.

His head tilted to the side, his chin jerking back into his neck. "'Scuse me?"

"You need to move on, Cormack."

"Do you two know each other?" Hayden asked, but I ignored her question, too busy trying to keep myself in check so I didn't choke the life out of this murderous son of a bitch in the middle of a crowded bar.

"She yours or somethin'?" he asked, an arrogant gleam in his eye, like he was in the mood for a pissing contest.

"Absolutely not!" Hayden proclaimed at the same time I answered, "Sure the hell is."

Her long hair slapped my arm and chest when she jerked around again to face me. "I am *not* yours, you arrogant dick!"

For the first time since the standoff started, I looked down at the little fireball standing in front of me, a smirk pulling at my mouth. "Know how hot your pussy gets when it's wrapped around my cock, and what your nails feel like, diggin' into my back when you come. Pretty sure that makes you mine."

She sucked in a gasp so big it was a wonder her lungs didn't burst. "I can't—you didn't just—that was—Oh my God! *You're unbelievable!*"

"You've said that before. That time when you were riding me while your hands were—"

"Enough!" she cried, slapping a hand over my mouth to silence me and looking back over her shoulder. "Greg, I'm so sorry, but maybe we can finish this conversation at a later date? You could swing by the shop one day next week."

His eyes actually gleamed with triumph as he stared me down before slowly turning back to Hayden with a goddamn toothpaste commercial smile. "That's a great idea.

I'll just leave you to handle this, and we'll see each other next week."

"Sounds good. Have a good night, Greg."

"You too, beautiful."

Motherfucker!

He walked away just seconds before I gave in to my urge to reach across Hayden and rip his throat out.

Shifting my glare down to her, I bit out, "What the fuck was that?"

"I should be asking you the same question!" she shouted, her sapphire eyes glazed with either rage or alcohol, I wasn't sure which. "I can't believe you just did that!"

"Well, you better start believing, Red. And just an FYI, there's no way in hell you're seein' that guy again."

"Oh my God," she said, reaching up and raking her fingers through her hair on a bewildered laugh. "You're insane. Completely certifiable."

"This isn't a joke," I grated, moving in closer and grabbing her arm as I lowered my voice. "I'm very serious, Hayden. You need to stay away from that guy."

She must have seen something in my eyes that gave her pause, because instead of throwing attitude back, she lifted her chin and said, "Tell me why. You can't issue a demand like that without an explanation, Micah."

"Because I said so." It took less than a second for me to realize that was the wrong thing to say.

The fight returned to her features in a venomous glare as she ripped her arm from my grasp. "God, I hate you."

I felt my defenses start to rise. It was ridiculous how this goddamn woman could turn me on and set me off at the same damn time. It was completely irrational how she was able to piss me off with just a look, but the way my body reacted to just the thought of her left me so muddled, my kneejerk reaction was anger.

"Don't recall sayin' I was the biggest fan of yours either, Red."

Her face twisted and scrunched with rage, but, goddamn it, that look made me want to kiss her. "You know what? Go fuck yourself, Micah. I'm done with you."

Spinning around on the heels of her insanely sexy boots, she started to stomp off. It just so happened, she was heading in the same direction I was, toward Leo, Dani, and her whole crew.

Every few feet, she checked back over her shoulder, frowning when she saw I was still trailing behind her. I had to bite the inside of my cheek each time to keep from laughing. Finally, we reached the cluster of tables, and I noticed everyone was staring at us in slack-jawed shock.

Hayden whipped around, planting her hands on her rounded hips, and hit me with that attitude I kind of got off on. "Who's the stalker now, asshole? Stop following me."

"Uh . . . do you two know each other?"

At Eden's question, Hayden caught on to the attention we'd garnered and looked back to the table in confusion. "Wait. Do *you* guys know him?"

"They do," I answered for the group. "Seein' as I've lived here for years."

Roxanne spoke up then, her shrewd eyes gleaming, a knowing smile on her lips. "What I want to know is how you two know each other."

"An unfortunate run-in that I wish had never happened," Hayden spit, skewering me with a murderous glare.

"This is the best night ever." That little gem came from Leo, who was having way too much fun with this disastrous situation.

Hayden pretended not to hear him and kept me in her sights, flames shooting from her bright blue eyes. "Wow, all you have to do to ruin a person's night is show up, huh?"

"Oh damn," Sage said on a giggle. "This is great. You guys, I think we just found the first woman on the planet who doesn't go stupid at the sight of Micah Langford. She's like our very own unicorn!"

"I don't know about that, Red," I said in a murmur, leaning in so only she could hear. "Think if I got you back underneath me, I could get you to go stupid?"

"You know, I was having a really great night before you showed up. Why don't you do me a favor and go jump off a bridge or something."

"If you consider being hit on by a limp dick like Cormack a really great night, we need to reevaluate your standards, babe."

An adorable little growl worked its way from her throat. "I hate you."

"So you've said. Might want to come up with some new material. Your insults are getting a little stale."

All the women gathered at the tables started laughing hysterically. "Oh, man." Dani giggled several seconds later, wiping at the wet under her eyes. "This is the best thing ever."

"Forget all those other suggestions, ladies," Roxanne announced to the group. "Pretty sure we found the guy."

I wasn't sure what the hell that meant, but my gut was telling me shit was about to get really, *really* messy.

NINE
MICAH

My plan to find a woman to help take my mind off all the stress in my life had been blown to hell the instant I'd laid eyes on a certain redheaded devil the night before. No other woman at The Tap Room held a candle to Red. None of them stirred something inside me that made me desperate to touch and taste. Only her. *Goddamn woman.*

This morning, I'd woken up alone after crawling into bed the night before and jerking my dick to the memory of Hayden's smart mouth and flashing eyes until I came all over my stomach. I'd gotten up and gone for an extended run, pushing my normal five miles to eight in the hopes of working her out of my head and from beneath my skin.

None of that had worked, so now I was hauling my lawn-mower out of the garage.

"Yoohoo. Mornin', neighbor."

I looked across the small picket fence through wild shrubbery into my neighbor's yard. Sylvia was there in the garden like she was almost every morning, her yoga mat stretched out on the lush grass, bright teal leggings on beneath a long, flowy, multi-colored top. I'd lived next door to her for more than five years now, and she was, without a doubt, one of my favorite people in the world. For a woman in her eighties, she was constantly on the go and the life of whatever party she felt like attending. She spoke her mind and wasn't afraid to give you her two cents' worth. And more times than not, that came from a place of wisdom and experience. She'd lived each day of her long life to its fullest, and she had some incredible stories as proof.

Most people would probably be surprised, but one of my favorite things to do was chill with her in her crazy garden, sipping the Tom Collins she'd make me—even though I wasn't a fan of gin at all—and listen to her tell me about the more adventurous things she'd done.

Moving to the fence, I tilted my chin and greeted, "Hey there, gorgeous. How's your morning so far?"

"Well, I woke up, so I'd say it's off to a pretty good start. How about you?"

My morning so far had been shit, but I wasn't going to share that with her. She'd just dig into why, and it was bad enough I couldn't get Hayden out of my head, the last thing I needed to do was talk about her as well.

"Darlin', you'll outlive us all, and you know it."

She grinned and gave me a cheeky wink as she abandoned her mat and came closer to the fence line. "So, how have you been, dear? Haven't seen you home much these past few weeks. It's the case, isn't it?"

I hadn't gone into detail about the Callo investigation with Sylvia, or anyone else for that matter, but gossip spread in Hope Valley like a nasty stomach flu. Everyone in town knew Leo and I were working lead on that case.

"Had to pull some late nights and weekends, that's all. Things will get back to normal as soon as we wrap up this investigation."

Reaching over, she patted my cheek with her small hand. "And I have every confidence you and Leo are up to the task. But you better be takin' care of yourself in the meantime. Don't make me lecture you on the importance of self-care."

Pretty sure *self-care* was what some might call what I'd done to myself in bed last night, but I wasn't about to go there with an elderly woman, no matter how cool she was. "Don't worry, sweetheart. I'm bein' careful," I assured her. "Now, enough about me. Tell me about you. Saw a new car has been in the driveway the past several nights. That mean your niece finally arrived?"

Sylvia's face split into a huge smile that made the creases in her weathered skin carve even deeper. "That she did. Just over two weeks now. I tell you, it's so nice to have her and her little one here. They've breathed life back into this old place."

For months, all my neighbor had been able to talk about was her great-niece coming to live with her. I wasn't sure I'd ever seen the woman so happy, which was really saying something, because she lived in a perpetual state of bliss—that wasn't *totally* due to the special brownies she made on occasion—as far as I could tell.

I'd heard one story after another about her gorgeous, talented, fiery niece. She'd told me about her from childhood to adulthood. Most of the stories were sweet or funny, but I'd also gotten an earful of her niece's piece of shit ex and bitch of a best friend.

I knew Sylvia well enough to trust her judgment in most everything, especially people, and if she said her niece was good people, I had no doubt. And if she was anything like her great-aunt, I couldn't imagine how a man could ever step out on that, unless he was lower than scum.

Several weeks back, I'd helped Sylvia move from the big house to the small, converted carriage house near the back of the property, and since then, she'd gotten the idea in her head that her niece and I would be an incredible match, saying constantly that we'd hit it off in an instant. It was a notion I'd tried strongly to dissuade her of.

"How's she and her girl settling in?"

"Oh, just wonderfully," she answered, her face glowing with pride. "Making friends, getting the house in order, and my darlin' girl's taking to the shop like a seasoned pro, just like I knew she would." She stopped waxing poetic, and her happy expression fell into a frown. "Although, this weekend was that rat bastard's weekend with sweet little Ivy, so that hasn't been very easy. But my girl, she pulled through. She's one tough cookie." She arched a single brow knowingly, and added, "And *very* attractive."

"Sylvia," I said sternly, "not this again. Like I've told you a million times, I'm not the kind of man you want your niece tyin' herself to. Trust me."

Her expression was full of exasperation. "Micah Langford, as I've told *you* a million times, you don't give yourself nearly enough credit. You're a good man. I don't buy for a second that you're the Lothario you're known around town to be."

She'd seen the women coming in and out of my house

more than I'd care for her to, so she knew better than anyone that wasn't true. "Sweetheart—"

"If a man wasn't a good man, he wouldn't start caring for the little old lady's lawn next door without bein' asked. You did that. Woke up one day and you were just out here, cutting and edging like my yard was yours."

It was ridiculous to think Sylvia could handle maintaining a yard her size. The lots in our neighborhood were massive, the houses set far back from the street so the front *and* back-yards were huge. Sylvia was a deft hand at all things gardening, so I let her handle that, but I took care of the grass, keeping it cut to a manageable length at all times, as well as fertilizing in the fall and spring so it always stayed lush and green. Every month for the past three years now, Sylvia had won Yard of the Month, and every month she insisted I stand with her when they took the picture to include in the town's little newsletter.

"Well, who else is gonna do it? I wouldn't expect you to get out here with a push mower by yourself. You keep your-self healthy, but that shit's dangerous for you. And those punk-ass kids in the neighborhood charge a small fortune."

"Because you're a *good man*. You'll see. One of these days, you'll meet a woman who's gonna knock you on your behind, and you won't know what to do with yourself. Personally, I can't wait to see that happen."

At that, my mind wandered for a moment, and I saw Hayden's smile. I pictured how she'd looked back at that bar in Richmond when she'd laughed with abandon.

"Unless . . ." Sylvia dragged out, pulling me back into the present. Her eyes were narrowed in intrigue as she studied me closely. "You've already met her, haven't you?"

"What are you talking about? Of course not," I semi-lied.

"Goodness me," she cooed, placing her palms to her chest. "You have! I just saw it written all over your face. Can't say I'm not disappointed it wasn't my girl who got you there, but I *am* happy some lucky woman's finally caught your eye."

"All right. This conversation's over. You need to get back to your yoga, and I need to mow your lawn before the grass reaches to your knees."

"By all means," she said on a tinkling laugh, waving her hand as she moved backward toward her mat. "Mow away."

Shaking off the discomfort caused by the turn in that conversation, I moved back to my lawnmower, determined to put the conversation out of my head as I checked the gas level and cranked it up.

Then, pretending Sylvia wasn't watching me, laughing her ass off at the scowl etched into my face, I got to work.

———

Hayden

It felt like someone was drilling into my skull. My eyeballs were actually pulsating, and my mouth tasted like I'd eaten hot garbage.

"Oh God," I groaned as I gingerly rolled to my back, and slowly peeled my eyes open, one at a time.

Needless to say, the drinks had gotten a bit ahead of me last night. In comparison to everyone else, I hadn't had all that much, but it had been *years* since I really drank, so I was the very definition of a lightweight. Everything that came after getting into yet *another* fight with that arrogant bastard was fuzzy.

I remembered he stuck close to the group the whole time, hanging out with the man I'd discovered was Dani's fiancé, a man by the name of Leo Drake. A few other guys had shown up as the night progressed, boyfriends, husbands, and the like of my new group of girlfriends, but I didn't remember names or faces. The one thing I *did* remember with almost perfect clarity was feeling Micah's eyes on me the entire night. They seared into my skin like a brand and made my heart race.

"Get your shit together, Hayden," I cursed to myself, staring up at the ceiling. "He was a one-night stand, for God's sake. Was he amazing? Yeah, sure. But you'll find another guy who'll do those same things without making you want to commit murder."

I could tell myself that all day long, problem was, I wasn't completely sure it was true. There was actually something . . . I don't know, almost *fun* about how we fought.

"God, there's something wrong with me."

Pushing up to sitting, I brushed my hair back off my forehead and blew out a steady breath. Once I felt like I was no longer at risk of my head splitting open, I climbed out of bed and padded across the floor to the bathroom. Halfway there, the loud, teeth-clattering roar of a motor sliced through the peace and quiet—*and* my skull.

"What the living fuck?" I rushed to the big bay windows that faced the back of the house but couldn't see anything past the huge garden. Moving as quickly as my pounding head would let me, I stormed to the bathroom and pulled my satin robe off the hook behind the door.

I stabbed my arms through the sleeves and cinched the belt at my waist as I charged down the stairs and out the back door.

"Sylvia!" I yelled over the grinding noise as soon as I saw her, rising up from half-moon pose. That was a mistake. Hell, this whole scene was one huge mistake. I'd shot down there in an indignant rage, and now the evil sun was making my brain feel like an egg being scrambled.

"Oh dearie. Someone looks like their feelin' the effects of a good night this mornin'."

"Yes," I gritted, lifting my hand to shield my poor eyeballs from that bastard, daylight. "So can you please explain to me what the hell is going on?"

"Of course!" she smiled brightly, rubbing her sunny disposition in my hungover face. "My—well, now *our*—neighbor cuts my—our grass every once in a while. Isn't that just the sweetest? He really is quite the gentlemen. I'd been hoping to set the two of you up, but it seems he's already smitten with another woman." She stuck her bottom lip out in an exaggerated pout. "Such a shame, really."

"Oh my God," I groaned, closing my eyes and rubbing my temples. "This isn't happening. Look, any other morning, I'd be the first one out here to thank him for doing me a solid, but right now it feels like someone's using my head as a piñata. So please, *please*, can you just ask him, really politely, to knock it the fuck off?"

I'd been so busy trying to keep my brains from leaking out of my ears that I hadn't noticed the mower had cut off.

That was, until I heard a rich, sinful voice come from behind me. "Are you fuckin' kidding me? *You're* Sylvia's niece?"

I slowly turned and faced a sweaty, *shirtless* Micah, holding on to the handle of a lawnmower, looking too freaking good to be legal. It took a few seconds for my alcohol-soaked brain to catch up. "Wait . . . *you're* my neighbor?"

Those grassy green eyes did a full-body sweep, reminding me I was standing out in the back garden in nothing but a nightie and short satin robe—which had come untied. *Son of a bitch*! "Looks like," he answered, a sinful grin stretching across his lips.

In reaction to that news, I threw my head back and looked up at the sky, shouting, "What the hell have I ever done to you, huh?" at the top of my lungs.

Me and the man upstairs were about to have some serious words, because this shit was getting ridiculous!

Ten
Hayden

"Oh my." Aunt Sylvia looked far too pleased when I righted my head and pointed an unhappy frown in her direction. "Well, isn't this an interesting new development?"

I didn't see it that way, but *of course* she would.

"Sylvia," Micah said, his tone holding a hint of warning, but also humor, like he and my aunt were the best of friends. *And isn't that just freaking great?*

"What?" she asked innocently. "I didn't say anything. I certainly didn't say how pleased I am to find out the best sex my precious niece ever had just so happened to be with my strapping young neighbor."

"*Sylvia!*" I yelped.

"And I most certainly didn't say boo about the fact the woman that very same strapping neighbor is completely hung up on is my niece. Nope. Not me. Not a word. I'm just here, minding my own business."

"That's it!" I threw my arms up and spun around, my bare feet slapping on the cobblestones as I headed back for the house. "I'm drinking an entire pot of coffee and pretending this morning never happened. This has all been an alcohol-induced nightmare."

Slamming the door on my aunt's laughter, I moved straight to the coffee maker and hit the switch, glaring at it as it gurgled and began to spit out the much-needed liquid, like my anger might actually make it work faster.

I heard the creak of the back door opening, but didn't bother turning around as I stated, "Now's really not a good time, Sylvia. I think it's safe to say I'll be skipping yoga this morning."

"Gotta say, that's some nightie."

At *that*, I spun around so fast my poor, abused head wobbled like it was at risk of falling off my shoulders. "Did you seriously just walk in here without even knocking?" I asked as I slapped my robe closed and retied the belt.

"Look, Red, we need to talk."

He'd put his shirt back on before he followed me inside, but it was clinging to his sweaty skin, showing off those slabs of defined muscle I'd spent hours licking. *I want to lick them again*, the devil on my shoulder said on a dreamy sigh.

Pushing that thought to the back of my head, I crossed my arms over my chest protectively. "Pretty sure we don't, Micah."

His eyebrows lifted as he moved deeper into the kitchen, rounding the counter between us and resting his hips back against it. "So, what? We're just gonna live next door to each other and pretend the other person doesn't exist?"

"Sounds like a brilliant idea," I muttered. "How about you get the hell out and we start now?" I was acting like a brat. I knew it and I *hated* it, but there was something about this man that pushed every one of my buttons, turning me into a petulant little shit, and I couldn't seem to stop it.

Letting out a beleaguered sigh, Micah reached up and pinched the bridge of his nose before he started speaking again. "Us ignoring each other wouldn't make Sylvia happy, and I don't know about you, but I'm not a big fan of making her unhappy. For her sake, we at least need to pretend to get along. It's what she wants."

"Oh, is it?" I asked snidely. "So you think you know what my aunt wants more than I do? Why? Because living next door makes you an expert?"

I regretted the nasty words almost as soon as they spilled out of my mouth. This wasn't me. I wasn't a bitch, and I really hated that, whatever it was about him, it brought out this kind of behavior in me.

His vibrant green eyes flashed with something unpleasant as he uncrossed his arms and braced his hands on his trim hips. The wall of anger radiating from him slammed right into me, nearly stealing my breath as he pushed off the counter and took a step closer.

"*Exactly,*" he seethed with his brows drawn. Just like that, he'd gone from sexy—in a wildly irritating way—to intimidating, and if I'd been able to, I would have taken a step back. "Because *I'm* the one who's been cuttin' her grass, and carryin' her groceries in every goddamn weekend. *I'm* the one who sits out in her garden drinking Tom fuckin' Collins with her when I hate gin, but she likes it, so I suck back the foul-tasting shit every time she makes me one. *I'm* who has dinner with her twice a week just so I can keep my finger on her pulse and make sure she's doin' okay, in this big house all by herself. Meanwhile, you've lived less than an hour away, and I haven't seen your face *once* in the past five years. So yeah, I'd say I'm an expert on your aunt. Certainly more of one than you are, 'cause *I've* been here while you couldn't take the time outta your precious life to visit."

By the time he finished his little diatribe, my chest was rising and falling like I'd run a marathon at a full sprint, my sinuses were burning and my vision had grown blurry thanks to the dampness building up in my eyes. "You don't know what you're talking about," I whispered, feeling each word he'd said like a slap against my skin.

His chin jerked back in mock surprise. "I don't? I find that really fuckin' hard to believe, Red, since *I'm* the one who's spent the past five years listenin' to her go on and on about how incredible her niece is. You know, she's done nothing but sing your praise constantly since the moment she found out you were moving here, and I gotta tell you, the woman she described isn't the woman I see standing in front of me. All I see is a spoiled selfish brat who couldn't be bothered to spend time with her own flesh and blood until her world fell apart and she had nowhere else to turn."

After landing that well-placed blow, he turned and started for the back door, stopping once his hand landed on the knob to look back at me over his shoulder. "You know what? I think you're right. It's probably best we pretend the other person doesn't exist."

With that parting shot, he slammed the door behind him, leaving me standing there, feeling like I'd just been cut right open.

———

I'd spent the better part of the day stewing over my confrontation with Micah. During my first two cups of coffee and all through my shower, I'd been outraged that a man who didn't know me at all would accuse me of being such a selfish, inconsiderate person. It was halfway through my failed attempted at yoga, where I was trying to calm my swirling thoughts, that I realized I had no right being angry at anyone but myself.

Falling back onto my mat, surrounded by the stunning beauty of the garden my aunt had created, the truth hit me like a slap to the face as I stared up at the perfect blue sky. Micah was right. My stomach sank like a rock being dropped in the middle of an ocean.

Shoving up to my feet, I took the path, not back toward my new home—a home my aunt had so generously given to me—but to the apartment behind.

"Sylvia?" I called as I rapped my knuckles against the door. "Sylvia, you there?"

My aunt's figure appeared through the wavy glass set into the door. "Hayden, what on earth—?"

"I've been a selfish asshole," I blurted, pushing my way inside the adorable little apartment. It was decorated just as bright and crazy as the main house, every inch of it screaming my aunt's—and now my—name.

"What are you talking about, sweets?"

"Micah said something this morning, and at first it really pissed me off. But then I realized he was totally right. I'm a selfish asshole!"

"Come on, darlin'. Sit down and I'll make you a cup of tea." She guided me to a stool at the small kitchen island upholstered in a paisley fabric with tassels hanging all along the edges. "You'll have to explain what you're talking about, because I'm afraid I don't follow," she said as she filled a kettle with hot water and placed it on the stovetop, lighting the gas burner beneath it. "Are you tellin' me Micah called you a selfish asshole?"

"Yes—well, no. Not in those exact words. More like, he pointed out some ugly truths I'd been avoiding."

"And those would be?"

Letting out a sigh, I slumped my shoulders and looked down at my hand, pulling the sleeves of my tight-fitted yoga jacket down past my fingers. "I should've made a better effort to come see you the past several years," I admitted. "Or *any* effort, really. I let Alex dictate every aspect of my life, and that's not who I am. It's not who I ever was. And honestly, I'm kicking myself for not seeing it all as it was happening. I let him turn me into someone else entirely, and I did it at the expense of the *one* person who's always been there for me. You."

She placed two delicate china tea cups on the island, dropping a teabag into each one before looking back at me. "Oh, honey. I never felt that way."

"I know, but that doesn't make it any less true."

"Hayden, you don't—"

"Please, just let me get this out."

I waited for her to give me a nod before continuing. I leaned deeper into the island, placing my palms on the top of it. "I want you to know, I appreciate everything you've done for me. Every *single* thing. And not just recently, but my entire life. I've always known I could count on you, and I think a part of me took that for granted. But that's done."

She didn't say a word once I finished, and I found the silence we lapsed into pretty damn uncomfortable.

"Uh . . . are you gonna say anything, or just stand there looking at me?"

"Well, I wanted to make sure you were finished first."

"Oh, okay. Um . . . I'm finished."

"Good. Then it's my turn." The kettle began to whistle, cutting her off. She moved casually, extinguishing the flame and pouring the boiling water into both cups before returning the kettle to the stove. Once she finished, she came back to the island and scooted my cup in front of me, picking hers up and dunking the bag a few times before blowing on the steaming liquid inside. "Right, where was I? Oh, yes. Darlin' girl, you're being completely ridiculous."

I paused with my tea cup partway to my lips. "I—huh?"

She rolled her eyes and scoffed. "Hayden, you couldn't be selfish if you *tried*. You don't have a selfish bone in your body."

"But I—"

"Still talkin', lovely." I quickly clamped my mouth shut. "As I was saying, you aren't selfish. You think for one second I'd bend over backward to help you if I truly thought you were just takin' advantage?"

"Well . . . no. I guess not. But then—"

"You were flounderin'. You were stuck in this life that was pullin' you down, and you were fighting to stay afloat. And yes, while you were stuck in the midst of that, there were other aspects that got pushed to the wayside. That doesn't make you selfish. People do bad things sometimes, that doesn't mean they're bad people, and sometimes people do selfish things without actually being selfish, simply because they're tryin' to keep their heads above water. You see what I'm sayin'?"

"I-I think so."

"You were pre-occupied. I get that now, and I certainly got it then. Let the past stay where it belongs, Hayden. Enjoy the present."

Enjoy the present. I was pretty sure I could do that. Hopefully.

"Now, are you finished with this silliness? 'Cause there's a marathon of *Supernatural* on right now, and you know how I love those Winchester boys. You'll stay and watch it with me."

It wasn't a request so much as an order, but even if she'd asked, my answer would have been yes. Because I too loved those Winchester boys.

———

I moved down the front walk the moment I saw the Mercedes, meeting the car at the curb just as it came to a stop. Ignoring the woman up front, I kept my eyes on the back seat, smiling big and waving the moment Ivy came into view.

As soon as Alex put the car into park, she undid her seatbelt and smooshed her face against the window. "*Mommy!*"

I moved to her door and pulled it open, scooping her up and resting her weight on my hip. The moment her tiny arms closed around my neck I felt that tightness that had taken up residence in my chest the past couple of days start to loosen.

"Hey there, love bug!" I gave her a big squeeze, burying my nose in her mess of hair and breathing in her scent before pulling back to get a look at her face. "Did you have fun?"

"Uh huh! We watched movies and made a fort and ate ice cream and went shopping!"

I looked to Alex and arched a questioning brow.

"We got her some clothes and stuff to keep at our place so you don't have to pack her a bag every other weekend. Make things a bit easier, you know?"

"Well, thanks," I mumbled as I bent to put Ivy on the ground so I could take the unicorn backpack he was holding out to me. "Ivy, give your dad a hug goodbye," I ordered, keeping my tone gentle, even though all I wanted to do was grab her hand and drag her away from Alex and Krista and that part of her life.

Alex picked her back up, giving her a squeeze much like the one I'd just given her. "Love you, little monkey. See you soon, yeah?"

"Love you too, Daddy."

He put her down once she gave him a smacking kiss on the cheek, and looked to me. "Well . . . I guess I'll see you in a couple weeks."

"Yeah. Drive safely."

With that, I took Ivy's little hand and began leading her up the front walk toward the house, not bothering to turn and look back.

ELEVEN
MICAH

My phone sounded with an incoming text just as I pulled into the garage and shut my truck off. Grabbing it from the cupholder, I swiped my thumb across the screen, bringing it to life. My teeth clenched and a tick formed in my eyelid as I read and reread the message Charlie had just sent.

C: *Can't talk but am safe. Will call when I can. Call off your bloodhound.*

I'd been trying to reach her since Monday, worried my little showdown with Greg Cormack at The Tap Room had set him off in some way. He called off sick Monday and Tuesday, which set me on edge, and when he got to the station this morning, it was obvious he was in a foul mood.

My anxiety had spiked to an all-time high when I hadn't been able to get ahold of Charlie for the past two days. I'd called her burner, using our code, letting it ring once before hanging up, but when she didn't call back, I'd thrown protocol to the wind, and Leo and I both had started blowing up her phone. When we hit the twelve-hour mark, I'd officially lost my mind and called Linc, telling him to put Dalton on it.

It hadn't taken him long to track her down, and once we got word she was still breathing, his orders were to track her every goddamn move.

I started typing at a rapid clip.

M: *Not fucking happening. This is your fault for ghosting me for two goddamn days. You either let him tail you, or he's been instructed to pull your ass out. End of story.*

The bubbles popped up, telling me she was typing some-thing. It blinked on the screen for several seconds before her message came through, calling me, Leo, and Dalton every name in the book, spelling out her displeasure at the new turn in the operation with perfect clarity. But I noticed she hadn't said anything more about calling Dalton off, so I took that as a sign she was getting with the program and decided not to message her back. We *both* needed a chance to cool down.

If we didn't wrap up this case soon, I was going to die of a heart attack. As it was, I was sure my blood pressure was already through the roof.

I climbed out of my truck and rounded the back of it, about to hit the button to close the garage door when I heard a little voice call out, "Hi."

Looking toward the picket fence between my property and the one next door, I spotted a little girl with long, wild red hair holding on to two of the pickets as she squished her chubby little face in the opening between.

I'd seen her one other time, a few days ago when her dad had dropped her off. I'd spotted Hayden through my window as she'd rushed to the curb, giving a little hop as a shiny Mercedes that probably overcompensated for a small dick pulled up in front of the house. My first thought was that she was going to give me a coronary if she kept walking around in those little yoga outfits all day every day. If I thought her ass looked outstanding in jeans and leggings, it was nothing compared to how yoga clothes not only showed off but also flaunted her incredible body.

Those thoughts flew out the window the instant I watched her whip open the back door of the car and nearly catch a little girl with the exact same hair color midair. The air actually expelled from my lungs at the sight of Hayden then. It was the look of sheer joy on her face, the love radiating from her as she clutched the child tight. I felt like I was witnessing the woman slowly being pieced back together after days of having lived broken in two.

The prick who got out of the driver side and rounded the hood had to have been the ex, and I saw it then, clear as day, he was missing what he'd thrown away, no doubt about it. It was all but chiseled into his face, even as his new bitch sat in the front seat, scowling at Hayden and her girl.

I hated the jackass on sight.

Moving toward the fence, I got my first up-close look at the little girl, and if the hair hadn't made it obvious who she belonged to, the blue gemstone eyes certainly did. She looked like a mini-Hayden, and I thought she was cute as hell. Especially when I caught a glimpse of her outfit.

Her black long-sleeved tee had a skull and crossbones on the front made out of bright pink sequins. She wore a big, puffy tutu in the exact same pink, and beneath that were black leggings, and shiny combat boots that looked like they were covered in pink glitter. She looked part diva, part princess, part rocker, and all wild with her wavy red hair hanging free, all the way down her back.

"Hey there," I said once I was within a couple of feet.

"I'm Ivy," she said, her big bright eyes full of curiosity and happiness. "Who're you?"

Jesus, this kid. I wasn't sure I'd ever seen one so damn cute before. But still, she needed to be a whole hell of a lot more careful. "I'm Micah. Hasn't your mom talked to you about stayin' away from strangers? It's not safe to go around givin' your name to just anyone."

Her little head cocked to the side, and I noticed then that she had a bright pink flower tucked behind her ear. "But you're not a stranger," she said, her Rs coming out a bit thick, sounding more like Ws—again, cute. "Auntie Siva said you're our neighbor, and people should know their neighbors. So I said hi."

"Fair point. Well then, hi back. Speaking of your aunt . . ." I scanned the area nearby. "She out here keepin' an eye on you?"

"Yep," she chirped. "We're lovin' the garden. Auntie Siva says dat means I get to tear all the dead stuff outta the ground so all the new, pretty stuff can grow. See?" She held up her hands, showing me they were caked with dirt. Upon closer inspection, so was her tutu. So, she was a rocker/diva/princess/tomboy then. Odd combo, but she seemed to make it work. "You wanna help us love the garden?"

"No thanks, kid. I had a shit day. I'm gonna go inside and crash."

Her mouth dropped open comically wide, and she

sucked in a dramatic gasp. "You said *shit*," she stage whispered. "You owe me a dollar!"

My chin jerked back in shock at that. "I'm not givin' you a fuckin' dollar," I declared, the words tumbling out before I could pull them back. *Son of a bitch*. I wasn't used to being around kids, hell, I wasn't even *good* with kids, so I hadn't been prepared to keep my language in check.

Her chest puffed and her whole body swayed backward on another gasp. "Dat's *five* dollars! 'Cause Mommy says dat's a *really* bad word."

Sylvia joined us at the fence line. "Evenin', Micah. Glad to see you made it home before the moon came up tonight."

"Auntie Siva! Mike said *alllllll* the bad words!"

Sylvia arched a single brow. "Did he now?"

"It's Mic*ah*, not Mike," I corrected.

"Dat's what I said."

Deciding it was best to give up on that particular argument, I looked to Sylvia and saw a look of reproach on her face. "Give me a break," I grunted. "I'm not used to kids. I fu —I messed up."

"He owes me six dollars!" the adorable little snitch exclaimed, looking up at her aunt and hopping in place with excitement. "I'm gonna buy ice cream!"

Well shit. She was just so damn enthusiastic about the idea of having six bucks, I couldn't bring myself to tell her no. Pulling my wallet from the back pocket of my jeans, I flipped it open and fished out six ones, handing it over to the little extortionist.

She actually fanned the bills out and counted, making sure they were all there before tucking them into the waistband of her tutu with a resounding nod.

Had to appreciate the kid's smarts. She played me with her super cuteness before showing her ruthless side and going in for the kill.

"All right, well I'm gonna go before this little monster cleans me out."

"Mike, wait!"

I looked down at the kid who looked so much like her mom, thinking, *Christ, the men in this town are so fucked when she gets older.* "Yeah, Monster?"

"Wanna have dinner with us? Mommy's makin' man-a .. . somethin'—"

"Manicotti, sweets," Sylvia assisted.

"Yeah, dat! And it's super good! You wanna come over? Please, please, *please*?"

Something told me she wasn't used to hearing the word no, especially from men, and I wasn't a big fan of being the one to burst that bubble. If the circumstances were different, I'd have told her yes in a heartbeat. But I had a feeling her mom wouldn't be thrilled with me just walking in and sitting down at the dinner table.

"Sorry, kid. Maybe some other time."

Her whole face fell like I'd just told her Christmas was canceled this year because Santa had gotten into a sleigh crash, Rudolph had died on the scene, and two of the other reindeer were in critical condition.

"Oh," she whispered, looking down at the ground as she stuffed the toe of her glittery combat boot into the grass. "Okay."

Shit. I hadn't technically done anything wrong, but I still felt like the world's biggest jerk. I needed to get the hell out of there fast before I gave her the rest of the cash in my wallet just to bring the smile back to her face.

"You ladies have a good evenin', yeah?" I told her and Sylvia. "And enjoy that manicotti."

I jerked my chin up to Sylvia before quickly turning and hustling toward my house like a goddamn coward.

———

Hayden

The back door opened as I was filling the manicotti shells with my special cheese mixture. "Hey, guys. Dinner'll be ready in a little less than an hour. I just need to . . ." My sentence trailed off when I saw the dejected expression on my daughter's face. "What's the matter, love bug?" She'd been out in the garden with Sylvia, pulling weeds and pruning the plants, so I couldn't imagine what could have happened to put that look on her face.

She hung her head, her sadness filling the air all around her little body. "My new friend Mike won't have dinner with us."

I looked to Sylvia in confusion. "Mike?"

"Micah," she clarified. "Our little princess spotted him when he got home from work and took an interest."

"He gave me six dollars for the swear jar."

"Wait . . ." I shook my head. "He gave you money? For swearing?"

"Yu-huh. He said a bad word, then a *really* bad word. So I told him he gots to gimme six dollars, and he did."

I put down a partially filled manicotti and wiped my hands on the dishtowel I'd hung over my shoulder. "Honey, that swear jar is something for you and me. You don't tell just anyone they owe you money for saying bad words."

I caught Sylvia curling her lips between her teeth to keep from laughing out loud.

"But—but he gave it to me."

I gave her a mom look and held my hand out. She heaved out a huge sigh and rolled her eyes so far back in her head she could probably see her spine before pulling the cash out of her tutu and handing it over.

"Thank you. Now, what was this about dinner?"

"I asked him to come. I told him your man-i-stuff was super yummy, but he said he would some other time," she moped. "I wanted him to eat with us."

Ah hell.

"Well, honey, maybe he's just tired. You know, he has a really important, stressful job." Or maybe he didn't want anything to do with me because he thought I was a bitch. Mainly because I'd been acting like one since that first run-in at the supermarket. With Alex, I might have thrown attitude once in a blue moon, but something about Micah had me on the offensive before a word was even spoken. I lashed out because I wasn't prepared to feel what I felt every time I saw him. The intensity of it scared the living hell out of me, especially since my marriage had been blown to shreds only months prior.

Still, I'd spent the past few days feeling fifty kinds of terrible for how our last encounter had ended. I'd told myself time and again that I was going to go over there and make it right, but each day I'd chicken out.

"Or maybe he doesn't wanna be my friend."

"Or maybe he needs an invite from someone else," Sylvia added, giving me a look of rebuke. That damn brow was arched again, managing to make her look dignified and judgy at the same time.

I paused, nerves rolling around in my belly like a pinball being smacked to hell by those damn paddles. "Oh, well, uh . . ."

Ivy began jumping in place. "Would you, Mommy? Please, please, *pretty please*?"

I wasn't going to win this time, that was for freaking sure, so instead of dragging this out, I relented on a weary sigh. "Fine. I'll go over and talk to him—but don't hold your breath," I added when my girl started to squeal excitedly. I didn't want her getting her hopes up. "But you guys have to finish stuffing these shells."

"Okay, Mommy! We can do dat!"

"And don't touch my sauce." I pointed right at Sylvia since she was a repeat offender when it came to stuff like this. "I have it exactly where I want it, and I don't need you going behind me and messing it all up. Got it?"

She held up her hands in surrender. "I won't touch your precious sauce. Although, I don't think a few bay leaves would hurt anything."

Yuck!

"Don't. Add. *Anything*," I stressed. There wasn't much about Sylvia that wasn't damn near perfect, but her penchant for putting bay leaves in almost everything definitely was one of her downfalls. Those things smelled and tasted *awful*. And so help me God, if she put them in my perfect sauce, I was going to lose it.

"All right. All right. Will you just go already? Then you can come back and watch your own damn sauce." She grumbled that last bit under her breath, purposely loud enough for me to hear.

With nothing else holding me in place, I let out a huff and started out of the kitchen toward the front door.

TWELVE
HAYDEN

As I walked up Micah's drive, I noticed that his ranch style home was completely different than my bungalow. Our neighborhood was much older and more established, meaning it wasn't full of cookie-cutter houses that all looked exactly the same. That was one of the many things I loved about this place.

Back in Richmond, Alex had moved us into a big house in a fancy gated neighborhood where every other house was identical, and every yard had the exact same stumpy, undeveloped trees. There was no originality and absolutely *no* personality.

I pulled in a deep, bolstering breath and knocked on the front door, trying not to fidget as I waited, hoping he would answer.

Micah's hair was damp from a recent shower when he came to the door, and the woodsy, spicy scent of his aftershave slammed into me, making heat pool in my belly. "Hayden?" he questioned when all I did was stand there staring like an idiot. "What's goin' on?"

"Oh, um . . ." I had to shake my head to get my thoughts back in order. "Sorry, I just . . ." I noticed then that the money he'd given Ivy earlier was still in my hand, so I thrust my arm out. "I believe this is yours." He looked at the crumpled bills in confusion. "It's the money you gave Ivy. I wanted to return it to you."

He looked back to me, his strong, dark brows lifting. "But that was for the swear jar thing."

I couldn't stop the smile pulling at my lips. "Yeah, but the swear jar is only for her and me. She knows that."

He still hadn't taken the money. "It's cool. She can keep it. It's only a few bucks, anyway."

"No, you don't understand," I insisted. "If you don't take this back, she'll know she's got you, and I swear, Micah, she'll fleece you for everything you've got if you aren't more careful."

That comment earned me a smirk, the effects of which felt like riding on a rollercoaster. "Yeah, I can see that. Your girl's pretty used to getting her way, isn't she?"

"Most of the time," I answered honestly, shrugging a shoulder. "But mainly only with men."

He let out a chuckle and finally reached to take the cash. "Fine, I'll keep this, as long as you tell her I only took it under duress."

"You got it."

He watched me for a beat, as if waiting for me to say something else. I struggled to get the words from my throat for several seconds before he gave up, taking a step back. "Okay, well, thanks. I guess I'll see you around."

"Wait!" I cried, slapping my hand on the solid wood door as he began to close it on me. "Micah, I—"

"You what?" he pressed when I didn't finish my sentence.

"Okay, look. I know things between us have been . . ."

"A shit show?" I curled my lips between my teeth to hide my grin while nodding. "Yeah. That's one way to put it. Anyway, I've been meaning to talk to you." I stuffed my hands into the pockets of my jeans and began fidgeting in place. "I wanted to apologize for how I've been acting around you. Despite what you may think, that's not me. I'm really not a mean person, I promise. Even though I've been acting like one lately."

He crossed his arms over his chest and rested a shoulder against the door jamb, like he was settling in. He was getting a kick out of watching me squirm, not that I could blame him. If the shoe was on the other foot, I had no doubt I'd be doing the exact same thing.

"So . . . I'm sorry. That's what I wanted to say."

"That it?"

"Yep—oh, actually, no," I blurted, suddenly remembering the real reason I was there. "I also wanted to invite you over for dinner. Ivy told me she asked you, but you turned her down. And, well if you'd like to come, the invitation's still open."

His lips curved, revealing those pearly white teeth. "That so?"

His grin was infectious. "Yes, that's so." I started walking backward, adding, "It'll be done in about forty-five minutes. And I know a particular little redhead, about this tall"—I held my hand out at my hip—"who'd be really happy if you showed."

"Yeah? She the only redhead who'd be happy if I

showed?" he called back as I turned and started back toward my house.

"Baby steps, Micah," I returned. "Baby steps."

He let out a booming laugh as I crossed back into my yard and scurried up the front walk. I was smiling wide as I stepped into the house and closed the door behind me, hoping more than I cared to admit that he'd show up.

———

Micah

The door flew open before I finished knocking.

"You came!" I was rocked back a step when the full force of a little four-year-old plowed into my legs, locking them in a vise grip. My arms shot out at my sides as I fought to keep my balance, looking down into a pair of big, sapphire doe eyes. "Mommy said she didn't know, but I told her you'd come, 'cause we're best friends!" she declared.

"We are?"

She released my legs and took a step back. "Yu-huh! You're my best friend, Mike, who gave me six bucks!" I gave up trying to get her to say my name correctly, accepting that I would probably forever be known to her as Mike. All of a sudden, her smile drooped. Her bottom lip poked out, and her chin began to quiver. "But Mommy took my money away." Her big blue eyes grew even brighter as tears welled up in them.

Oh shit. Oh fuck. No, no, no, no. "What's happening right

now?" I asked, panic starting to clench my chest. "What are you doing? Stop it."

She sniffled. "N-now I c-can't get ice cream."

"Oh God. No. Please don't. Look." I quickly pulled my wallet from my back pocket. "I'll give you the money back, okay? I'll give you all of it. Just . . . stop whatever you're about to do."

Hayden suddenly appeared out of nowhere, grabbing hold of my wrist to stop me before I could throw all the cash I had—a hundred and twenty dollars—at her kid. "Ivy," she clipped in a scolding tone. Almost immediately, the chin quivering stopped and the tears dried up. "What have I told you about that face?"

The little monster let out a huffed breath. "Not on easy targets."

"That's right. Now go help your aunt set the table." The girl literally skipped off with a wicked smile on her face.

I turned to look at Hayden, slow blinking as I muttered, "She just played me, didn't she?"

"With hardly any effort." She shook her head in mock disappointment while bracing her hands on her hips. "Really, Micah, I'd have expected better from you. I *told* you she'd clean you out if you weren't careful. You gave in within thirty seconds of that door being open. That's a new record, even for her."

"Wait a minute." I lifted my hand, finally registering what she'd said. "Easy target?"

Her response was to shrug her shoulders on a sweet, melodic giggle. "If the shoe fits."

I couldn't argue that. "But . . ." I looked back into the

house. "*That face*. Christ, it was the worst thing I've ever seen. I'd have signed over the title to my truck if she'd asked."

"Yeah," Hayden said on a weary sigh. "She's gotten way too good at it."

My head whipped back to her, my tone almost accusing as I asked, "How the hell are you not affected by that face? Is your heart made of stone or something?"

She brushed me off like it was nothing and started into the house, waving for me to follow. "Oh, please. Where do you think she learned it? That face has been passed down for generations," she said as I followed her toward the kitchen. The house was still as bright and insanely decorated as it had been when Sylvia lived in it, but I noticed Hayden had made some additions. There were new framed photos everywhere, almost all of them containing Ivy, either by herself or with Hayden and/or Sylvia.

"Fuck," I hissed under my breath. "I just stepped into the lion's den, didn't I?"

She turned and threw a beaming smile over her shoulder that hit me straight in the chest before traveling south— along with all the blood in my body—to my dick. Christ, she had an incredible smile.

"Just watch where you step," she teased with a wink.

"Ah, there he is," Sylvia crooned as soon as Hayden and I entered the kitchen. She moved from the stove, coming around the counter to place her hands on my shoulders, her way of communicating silently that she wanted me to bend so she could give my cheek a kiss, which I did. "Heard you got hit with *The Look*. You managed to survive the first time, which is more than I can say for some men."

"Let me guess. You're the one who taught Hayden, who taught that little devil child."

Ivy grinned happily, completely unfazed at being called a devil.

"It wasn't so much taught as it was passed down through the genes. You can't blame me for genetics."

"I'll find a way," I grumbled in mock seriousness.

Then I noticed the delicious smells filling the air around me. My stomach let out a loud growl, reminding me I hadn't put anything in it since the donut I'd gotten at Muffin Top that morning. If dinner tasted anywhere near as good as it smelled, I couldn't wait.

"Mike. Come sit here." Ivy patted the cushioned stool next to hers at that bar. "You can draw with me till supper's done."

"I don't know, kid. I'm not very good at drawing."

"Dat's okay. Just try your best. Dat's what Mommy always says." She patted the seat again, giving me no choice but to join her. As soon as I sat, she shoved a piece of yellow construction paper in front of me and slid a box of crayons between us.

I looked across the counter to where Hayden was standing at the stove, her lips curled between her teeth in a failed attempt to hide her smile as she watched us. When she caught me staring, she uncurled them and grinned, mouthing *sorry*.

"Let me get you a drink, Micah," Sylvia decreed, shuffling toward the drink shaker she always made her Tom Collins in. "I'll have you set up in no time."

Before I had a chance to fight back a wince at the thought of having to drink that disgusting cocktail, Hayden spoke up.

"Actually, I was gonna offer Micah a beer," she said quickly. "I bought a six pack the other day, and I ended up not liking it. It'll go to waste unless he drinks it for me."

"All right, dearie. More gin for you and me, then." Undeterred, Sylvia whipped up a new batch while her niece moved to the bright, lemon-yellow fridge and pulled out a beer. She popped the top as she headed toward me and slid the bottle across the bar.

"Thanks," I murmured under my breath, picking it up and taking a big gulp.

"No problem," she returned, just as quietly. "I remembered what you said the other day, and I know you'd drink it just to make her happy, but I figured this would be a safer bet."

I was quickly coming to realize she hadn't been lying when she said she wasn't normally a mean person. Sitting in her kitchen with her aunt and daughter, I was seeing the side of Hayden I'd seen that night in the bar, the side I'd thought was just a fluke. I'd only had brief glimpses of it then, but it had been more than enough to make me want to fuck her. And I'd be damned if seeing this lighter side of her now wasn't making me want the same damn thing.

"Appreciate it, Red."

I caught a peek at the pink that was blooming across her cheekbones just as she turned her back on me, and I knew then how completely fucked I was.

Because there wasn't anything I wouldn't do to have this woman under me again.

THIRTEEN
HAYDEN

Dinner turned out to be surprisingly fun. Between Ivy filling any silence with her usual chatter and Sylvia sharing stories of me as a girl and stories of Micah in the time she'd lived beside him—most of the stories embarrassing as hell—there hadn't been a single lull in the conversation. I laughed almost as much as I had the night Micah and I first met.

I managed to find out more about Micah as we ate. I learned he'd been with the Hope Valley Police Department since the start of his career as a police officer over thirteen years ago. I learned his drive to become law enforcement came from his father, who was a cop in Richmond, but he preferred the slower pace of a smaller town and had left the city specifically for this job.

The better I got to know him, the more I liked him. He was funny and down-to-earth, and he didn't seem to mind that my baby girl had latched onto him like a suction cup. But that was part of the problem. It wasn't *just* about wanting to strip him naked and climb him like a jungle gym.

That attraction I'd felt the very first night, the one that hadn't faded even while we were fighting, was there in spades, only now it was more intense, because I was getting glimpses of the real man beneath the surface. He loved his job, he cared about the people in this town, and he was loyal to his friends and family. That was a side of him I'd never seen before, and damn if it didn't make him even *more* attractive.

When dinner wrapped up, he offered to help clean, but I quickly shooed him out of the kitchen to join Sylvia and Ivy in the garden while I took care of everything.

Truth was, I needed a few minutes to myself to get my head straight. I was discombobulated and off balance. As I washed the dishes by hand, scrubbing the hell out of the baked-on cheese in the casserole dish, I practiced my yoga breathing, hoping to find my center, as Sylvia would say.

I'd almost gotten myself there when a hand came down on my shoulder, scaring a yelp from me and making me jump around, slinging sudsy water all over the place. "Holy shit," I exclaimed, placing a wet hand over my heart to keep it from beating out of my chest. "You scared the hell out of me."

"Sorry about that," Micah said, holding his hands up in surrender. "I thought you heard me." One corner of his mouth curled up in a smirk. "So how much do you owe the swear jar?"

"Real funny," I deadpanned, turning back to the casserole dish. "Do you need something?"

"Nope. I was just wonderin' what was taking so long. Then I saw you scrubbin' that dish like you were trying to get a genie to pop out of it or something. Didn't even hear me call your name."

"Oh. Uh . . . yeah. Um, baked-on cheese is a real bitch. If

you don't get it all off the pan right away, you might as well buy a new one."

"Well, I think it's safe to say you got it all."

I looked down at the dish that was now so clean it was practically sparkling beneath the soapy water. "Oh."

"You good, Red?"

Was I? He wasn't standing close, but I was still able to smell his intoxicating scent, and that was enough to make my body react. Goosebumps had broken out across my skin, my pulse was thrumming, and my breasts felt heavy, my nipples tightening to stiff peaks beneath my bra.

"Mmmhmm," I hummed, keeping my eyes on the sink as I pulled the plug and turned on the water to rinse the stupid dish. "Just finishing up here. I'll be right out. You need another beer? I'll bring one out for you in—"

The rest of the sentence got stuck in my throat when Micah's chest pressed into my back and his arm came around my front, taking the dish from my hands and dropping it back into the sink before shutting off the water.

I spun around in surprise and had to lean way back in order to look up at him. I'd forgotten just how big he was. Big enough to make me feel small and protected. *Damn it, Hayden! Get your head in the game.* "What are you—?"

"What's the deal, Red?"

"What are you talking about?"

"You come over to my place and apologize, invite me to dinner, then act like I'm a walking case of typhoid. What was all that stuff about earlier? Was it just bullshit?"

"No! Of course not!" He was standing so close. *Too* close. "Could you maybe take a step back?"

He moved, but only to brace his palms on the edge of the sink beside my hips. "Then what's with the avoidance?"

His gorgeous face and clear green eyes were all I could see. His musky, manly smell invaded my senses. "I'm not avoiding you, I swear."

"Bullshit."

"Micah, please." My chest was beginning to heave. "Please just step back."

"Not a chance. Not until you tell me what the fuck is goin' on with you."

I tried to keep my eyes from straying, but they drifted down to his mouth and those perfect, plump lips of their own accord. Just staring at them made the skin on the back of my neck prickle. My tongue peeked out to swipe over my bottom lip before I pulled it between my teeth and bit down.

A deep rumble worked its way from Micah's chest, giving me a start, and when my gaze flew back up to his, I knew I was busted.

"Ah. I see what the issue is."

"Micah," I said on a breathy whisper. "Move back." A gasp was ripped from my throat when he closed the last remaining inches between us, pressing his body against mine from hip to chest, the unmistakable impression of his steely erection prodding into my belly. My body jolted at the feel of it, an electric shock zipping its way through my limbs and coming to a stop at my core.

"You still want me," he murmured, the green in his eyes darkening as his pupils expanded. "That's it, isn't it? You want me, and it's freaking you out."

"No, I-I don't—That's not . . ." I let out a tiny growl of

frustration. "Please move. I can't think when you're this close."

Instead of giving me space, he lowered his head, dragging the tip of his nose along the column of my neck until my whole body shivered against his. "What if I told you I still want you?"

Ah hell. There was only so much strength one woman was expected to possess. "We can't do this," I insisted, but the fight sounded weak, even to my own ears. "It's not smart."

Screw smart! That little devil shouted. *Think of all the orgasms!*

He made his way up, trailing his nose along my jawline and cheekbone before bringing his lips to mine, hovering millimeters away so they gently brushed against mine as he asked, "What would you do if I kissed you right now?" He knew what he was doing. He knew how to tease so damn well I felt like I was about to come apart. "Would you push me away or kiss me back?"

"I—" didn't have a freaking clue. "This is too messy, Micah. We're neighbors."

"And apparently, I'm your kid's new best friend," he said, humor laced through his words. "But I don't give a shit. You're still the best I've ever fuckin' had, and I'm dying for more."

"B-But . . . we hate each other."

"If I recall, those words never came outta my mouth, Red."

He was right. "Well, no, b-but . . . I hate you." I was so turned on, I couldn't even make that lie sound believable.

His chest shook on a low, raspy chuckle. He knew as well as I did, that I was completely full of shit. "You can hate me all you want, Hayden. Just as long as you come undone for me again and again, the way you did in that hotel room."

My panties were soaked, my nipples throbbed, and my pussy pulsated, wanting him almost to the point of desperation. I was about to close the last remaining bit of space between us, sealing his lips with mine, when my daughter's voice carried in from outside. "Mommy! Can I have a popsicle?"

Micah and I flew apart like our bodies had given each other an electric shock. The spell was shattered, the air around us, humid and thick with lust only a second ago, now felt chilled.

"Uh, yeah, love bug," I shouted back so she could hear me through the closed back door. "Be right out." Moving as far away from Micah as possible, I opened the freezer and pulled out a popsicle, hovering in the open door for a few seconds to let the cold slap against my cheeks and cool the heat that had built inside me.

When I had no choice but to turn around, Micah was right where I'd left him, watching me like a hawk might watch its prey. "What just happened here, or almost happened, or . . ." I shook my head to piece my thoughts together. "Whatever *that* was. It can't happen again. Not when we're living right next door to each other. It isn't smart."

He moved in, taking the popsicle from my hand and bending low so his face was all I could see. "You might be right, Red. But smart or not, we're inevitable, so you may as well wrap your head around that now."

With that, he turned on his boot and headed out the

back door, taking my daughter her popsicle while I tried to get my knees to work.

———

Micah

Lying on my back, legs spread, one knee bent, my hips lifted off the mattress as my grip tightened around my aching cock. My hand moved faster up and down the shaft as images of Hayden flashed across my eyelids like a slide show. Images of her smiling, of her full, pouty bottom lip glistening from where she'd just licked it. The way her eyes glazed over as she stared at my mouth.

Pre-cum leaked from the tip, making my hand slicker as I jacked myself harder, twisting my wrist each time I reached the swollen, purple crown. I was so close, but I didn't want to blow just yet. I wanted to make this last as long as possible.

The pictures of Hayden shifted, going back to that night. I let out a grunt as I remembered how tight her pussy had squeezed me. When I recalled the little mewling sounds of desperation she made as she clamped down tighter around me, my eyes rolled back in my skull.

I hadn't been lying when I told her she was the best I'd ever had, and weeks upon weeks of coming from my own hand to the memory of *one . . . fucking . . . night* were proof of that.

I pictured her mouth as her lips formed around my name, the way her eyes widened for just a second before falling to half-mast every time an orgasm washed over her. I imagined I could feel her nails digging into my skin and raking down my back.

And that was as long as I could hold off. On a groan, I went off, shooting all over my hand and stomach. I came until I was out of breath, until stars danced in front of my vision. Each time I thought I was finished, my dick would twitch and leak more cum until my balls were completely drained from nothing more than a goddamn memory.

That was how good she'd been. And *that* was why I'd laid it out for her earlier. I hadn't been bluffing when I told her we were inevitable. If I had to handcuff her to my bed to keep her from running, I *would* have her again. And again. And a-fucking-*gain*.

A minute later, still feeling breathless, I got up and shuffled into the bathroom to clean myself up. Once I finished, I pulled my underwear back on and fell into bed.

After the exhausting day I'd had, coupled with a good meal and a release that nearly made my head explode, it didn't take me long to find sleep. And for the first time in what felt like an eternity, when I crashed that night, I did it hard and uninterrupted.

FOURTEEN
HAYDEN

"That's right, dearie. You're a natural, just like your mommy and me."

I blinked my dry eyes and turned from the computer screen to where Sylvia was helping Ivy make her very own fairy garden in a big glass bowl to keep in her room. Some days I liked to take her with me to the shop instead of sending her to daycare because I wanted my little girl to have as many memories with Sylvia as possible. I wanted her to cherish them just like I cherished the ones I'd made with that spectacular woman.

As much as I wanted to believe my aunt was going to live forever, I realized our time with her was limited and getting shorter every year.

Watching them together, seeing the joy on my baby girl's face and knowing it was my aunt who'd put it there, made warmth bloom in my chest. All I could do was hope and pray for many more days and months and years just like this.

That's why I was doing the mind-numbing administrative work at the computer in the front of the shop instead of the one at the cozy desk in the back office. I preferred to be up here, especially on the days I could watch my two favorite people interact.

"Hey, so what do you think?" At Sonya's voice, I turned from my family to the floral arrangement our assistant set on the wide counter in front of me.

Two other employees worked at Divine Flora. Raul, a young twenty-something who didn't care much for flowers and plants, but needed a job. He dug my aunt, so she'd hired him to do the heavy lifting—literally—and deliveries. And Sonya, a fresh-out-of-school eighteen-year-old who was trying to discover what she wanted to do with her life, so she was taking a year to do her own thing before college. She mainly helped keep the shop clean and handled the transactions, but she was also learning from Sylvia—and now, me.

"Does it look okay?" Sonya chewed nervously on her thumbnail as I grabbed the fat, squat vase and slowly turned it so I could see all sides. "I remembered to snip the stems and pull the wilted petals off. And I added just a bit of Sprite to the water like you suggested."

"It looks beautiful, honey. You did a fantastic job."

Her face lit up. "You really think so?"

"Absolutely. In fact, if you're willing, I think we could sell it."

"Totally! That'd be so cool!"

I smiled at the girl's enthusiasm. "Mark it up and add it to the display case. I bet we'll have it sold in no time."

She skipped off excitedly, and I turned back to the computer, catching Sylvia's wink before focusing once more on the dull spreadsheets. I lasted all of thirty seconds before my vision grew fuzzy and mind drifted to Micah . . . again. It had been doing that since last night, making it harder than usual to fall asleep. To make matters worse, when I woke up this morning, I was all kinds of tense and antsy. I hadn't been this sexually frustrated during what I'd *thought* was a dry spell with Alex. Which had to be telling.

I was pulled from my daydreaming when the bell over the door jingled. I sat up straight and smiled big when Sage and Dani came waltzing through. "Hey, guys. This is a nice surprise. How's it going?"

"It's good," Dani said brightly. "We're on our lunch hour and thought we'd stop in to say hi."

"Well, I'm glad you did."

Ivy came skipping over, stopping beside Sage and tugging on the hem of her shirt. "I like your boots."

Sage was wearing kickass biker boots with a pair of black leggings and a long, loose-weave gray sweater that fell to her hips and had a wide, droopy neckline, showing a metallic camisole underneath. Her whole look screamed *biker babe in the fall*, so it wasn't the least bit surprising my girl had taken a liking to it.

As it was, my girl looked like a mini-biker chick in flashy colors. Her leggings were covered in pink and silver sugar skulls that matched her shimmery silver sweater and glittery silver Dr. Martins.

"Oh my God," Sage said on a squeal. "Aren't you just the most adorable thing *ever*?" In reaction, my girl beamed big and let out an enthusiastic giggle.

"Is this your little girl?" Dani asked.

She and Sage both looked like they were about to melt from cuteness overload, when my daughter said with that adorable little toddler lisp, "Hi. I'm Ivy. Are you friends with Mommy?"

"That they are, love bug. This is Ms. Dani and Ms. Sage."

Sage crouched down in front of Ivy and held out her hand to shake. "I like your boots too, munchkin. I think I need to get me a pair just like them."

"We can be matchy buddies!" Ivy declared excitedly.

"She's so cute," Sage squeaked, looking up at me. "I want her to be my bestest friend ever."

"I can't be your best friend 'cause I already told Mike I'd be his best friend, and he'd be really sad. But we can be second best friends."

Dani looked at me with a teasing smile. "Ooh, who's Mike?"

"He lives next door," Ivy informed them. "He had supper with us last night and almost kissed Mommy at the sink."

My head shot down, my eyes nearly bugging out. "*What*?"

Sylvia joined us then, grinning like she knew a secret. "Next time you feel like neckin' with the neighbor, maybe don't do it standin' in front of a window."

Shit! Shit, shit, fuck!

"Wait." Sage's eyes bounced all over the place. "Who's Mike?"

Dani didn't say anything, and when I looked at her she was watching me so intently I began to squirm. "What?"

Her brow's lifted high onto her forehead, nearly kissing her hairline as a smile tugged at her lips. "Doesn't Micah live next door to you?"

"I—" *Merciful hell.*

Sage stood to her full height, her smile matching that of Dani's as she crossed her arms over her chest. "I'm *so glad* we decided to stop in here today," she proclaimed.

"Look, it isn't what you guys think. It's not like that. We just . . . well, we came to an understanding yesterday, that's it."

"An understanding that required his mouth on yours?" Sage asked.

"We didn't *technically* kiss," I insisted. "I wasn't going to let it go there."

"Sure as heck looked like you were to me," Sylvia added unhelpfully. "In fact, it looked like *you* were the one about to take it over the finish line."

Ivy's gaze bounced around the group like she was watching a tennis match. "Mommy, was you and Mike gonna race?"

"Nah. From what I hear, Micah's the type to let the woman finish first," Sage teased.

Dani and Sylvia both started cracking up while I threw my hands up in exasperation. "Okay, this conversation's over. Nothing's happening between Micah and me, and that's how it's going to stay. End of story. Now, if you'll excuse me, I have work to do." I lifted my chin haughtily and turned back to the spreadsheets I had no interest in.

"All right, we'll cut you some slack," Sage said, then added cheekily, "for now."

The bell over the door rang, alerting me to a new customer. It took a second for my brain to register where I knew the man, but once recognition clicked into place, my stomach sank.

"Greg, hi," I greeted, pinning a smile on my face. The air

in the shop suddenly changed, growing heavy and charged. My eyes did a quick sweep, and I noticed the shift was coming from Dani. I didn't know what was going on, but she suddenly looked tense and on alert.

"Hey, beautiful." He gave me a wink before scanning the group. Tilting his head he offered a somewhat distracted, "Ladies," before leaning his elbows on the counter and focusing solely on me. "You having a good day so far?"

I'd totally forgotten about meeting Greg that night at The Tap Room and inviting him to come see me at the shop. In my defense, I'd been pretty buzzed that night. But the only reason I'd led him to believe I was interested in talking to him again was because Micah had pissed me off, and I wanted to get back at him. Not my finest hour.

It didn't sit well with me that he'd all but disregarded the other women around us, but I did my best to remain cordial. "I've got no complaints so far." Ivy rounded the counter just then, squeezing up beside me and wrapping her little arms tight around my thigh. "Greg, this is my daughter, Ivy." I looked down at my girl and brushed my fingers through her hair. "Can you say hi, honey?"

Instead of being her usual loud, personable self, she gripped my leg tighter, like she was trying to fuse herself to me as she mumbled, "Hello."

"Well, hey there, Ivy. My, aren't you a pretty girl? You look just like your momma," he said, looking up to shoot me another wink. "It's real nice to meet you."

She turned her face away, burrowing into my skin. The sudden shift in the happy vibe that had filled the shop coupled with my daughter's strange reaction to Greg left me feeling a bit unsettled. I let out an awkward laugh. "Sorry about that. Guess she's feeling a little shy today."

"Didn't realize she had a shy bone in her body," Sylvia muttered under her breath. My gaze shot to her and I saw she was watching Greg closely, her expression closed off in a way I'd never seen before. It was almost as if she didn't trust this man.

"Yeah, well . . . Maybe it's just one of those days." I attempted to brush her off, knowing full well she was right, and that my girl had never, in her four years, had *one of those days*. "So, what brings you by? You in the market for some flowers?" I'd tried to make my tone teasing, but everything about this situation felt uncomfortable and awkward.

"Not today, but maybe soon." That got me another wink, as if he were sharing a secret, when in all honesty, the wink was getting a little played out. Three in less than five minutes was too much. "I don't have long before I have to get back to the station; I just stopped in to see your gorgeous face."

"Oh, uh . . ." That comment threw me. It felt far too intimate for a man and woman who'd only spoken one other time, and for less than ten minutes. "Thank you. That's sweet."

"Actually, I came by to see if you were free Saturday night. I'd love to take you to dinner."

"Oh. Well . . ." Micah's command to stay away from this guy came back to me all of a sudden. I'd initially thought he was marking his territory in some alpha caveman sort of way, but I remembered the look on his face when he'd issued the order, and I could have sworn I'd seen something other than jealousy there.

My gut instinct was screaming that something was majorly off here. I just didn't know what it was.

Before I had to make up a lie or turn him down in front of an audience, Sylvia spoke up. "How sweet. Unfortunately, she already has plans on Saturday." She looked at me with that arched brow. "Remember, sweets? We have you and Ivy's welcome cookout. Practically the whole town's coming."

"Of course!" I said loudly as relief washed over me. "Things have been so crazy, that totally slipped my mind."

"I bet they have," Sage murmured under her breath with a mischievous grin.

I chose to ignore her and looked back to Greg, who was staring unhappily in Sylvia's direction. The expression on his face sent an unpleasant chill down my spine. "I'm sorry. But I really appreciate the invitation," I told him, trying to lighten the sudden tension crackling in the air, while hoping to move him out the door faster.

He turned back to me, the displeasure gone from his features in an instant and replaced with the charming smile he'd walked in wearing. "That's all right, beautiful. There'll be other weekends." He took a step back, rapping his knuckles on the counter. "I'll see you soon. Enjoy the rest of your day."

"Yeah, you too."

He turned and headed out of the shop without acknowledging anyone else.

Ivy went back to acting like her normal self almost as soon as the door closed behind him, and Sylvia didn't say anything about her odd behavior, so I chose to brush off the uncomfortable feeling clinging to my skin and pretend everything was perfectly normal.

Ivy pulled Sage across the shop to show her the fairy garden she and Sylvia were making, leaving me and Dani alone at the counter. I twisted my head, prepared to speak, when she started before I could.

Leaning in close, she lowered her voice to a whisper and said, "Be careful, Hayden. That's the kind of man you don't want attention from."

A chill burrowed its way beneath my skin. "What do you mean?" I asked, keeping my voice as quiet as hers.

"I'm sorry but I can't say. Please, just stay away from that guy, all right? He's dangerous."

I felt the tiny hairs on the back of my neck stand on end. I wanted to probe further. I wanted to demand answers, but I could see worry etched into her pretty face. She wanted to say more, but for whatever reason, she couldn't.

Instead of pushing, I nodded, promising, "Okay, sweetie. I'll stay away." I reached across the counter to give her hand a reassuring squeeze, causing her shoulders to sink in relief.

"All right, good." The concern quickly melted away, just like that, replaced by feminine curiosity. "Now tell me about you and Micah."

FIFTEEN
MICAH

The crime scene was lit up by the time I put my truck in park and killed the engine a little after one in the morning.

The area had been taped off and there were uniformed officers and crime scene techs canvasing the area.

I climbed out of the truck and slammed the driver side door. Leo was already heading for me by the time I ducked under the tape. "They got an ID yet?" I asked as soon as he was within hearing distance.

My partner's jaw clenched, the muscle in it ticking violently. "Victim's name is Evan Webb. Meth dealer out of Grapevine."

Goddamn it.

Evan Webb was one of the names Charlie had given us, the dealer who was working in Cormack's operation. If Leo and I had pulled him in without cause, it would have sent up red flags, so we had Linc send in a few of his guys. The lead hadn't given much in the way of names, but we found out the operation was much larger than we'd originally anticipated, spanning across three towns, with cops from Hope Valley, Hidalgo, and Grapevine involved, as well as your run-of-the-mill, low-life dealers.

Linc's team cut the kid loose with a warning they'd be back for more, so he needed to do a little digging unless he wanted them to rain holy hell down on his life. Evidently, Evan Webb hadn't been very good at covert.

"How was it done?" I asked as we moved toward the body.

"Single shot to the head, execution style. He was dead before he hit the ground. We have to wait for ballistics, but looks like he was done with a .45."

Same caliber as the gun that had killed Darrin Callo. Someone was tying up loose ends.

I let out a curse under my breath and raked a hand through my hair as I scanned the faces around the crime scene. Greg Cormack wasn't anywhere to be seen. "All right. Let's work the scene." I lowered my voice and added, "Put in a call to Linc. Know it's late, but we meet in an hour."

"And her?" he asked, referring to Charlie in a hushed voice. "You think she's safe?"

I didn't have a fucking clue at that point, and it was twisting me into knots. "If she's not, she will be. As of this moment, she's done. Even if that means we gotta have Linc lock her ass down somewhere until it's over."

———

As it turned out, Charlie had been safe. She'd been asleep in her bed when Dalton let himself into her house and all but threw her ass in his truck and drove her to Alpha Omega where the rest of us were waiting.

You wouldn't have known it by looking at her—what with her petite frame, long dark blonde hair, button nose, and pixie features—but this girl could be hard as stone when she was in the mood to be, and judging from the way she burst into the conference room in Lincoln's offices, she was in the mood.

"What the hell?" she snapped the minute her eyes landed on Leo and me. "You know, cops or not, having your boy break into my place in the middle of the night and take me against my will is *still* illegal. And a felony!"

"Sit down," I grated, curling my fingers into the arms of the chair I was sitting in.

"Screw that! Are you trying to blow my cover? Cormack could've had one of his goons watching my house!"

"And they wouldn't have seen a thing," Dalton gritted out.

She shot him a scathing look. "Yeah? You and Harry Potter tight? He let you borrow his invisibility cloak or something?"

One of the most annoying things about Charlie Belmont was her ability to be funny while still pissing you off. I wanted to laugh at the same time I wanted to cuff her to the table so she couldn't get away.

"Lose the attitude, Thumbelina," Dalton clipped.

"Eat me, man bun," she fired back.

I finally snapped when the two of them started going at each other. "Enough!" I bellowed, shooting up and slamming my hands down on the table. She clamped her mouth shut instantly, giving me wide eyes. "Sit the fuck down and listen, Charlie."

To my complete and utter shock, she yanked out a chair and plopped down in it with a huff, crossing her arms over her chest and sulking petulantly.

Leo spoke while I took a few much-needed seconds to calm the hell down. "Some shit went down tonight and it's changed the state of play."

"What happened?"

"Evan Webb was shot at point blank range in the back of his head while he was down on his knees," I growled. "*That's* what happened."

Her whole frame jerked back while the color slowly leeched from her face and her chest heaved with rapid breaths. "What?"

"I take it you didn't know."

"Of course I didn't know!" she cried. "Oh my God. He was asking questions. I didn't know what he was doing, and I wasn't gonna ask. I've been keeping my head down, trying not to draw too much attention, but I wondered what the hell he was up to."

"So it's like we suspected," Leo said on a low grunt. "The kid showed his hand and got himself caught. Now he's dead."

"You're out, starting now," I demanded.

"What? You can't do that," she cried, slapping her palm onto the table.

I sat back down and leaned back in my chair, faking a calm I most certainly wasn't feeling. "It's already done."

"This is bullshit!" she argued. "Now that Evan's dead,

I'm the only eyes you have on the inside. I'm not quitting now."

"That's not your call," I replied flatly. "As of an hour and a half ago, it stopped being your decision to make, mainly because you were making all the wrong ones by not getting yourself safe."

Giving up on me, she looked to Leo imploringly. "Leo, please. You can't—"

"You're out," Dalton snarled. "Don't fuckin' test me on this. If I have to tie you up and lock you in my basement, I will."

She ignored him and shifted her focus back to me. "Micah, come on. I can do this. I know I can."

"People are dying, Charlie," I stressed. "This motherfucker didn't just kill a fellow police officer, he murdered his *partner*. You think he'd hesitate for even a moment to squeeze the trigger if he thought you were a threat to him? Not a chance. He'd put a bullet in your head without losing any sleep. I can't let that happen. You might not care what happens to you, but I sure as fuck do. And so does Leo. We can't sit back and watch you put yourself at risk like this. Not anymore."

She surprised me again, and not in a good way, when she lowered her head on a sniffle.

"Sweetheart—" Leo started.

Then she looked back up at us, her chin trembling and her eyes glassy with unshed tears. I'd never seen this kind of emotion from Charlie before. I'd always pictured her too hard, too tough to cry, but clearly, I'd been very wrong.

"I haven't done a lot of good in my life," she said in a wobbly voice. "I put my trust in the wrong people over and over, and when they finally showed their true colors, instead of doing the hard thing or the *right* thing, I ran. I *always* ran."

"Darlin' this isn't—" I tried, but she wasn't finished.

"As long as I wasn't the one being hurt, it wasn't my problem these assholes were out there, breathing free and clear, able to do whatever the hell they wanted. It didn't affect me, so it wasn't my business, right?" She let out a self-deprecating laugh and shook her head in disgust. "The only person I've ever looked out for my whole life was *me*. Then I saw Darrin Callo's girls." All the air whooshed from my lungs, but she kept going. "If they'd had a mom as worthless as the one I'd been born to, more than likely, they'd end up on the very same path I've spent most of my life on. I saw them and I decided I was done running. I was done looking out for only myself. Greg Cormack took a good and decent man from this earth. He doesn't get to breathe free and clear."

Jesus, she was killing me. "You've done enough," I told her, my voice low and gentle. "You don't need to risk your life for anything else."

"Better my life than someone who'd leave people behind," she replied vehemently. "Micah, I've got no one. If something were to happen to me, it wouldn't be any great loss. There's no one to care if I'm not around anymore."

"Jesus Christ," I rasped, my chest feeling like it had been sliced open as I stared across the length of the table in bewilderment. "You really think that, don't you?"

She straightened her shoulders and lifted her chin. "Just saying it like it is."

"You think it wouldn't fuckin' torment me if something

were to happen to you? You think Leo wouldn't care? Or any of the goddamn men sitting at this table right now?"

"You might feel guilty for a little while 'cause I was your informant, but it wouldn't—"

"Bullshit!" I thundered. "It wouldn't have a fuckin' thing to do with guilt or responsibility or any of that other fucked-up shit floating around in your head right now. It would just be *loss*, plain and goddamn simple, Charlie. You think just 'cause you started this as a CI we don't care about you? We got to know *you*, and what we came to know, we grew to care about simply because you're *you*. That means, informant or not, you get hurt, or God forbid, worse, it's gonna fuckin' destroy me. And I'm not the only one. You're *family*, Charlie. And if something happened to you, you'd be leaving all of us with that pain."

Her lips parted on a broken exhale as her eyes went wide in shock. I didn't know if it was because she'd been stunned speechless or what, but she didn't say a word in response.

"Same goes for me," Leo grunted, and when I looked over, I could see how pissed he was that she'd be dumb enough to think she didn't matter to him or any of us sitting in that room. "And you can call it selfish if that'll make you feel better, I don't give a damn. But that's why you're out."

I looked across the room to where Dalton was standing, his back pressed against the wall, the sole of one booted foot propped on it, and his arms crossed over his chest. His stance might have appeared casual, but the rage rolled off his body in big, heavy waves. Out of everyone in this room, he might be the one most affected if something happened to her.

"It's not as easy as just walking away," she finally said in a small voice after a long, silent pause. "Cormack will know something's up if I just up and quit taking his calls."

"Then you've got two choices," Lincoln stated, speaking for the first time since she entered the room. "The first one, we take you somewhere and keep you hidden 'til this shit's over and done with. You'll be safe, and no one'll be able to find you."

Her gaze shot to his and she gave her head a jerky shake. "That's the same as running. If I disappear, he'll freak. He freaks, other people could get hurt. What's the second option."

"You aren't gonna like it," I informed her.

"As long as it doesn't involve running, I'll be fine."

"You and Dalt are gonna get close," I explained. "We'll make it look like it happened naturally, but you two are gonna be seen spendin' more and more time together. Cormack knows he's part of Linc's crew, so if he's smart he'll start putting some distance between him and you without getting suspicious." I was right, I could tell by the pinched look on her face she wasn't happy with that, so I added more, hoping to keep her head from exploding. "This way, you might be able to keep your finger on the pulse without getting any deeper, and you'll have a reasonable excuse to have Dalton at your back if anything goes down. But we're gonna make damn sure nothing goes down. That work for you?"

"It's that or a safehouse in the mountains with no cable or internet," Linc grunted.

Charlie's nostrils flared like an angry bull as her eyes skittered around the men at the table before finally turning to look at the one standing behind her. "Fine," she grumbled as she faced forward in her chair. "Option two it is." She threw her arm out and pointed behind her. "But if he pisses me off, I can't be held responsible for shooting him."

With that said, everything was as settled as it could possibly get, given the shitstorm swirling around all of us.

We ended the meeting shortly after that, with Dalton driving a fuming Charlie back to her house to make sure it was clear.

I stood from the conference table and started toward the doors when Leo called my name. "Look, brother, I hate to pile more on your plate after the night we just had, but there's something you gotta know."

I watched the rest of the men clear out of the room before looking back to my partner. "What is it?"

"You know Dani knows what's goin' down to a certain extent." I nodded. It was something he and I had talked about when we discovered we had at least one dirty cop in the department. We agreed he could talk to Danika about the case because she was his woman, and we both knew we could trust her. As far as I was aware, she hadn't breathed a word of what she knew to anyone else. "Well, she was at Divine Flora earlier today, visiting Hayden, and Cormack came in." My back went straight. Unfortunately, he wasn't finished. "Your little showdown at The Tap Room last weekend didn't do a damn thing to get him off her scent. He made his move right there in front of her aunt and her girl, as well as Sage and Dani."

"He *what*?"

"Asked her out in front of an audience. He's got her in his sights and he's not shiftin' target."

"God *damnit*," I snapped. "I told her to stay away from that son of a bitch."

"Well, the way Dani says she saw it, Hayden didn't look too excited to have his attention. My woman did her best to warn her away from the prick without lettin' anything slip, but Dani's still worried. Hayden's part of their crew now, and she wants to make sure her new friend's got someone lookin' out for her."

"I'm on it," I grunted, heading for the door. Greg Cormack wasn't going to get within fifty feet of Hayden again. I'd make goddamn sure of it.

SIXTEEN
HAYDEN

I thought my aunt had been exaggerating when she said nearly the whole town was coming to the party she'd decided to throw on a whim. That just went to show what I knew, because it felt like every single resident in Hope Valley was currently standing in our backyard.

I'd woken up this morning frantic that nothing had been done in preparation. I'd hightailed it out to Sylvia's to find out what I could do, only to be told "Everything will work itself out, my precious girl. Just relax." I hadn't bought it, but sure enough, she'd been right.

Everything was running like a well-oiled machine. Other than making a big helping of potato salad and two apple pies —my contribution to the potluck aspect of the whole thing —there'd been nothing else for me to do. There was no setting anything up ahead of time, no preparing for our "guests".

People showed, some with folding tables, some with chairs, others with yard games, and they set stuff up wherever there was an empty space. Each person came with at least one dish, so the spread was more impressive than the catering at my wedding. There were a few kegs off to the side, and coolers full of drinks had appeared out of nowhere.

And people milling about everywhere. Micah had dragged a grill over earlier and spent the past hour standing around it with a bunch of other men, talking and drinking beers while grilling up hamburgers and hot dogs.

I didn't recognize three quarters of the people, yet they all seemed to know exactly who I was, giving 'hellos' or waves, some even stopping to chat with me for a bit. There wasn't a single stranger in sight. Everyone had made themselves right at home, kicking back and enjoying a beautiful fall day before the weather got too cold, hanging out with good friends, good food, and lots of laughs.

Eden sidled up to me, a clear plastic cup with what looked like lemonade clutched between her hands and propped on her baby bump. "Hey, babe. You having a good time?"

I let out a small laugh. "This is certainly not what I was expecting. The last time I hosted a barbecue, it had been planned weeks in advance, there were no kids allowed, and everyone came dressed in 'garden party chic'."

She turned her face to me, her brows raised in confusion. "I'm not even sure what that means."

"Lightweight dresses and heels for the women. Sport coats and chinos for the men."

"That sounds . . ." she scrunched her nose up adorably.

"Awful?" I added on a giggle. "Yeah. It really was. It was an event for Alex's clients and work associates. I was bored out of my mind."

"And now?"

I looked out at the sprawling yard. My baby girl was easy to spot with her long, wild hair and the purple tutu and T-shirt sporting a sequined Eiffel Tower she'd paired with her combat boots. She was in the middle of a Frisbee game with a group of kids of all ages. She looked like she was having the time of her life.

A smile slowly stretching across my lips. "Now I'm having the best time," I admitted in a quiet voice. "Everybody knows everybody. There's a comfort in that I've never experienced before. There are no pretenses, no one's trying to show anyone else up. The only thing anyone cares about is that the person next to them is having fun."

Eden grinned big. "Welcome to small-town living, honey."

"It really is the best."

A woman who looked to be around Sylvia's age shuffled her way in front of Eden and me. Her short, gray hair was tinted blue and, while she was far less spry than my aunt, there was a shrewdness in her eyes telling me this woman still had her wits about her, and then some.

"So, this is the new one, huh?"

My chin jerked back at her bluntness while Eden let out a giggle before introducing us. "Ms. McClintock, this is Hayden Young. Sylvia's niece. Hayden, this is Ms. M. Don't let her fool you, she's actually sweet as pie. You'll love her."

The old woman harrumphed before stating flatly, "What are you tryin' to do, Eden Sheppard? Scare the girl off? Of course she'll like me. *Everyone* likes me. I'm a ray of freakin' sunshine."

My attempt to swallow my laughter resulted in a loud, indelicate snort. "It's nice to meet you, Ms. M."

She looked me up and down, mumbling, "Mmmhmm," and giving me the impression she was still waiting to see what I had to offer before casting judgment. "So, you're a pretty thing," she stated in the same tone someone might use to announce they had food poisoning, almost accusingly.

"Um . . ." I looked to Eden for direction, getting only a shrug in return. "Thank you?"

"I'm assumin', seein' as you're pretty and this town's full of good lookin' men, you've got your sights set on one already." She looked out toward the yard like she was weighing the options. "So who's it gonna be?"

"Oh, uh . . ." I cast big eyes to my friend, silently begging her to save me from whatever the hell this was, but I got nothing. "Actually, I'm not really—"

"Don't gimme that BS about not lookin' for a man. Every single woman's lookin' for a man. Hell, *I'd* be lookin' for a man if they weren't already beatin' down my door."

My head fell back on a deep belly laugh. "You know what, Ms. M? Eden was right. I do like you."

"Of course you do," she said snidely. "Now stop avoiding the question."

"Ms. M—" Eden started, but the old woman waved her hand, silencing her. "You got yours, and he already popped a bun into that oven, so you know. Don't act like your friend doesn't need a man of her own. At the very least, she should find someone to sleep with. I read somewhere that orgasms actually extend a woman's life. It's science! It also means I'm gonna live forever," she added with a cheeky wink that had Eden choking on the sip she'd just taken.

"For the love of Pete," Sylvia decreed, coming to a stop next to Ms. McClintock and grabbing hold of the woman shoulders. "Will you leave the youngins alone already, Pearl? They don't need you scarin' the life outta them. Come on. I'm trying to get enough people to start a game of bingo."

Ms. McClintock gave my aunt a scathing glare. "I'm old, not dead. Bingo is for people who don't have a life."

"Not how I play it. Each time a person yells bingo, you have to take a shot. And I got a bottle of Maker's Mark just for you."

"Well why the hell didn't you start with that?"

The two of them scuttled off, leaving us standing there, slack-jawed.

"Is my aunt really organizing a drinking game at"—I looked down at my watch—"two in the afternoon?"

Eden wrapped her arm around my waist and pulled me against her side. "It's gonna be a long day, sweetie. And just a warning, it's highly likely that, at some point, at least one old person's gonna get wasted enough to start taking their clothes off."

Sweet merciful hell.

———

"You know what? This might be the best party I've ever been to in my entire life."

I looked to McKenna. She was staring out into the yard at her man Bruce with a glazed look in her hooded eyes, and burst into laughter.

At some point in the afternoon, someone had come up with the brilliant idea of starting a touch football game in the side yard. The longer the game went on, the sweatier the men playing became, until one by one, they started stripping out

of their shirts. Ms. M hadn't been wrong. This town was full
of *seriously* good-looking men. I was surrounded on all sides
by my new girlfriends, and as I watched their men running
plays, I was seriously happy that these incredible women were
going home to the likes of *all that*. Seeing them all now in
their full glory, it was a wonder Eden was the only one
currently knocked up. I made a silent bet with myself that
there were going to be at least two more pregnancy
announcements before the spring.

I bumped my shoulder against Mac's. "You act like you
don't see your man without a shirt every single day."

"It's not about seeing *our* men shirtless," Gypsy insisted,
fanning her face as her gaze remained riveted to the makeshift
field. "It's more the group as a whole. All these fine men, half
naked, glistening with sweat . . ."

She trailed off on a dreamy sigh, so Tempie finished. "It's
like some sort of witchcraft. I mean . . ." She waved her hands
in front of her. "Behold."

She wasn't wrong, it was definitely something to behold.
And we weren't the only ones *beholding*. As soon as the game
started, the old ladies lost interest in drunk bingo, and pulled
their lawn chairs over to watch while they sipped their cocktails, rooting for their favorites. Or in some instances, heck-
ling the players.

"You call that a throw?" Ms. M. had yelled at Eden's
husband, Lincoln, a big, blond Viking-looking dude. "I could
throw better than that, and I got arthritis in my entire body!"

"Get it together, Castillo!" a woman Gypsy had introduced to me earlier as Odette yelled at her man, Marco. "I
put money down on this game. Don't you go blowin' my
social security check!"

I looked back to the game—or to one player in particular —and felt my pulse begin to race. My libido was in the red, warning sirens were going off left and right in my head. Micah was dead center of the fray, his ripped chest and thick arms shining with sweat under the bright sun. The nice seventy-something degree weather began to feel almost sweltering the longer I stared.

"Go, Mike, go! Go, Mike, go!" Ivy chanted from her chair right beside Sylvia. She jumped up and down, cheering for her best friend at the top of her lungs as one of the guys called out the play.

Someone snapped the ball, bodies started crashing together, and I used that as my opportunity to duck away and grab a drink, hoping a few minutes by myself would help tamp down the heat building in my blood.

Moving to the coolers, I flipped the top on the one with the beer and pulled out an ice-cold bottle. I'd just popped the cap and taken a refreshing swig when a pair of hands landed on my hips from behind.

Jumping in fright, I whipped around, nearly choking on the beer I'd just swallowed. "Jesus, Greg," I croaked, placing a hand over my pounding heart. "You scared the shit out of me."

He held his hands up in apology while giving me that charming smile that, the more often I saw it, the more I felt it was strictly for show. Nothing genuine seemed behind that smile. "Sorry, beautiful. Didn't mean to scare you."

"It's all right." I gave him a small, shaky grin and took a step back, trying to put some space between us. "I-I didn't know you were coming."

"Well, I wasn't planning on it at first, but if I can't take you out on a date, at least we can still spend some time together here."

"Oh, um . . . That's nice." I looked around, trying to find any reason to get away from this guy. The other day at Divine Flora, my gut was telling me something was off, and after talking to Dani, that instinct had turned into a sick, queasy feeling. "Well, uh, there's still plenty of food if you want to make yourself a plate. And we've got all kinds of drinks—"

"I'm good. But maybe you and I could go somewhere a little more private? You know, just to talk for a bit." He took a step closer, reaching out and running his fingers down my forearm before wrapping them around my hand and giving it a tug. "Maybe get to know each other a little better?"

"Greg." I pulled my hand from his and took another step back. "Look, you're a sweet guy, but I think we're looking for different things right now. See, I *just* got divorced. Right now, I need to concentrate on my daughter and building our life here. I'm not looking to start something with another man right now. I'm so sorry."

That smile fell, taking all the charm with it. His brows slashed down into a deep, unhappy V. "Then what was all that shit at the bar the other night?"

"I'm sorry, but I think you might have gotten the wrong idea."

"Or maybe you're just a cock tease." I rocked back on a foot at the venom in his voice. "I didn't have the wrong idea. You put it right out there, practically throwin' it at me."

I thought back to that night, and could say with absolute certainty, I hadn't thrown *anything* at him. "Okay, you know what? I think maybe you should go."

"Yeah, I'm thinkin' you're right." He looked me up and

down, his top lip curling in a nasty sneer. "Waste of fucking time."

I didn't bother taking offense. I'd known more than enough men like him in my lifetime. A single blow to their ego, and they lashed out in an extreme and unwarranted way. His insult didn't even faze me. In fact, all I felt as he stomped through the backyard toward the driveway, was relief.

Until I turned around and noticed the football game had stopped, and almost everyone was now staring in my direction . . . because a seething Micah was storming through the yard, looking like a raging bull as he headed right for me.

SEVENTEEN
MICAH

I finished yanking my shirt back over my head just as I reached her. "Inside. *Now*," I ground out, but instead of waiting to see if she'd follow, my hand lashed out and gripped her arm. I all but dragged her up the path and into the house, slamming the back door with so much force the glass inside the frame rattled.

"Micah, what the hell?" Hayden yelped, trying to pull her arm from my grasp, but I held tight as I continued through the kitchen and down the hall.

I knew the layout of this house almost as well as I knew my own. Years of helping Sylvia out, making repairs whenever they were needed, had given me a perfect lay of the land. I knew Sylvia had moved her niece into the master bedroom, so I took the stairs at a clip so fast Hayden practically had to run to keep from tripping as I hauled us up them and down the hall toward her room.

She struggled against my hold, pulling at my hand the entire way, finally wrenching herself free once we cleared the doorway, but it was too late. Slamming the bedroom door closed, I stood between it and her so she had nowhere to run.

Her mouth opened and closed on a sputter before she finally managed to get her words out. "Have you lost your mind?" she shouted. "What the hell was that?"

"What was *that*?" I asked incredulously. "Are you fuckin' serious?"

"Yes, I'm *fuckin' serious*," she threw back. "You just dragged me through the yard and into *my* house, making a scene in front of the whole freaking town for no damn good reason!"

I took a step toward her, planting my hands on my hips. "Oh I had a perfectly good reason for that scene down there, and you know it," I seethed. "I told you to stay away from that guy, and you didn't listen!"

"Oh my God," she said on a bewildered laugh. "So that's what this is about? You acted like an asshole in front of everyone because you're *jealous*?" Her vibrant blue eyes flashed wildly as she threw her arms wide. "You're unbelievable!"

"And you're so goddamn stubborn it's driving me insane," I barked. With each step I took forward, she took one backward until she slammed into the wall across the room, leaving her with nowhere else to go. "I told you to stay the fuck away from him because that man's dangerous, Hayden. I know him a whole hell of a lot better than you do. I've lived here a long time, and part of my *job* is reading people. So when I say to stay clear of someone, how about instead of throwin' attitude, you pull your head out of your ass and actually *listen to me*!"

She pushed up on her tiptoes until her chest pressed flush

against mine and her nose was only inches away. "Don't tell me to get my *head out of my ass!*"

With that, the last tenuous threat of my control snapped. My hand shot out, tangling in the hair at the back of her head and holding it in place while I slammed my mouth down on hers.

Her lips parted instantly, her tongue flicking out to rub across mine. The kiss became a battle the moment it started, each of us fighting against the other for control. Using my knee, I forced her legs farther apart and wedged my hips between them, using my weight to keep her pressed against the wall as I ground my aching hard-on between her thighs.

I emitted a growl when her teeth clamped down on my bottom lip, biting hard enough that the sting made me pull back. Her eyes were glazed over, the blue nearly swallowed up by the black of her pupils. Her chest was heaving with each breath. She was just as aroused as I was, possibly more, but we weren't soft or gentle when it came to taking our pleasure from each other.

"You're such an asshole," she panted before grabbing my hair and forcing my lips back to hers.

"And you're a pain in my ass," I grunted.

"Stop bossing me around," she continued to argue between kisses.

"Then stop making stupid fucking decisions," I ordered, pulling back. The small distance I put between us served two purposes. The first was so she'd know I was being serious, and the second was to make her wild by denying her what she wanted. "You stay the fuck away from Greg Cormack," I clipped.

"Stop telling me what to do!"

I bent my knees, using the leverage to drive myself harder against her, forcing a moan past her swollen lips. "*Twice* now he's touched what's mine. There won't be a third. Don't put me in the position of doing something that'll threaten my job, Red. 'Cause if his hands go anywhere near you again, I'm gonna break every one of his goddamn fingers."

She let out a soft growl that I would've found adorable if it didn't make me impossibly harder. "I hate you." Despite her words, her hips rocked harder against mine while her delicate hands fisting at the material of my shirt to keep me close.

Grabbing her dress at her sides, I bunched it in my hands until, inch by inch, those long, seductive legs were uncovered. I got the material up past her hips, revealing her tiny lace panties.

"Fine by me. You can hate me all you want, as long as you do it with my cock inside you."

Her back arched when I gently trailed my fingertips up her inner thigh. "Micah," she said on a whimper as I brushed a feather-light touch against the scrap of material between her thighs. "*Please.*"

I pressed against her just a bit harder, hard enough to feel how wet her panties were. "Fuck me," I groaned. "Already soaked. That all for me?"

Her eyes squeezed closed as her head fell back. "Yes," she breathed.

I increased the pressure, pressing even harder against the fabric. "What do you want, Red? Give me your eyes and say the words."

She peeled her eyelids open with extreme effort, her breathing labored as she worked to focus on me. "Micah," she finally panted, "if you don't fuck me right now, I'm gonna lose my mind."

I was sure the smile I gave her just then radiated with male pride. "Is that right?" I teased, loving how hot it made me when I pressed her buttons.

But the little minx gave as good as she got. Her hand shot down between us and her fingers wrapped around my dick as best they could through my jeans. Feeling how hard I already was, she grinned in much the same way I had seconds ago. "This all for me?"

Thrusting against her palm I growled, "I told you we were inevitable. Now take me out."

She didn't give me any attitude. Instead, she made quick work of the button and zipper on my fly. Her long fingers dove beneath the waistband of my underwear and gripped my shaft tightly, wrenching a grunt from deep within my chest as I ripped her panties down her thighs until they pooled on the floor at her feet.

"Condom," she rasped as she guided my rock-hard cock out of my pants and stroked her palm up and down the shaft.

I let out a frustrated moan, wanting to feel the slick of her pussy with no barriers. *Next time*, I told myself as I retrieved the condom from my wallet.

As soon as I tore the package open, she snatched the rubber disk and deftly worked it down my length.

We moved in perfect sync after that, desperation clawing at both of us. I shoved the thin cardigan off her shoulders and tore the flimsy straps of her dress down her arms, baring her perfect breasts that spilled past the top of her bra. With a rumble of appreciation, I reached down and grabbed her ass with both hands.

Her long legs wrapped around my waist as soon as I lifted her off the ground, her ankles locking at my back. Fisting my cock, I lined it up with her center, and with one snap of my hips, buried myself deep.

Sounds of pleasure spilled past both our lips as I gave myself a second to feel her tight, wet heat closing around me.

"Like a goddamn glove," I grunted, lowering my forehead to hers while I breathed deep. If I didn't get myself under control, this was going to be over way too soon. "Jesus, you fit me perfectly."

"Micah, you need to move," she pleaded, circling her hips temptingly. "I need you to fuck me."

I could do that, but first . . . "How do you want it, baby?"

Her lids were half-mast, a lust-drunk smile pulled at her lips as she whispered, "Rough. Show me how much you want me."

I didn't need to be told twice. Pulling out almost all the way, I gave her just a moment to breathe before powering back in. Over and over, I slammed into her, driving so hard her back slid up and down the wall and her tits bounced in my face.

Holding her in place with one arm, I grabbed the cups of her bra with my free hand, jerking them down so those rosy pink nipples were revealed, making my mouth water.

Bending my neck, I sucked one stiff peak into my mouth, biting the tip before soothing the sting with my tongue.

"Fuck, *yes*," she cried, gripping my hair and giving it a yank as she ground against me. I switched to the other one, giving it the same treatment until both were red and throbbing beneath my tongue. "So good, Micah."

Her noises grew louder, spurring me on and making my

balls draw up tight. I could feel her pussy clamping down, telling me she was about to come.

Lifting my head, I stared into those incredible sapphire eyes. "Can feel you gettin' close."

She looked almost panicked at the intensity of what I was building inside her. "Oh God," she whimpered. "I'm gonna —" Her statement died when her head snapped back, slamming against the wall and she yelled as she began to come around me. I had to cover her mouth with my hand to muffle her screams. It rushed over her so hard she bared her teeth and bit into the side of my hand as she bucked against me, demanding every single ounce of pleasure my body could give hers.

The sting of her bite coupled with the vise-like grip of her pussy was too much. I tried to hold back as long as possible, but I couldn't. Burying my face in her neck, I groaned long and low as I blew. She milked every drop of release from me until my balls were completely drained.

I didn't think I'd ever come that hard in my life, and it was a wonder my knees hadn't given out.

The room was completely silent except for the sounds of our rapid breathing as we came down from what had to be the best sex ever had by two people.

"Holy shit," Hayden whispered seconds later as she untangled her fingers from my hair and brought her hands down to rest on my shoulders.

Once I was able to move, I lifted my head and pulled her away from the wall, moving toward the bed, careful to maintain our connection. I lowered us both down, resting my forearms on the mattress so I could look down at her. "You good?"

"I—" She stopped to pull her kiss-swollen bottom lip between her teeth and bite down. "I don't know. I mean, physically, hell yeah. But . . ."

"But what?"

She hesitated for so long I started to grow anxious. This wasn't just about the incredible sex, at least not anymore. This woman was under my skin, and there was no longer any point in denying how much I liked having her there. She was funny and fiery. She didn't take any shit. She loved her family fiercely. She had a good heart, and there was no doubt our sexual compatibility was off the charts. She was the only woman I'd ever been with who knew exactly what she wanted, but she didn't just ask for it, and she didn't take it either. No, she demanded *I* be the one to give it to her. And I got off on that in a *huge* way.

It wasn't about wanting to fuck her again. I just wanted *her*. I wanted to be able to touch her and kiss her, to tease or hold her whenever the hell I wanted. I wanted to show her there were men out there better than her dick of an ex-husband.

Everything I was feeling in that moment was completely foreign to me. They were the very things I'd insisted I'd never want, that I fought against feeling for as long as I could remember. But having her here with me now, all that gorgeous light red hair fanned out on the bed beneath me, the thought of something serious, something *permanent*, didn't terrify me at all. Not when it was Hayden I saw that with.

And just thinking of having something long-term with this woman had my dick swelling to half-mast. I decided right then and there, even if she fought it tooth and nail, it wasn't going to matter. The end result would be the same no matter what. I was keeping her. She'd just have to deal with it.

"I don't think that was very smart of us," she finally said in a tiny voice.

I raised my brows high on my forehead. "Really? 'Cause I think what we did was pure fuckin' genius."

Her lips curved up as she giggled. Hearing that and seeing her smile made my dick twitch, which caused her eyes to go big. "Wait. *Already?*"

"You have to ask that after the last time?" The muffled sounds from the party happening outside filtered through the window just then, reminding me we had other obligations and couldn't spend the rest of the day and night in this bed like I wanted. I let out a grumbled curse at having the moment ruined. "Looks like we'll have to take a raincheck on that."

"Micah." Hayden's voice was dripping with trepidation as she said my name. "Everyone out there is gonna know what we just did."

"Okay. So?"

She arched a single brow in bewilderment. "*So?* So our friends are gonna think there's something going on with us."

"Good," I stated simply. "Then we'll all be on the same page."

"Micah!" she cried agitatedly, giving my shoulder a weak shove that didn't budge me at all. "They're going to get the *wrong* idea! They'll think we're together or something. Like, a couple."

I grinned down at her, finding her cluelessness adorable. "Baby, that's not the wrong idea."

"Yeah, but—wait. What?"

"That isn't the wrong idea. This is happening."

"But—we haven't even talked—"

Lowering my head, I silenced her with a hard, hungry kiss, dipping my tongue into her sweet mouth for just the smallest taste before pulling back. She followed after me, a sound of displeasure rasping up her throat at me having stopped. "You just proved my point," I stated smugly. "One kiss, and you were chasing after me for more."

Her brows dipped and her face scrunched up in a scowl. "Don't be arrogant."

"Don't be so damn stubborn," I threw back. "What I'm getting at is that we're *both* drawn to each other in a way that's impossible to ignore. I've never felt about another woman the way I feel when I'm around you, and I want to explore that, Hayden. And you can argue all you want, but you want to explore this too. You know I'm right."

She blinked up at me slowly, the deep blue of her eyes full of fear. For a moment, I thought she was going to deny it, but she surprised me by nodding in agreement.

"Good. Then we're doing this."

"I-I guess we are," she replied, sounding hesitant and hopeful at the same time.

I hardened my expression, making my tone serious as I told her, "That means staying away from Greg Cormack. Got it?"

At my bossiness, her eyes flashed with fire once more. "For your information," she started snidely, "I told him I wasn't interested *before* you behaved like a Neanderthal. If you'd have let me explain instead of acting like a jackass, I could have told you that."

"If I'd let you explain first, we wouldn't have had that angry fuck against your bedroom wall," I countered.

Her gaze drifted up and to the side as she mumbled, "Hmm. Good point." When those vivid blues returned to me, she smiled proudly. "And that was a pretty exceptional angry fuck, wasn't it?"

"Christ, Red. That's an understatement. I thought the back of my skull was gonna blow off."

Her giggle reminded me of windchimes swaying in a breeze. "We're really good at that," she said in a conspiratorial whisper. "Like, *really* good."

A pained groan worked its way past my lips. "You gotta stop being cute, or we're never gonna leave this room." Her plump bottom lip jutted out in a tiny pout. I bent to give it a little nip before pushing off the bed and pulling her up with me, finally breaking our connection. "I know your game," I said accusingly as I removed the used condom and tied it off, tossing it in the trash bin beside her bed. I hiked my pants back onto my hips and tucked my semi inside. "You were about to use *The Look* to get your way, weren't you?"

She gave me a wide-eyed innocent expression as she righted her bra and pulled the straps of her dress back onto her shoulders. "I don't know what you're talking about."

The corner of my mouth twitched as I fought back a grin. "Bullshit. I just mentioned leaving the bed and that bottom lip came right out. You were totally about to use it."

She arched that brow and hit me with a seductive grin. "And if I was?"

I moved in and grabbed her by the hips, pulling her flush against me. "Two can play that game."

I could see the curiosity dancing in her gaze. "Meaning?"

I lowered my head and spoke against her lips. "Meaning, you pull that shit on me again, I'm not gonna let you come until you beg for it."

She sucked in a gasp, leaning deeper into me, and I knew right then that I had her.

And I couldn't fucking *wait* to get her in my bed.

———

Hayden might have been anxious when we rejoined the party, but I couldn't help but grin like a son of a bitch as we hit the yard, garnering attention and knowing looks from our friends.

Hayden tried pulling her hand from mine, but I wasn't having any of that. I tightened my grip and used it to pull her until she was pressed right up against my side. Only then did I release her hand so I could sling my arm over her shoulders.

Leaning in, I spoke quietly out of the side of my mouth as I guided us toward where Leo was standing with Dani, Hayes, Tempie, Eden, and Linc. "You keep actin' so stiff, people might start to think you don't like me."

She turned her head and tipped it back, hitting me with a glare that did a piss-poor job at masking the humor dancing in her eyes. "I *don't* like you. I hate you, remember?"

"Damn, Red. You just love to hate me, don't you?"

She finally got with the program, raising her arm and hooking it around my waist as she grinned. "You're finally getting it."

"Well don't you two just look cozy," Tempie teased as soon as we hit the group, but I was too busy scanning the yard to pay attention to whatever Hayden said in return.

"Hey, you guys know where Ivy is? I promised her earlier I'd teach how to throw a football."

Hayden's head spun around quickly. "Don't you think she's a little small to be catching a football?"

My arm around her clenched as I grinned down at her worried face. "For a chick who loves wearin' tutus, she's all tomboy. She'll be fine. That kid's tough as nails."

Lincoln lifted his beer bottle, pointing toward the back of the property. "Think I saw her hangin' with some of Gypsy's brood earlier."

Gypsy was married to one of his guys, Marco, and while they didn't have any kids of their own, they had custody of Gyspy's five siblings.

I shifted my attention toward the back of the yard just in time to see Gypsy's three-year-old brother Raleigh totter up to Ivy and grab her hair, pulling her face down so he could give her a big, smacking kiss.

Every muscle in my body locked tight as I grunted, "The hell?" I let go of Hayden and booked it across the yard with single-minded focus. I reached them just as Raleigh was going in for a second kiss—one that the little monster was already puckering up for.

"Nuh uh," I clipped, scooping Ivy off the ground and holding her to my chest as I twisted to shoot a murderous scowl at the little kiss thief. "No kissing allowed."

"But Mike!" Ivy cried. "He's my best friend."

I looked at her, my expression showing every bit of indignation I was feeling just then. "Like hell. *I'm* your best friend. And you're way too damn young to be kissin' boys," I scolded as I started stomping back toward Hayden.

I threw a finger out at Gypsy and Marco as I passed them,

ignoring the fact they were both cracking up. "You keep that handsy little toddler away from my girl, or he and I are gonna have some words."

That only made them laugh harder.

"Well, how old do I gots to be to kiss boys?" she asked, making my stomach sink like a rock.

"Seventy-two," I answered quickly, making her blue eyes go big.

"But that's *forever* away!"

"Exactly," I grunted under my breath just as we reached her mom's side. "I'll be dead by then so I won't have to see it."

"Think you might have over reacted just a bit?" Hayden asked as she took her daughter from me and balanced her on her hip.

"No. That boy's trouble. I can already tell."

"Mommy, Mike owes me two dollars!" Ivy declared excited. The she proceeded to snitch on me. "He said damn and hell!"

Instead of giving me a reproachful look, her head fell back on a long, loud laugh that worked wonders in unfurling the knot that had formed in my chest as soon as I saw that dirty rat's lips on Ivy.

I watched her for a second before I felt a pair of eyes on me. When I looked across our group I saw Leo watching me with a smug-as-hell grin on his face.

"You're so screwed," he mouthed.

I was. I *so* was. But I didn't care one damn bit.

EIGHTEEN
MICAH

Walking into the station Monday morning, I felt better than I had in months. Now that Dalton was sticking to Charlie's back like a leech, I could rest easier knowing she was safe. And after weeks of walking around in a near-constant state of arousal, all because of a certain redhead, that nagging ache in my gut—*and* groin— had been alleviated . . . at least temporarily.

I was counting down the minutes until I could slide back inside Hayden, but the pressure building inside me was no longer at risk of erupting at any moment.

I moved through the bullpen, not noticing that the noise all around me had dropped to a lull until I reached my desk. Leo was already at his, leaned back in his chair with his feet kicked up, grinning like the cat that caught the canary. I glanced over at the desk clump beside ours and noticed Hayes and Trick were watching me as well, both wearing expressions similar to my partner's.

"What's goin' on?" I asked, my voice coated with suspicion.

"Nothin'," Hayes replied, bringing his arms up to lace his fingers together behind his head, the picture of relaxation. "Just thinkin' of all the shit I'm gonna buy with my half of your paycheck."

My chin jerked back into my neck. "What the hell are you talkin' about?"

"The bet, asshole," Trick answered, looking way too pleased with himself. "We told you you'd find a woman one day and go ass over elbow for her. Your cocky ass was so sure that wouldn't happen, you bet your paycheck."

Goddamn it. I'd forgotten about that. "If I remember correctly, that bet was about getting married." I collapsed into my chair and sucked back a big gulp of coffee that I'd gotten earlier at Muffin Top. "And that's not on the table, so you guys can fuck off."

"It may not be on the table *yet*," Hayes said. "Did you forget we were there Saturday? We all saw how you acted when you thought Cormack was encroaching. You just quit runnin' in the middle of a play! Cost us the game and everything. All so you could whip your dick out and piss a circle around your woman."

"Jesus, man," Trick jumped in. "I thought for a second, if you'd had your gun on you, you'd have shot him."

Chances were, if I'd had my gun, I might have at least stopped to consider it. Especially knowing what I knew. I shared a quick, private look with Leo where he silently communicated he'd have considered the same damn thing.

"And we were *also* there when you two came back more than half an hour later, lookin' way too damn pleased with yourselves, and you couldn't keep your hands off her the rest of the night," Hayes added.

"Well, it's not an issue anymore." Not that it ever was. As far as I cared, Hayden had been mine since that night in Richmond. "Not like that asshole stood a chance." And soon it would be moot, because Leo and I were going to make goddamn sure that prick never breathed free air again.

Leo glanced at something past my shoulder, and whatever it was had him fighting back a grin. "Looks like word about you and Hayden's PDA fest the other night made its way through the whole town." He stopped fighting it and grinned full on as he turned his focus back to me. "Someone's pissed."

I turned to peer over my shoulder and saw Cormack was standing with a couple other uniforms at the entrance to the bullpen. They might have been engaged in conversation, but his focus was on me, and he was *not* happy. I didn't have it in me to give a single fuck.

"I gave him fair warning she was mine and he needed to back the hell off. Not my fault he didn't listen."

If it was the last thing I ever did, I'd make sure he never got anywhere near Hayden Young ever again.

———

Hayden

The trail of sweat starting at my scalp leading to the waistband of my fitted yoga pants probably looked about as sexy as I felt sliding down the pole. As soon as my butt hit the ground, I collapsed, my arms and legs spread wide as I desperately sucked in air.

McKenna's sleek blonde hair hung around her face as she stood over me. "You alive down there?"

"Barely," I wheezed. "I've got one foot in the grave right now, and it's all your fault."

"Well, if it makes you feel any better, you actually did pretty good today," she said on a laugh.

I peeled myself off the cool tile and sat up, taking the water bottle she was holding out for me and chugging half of it down in a few gulps. "It doesn't, but thanks anyway."

She sat down on the floor beside me and took a drink from her own bottle. Today was my first pole dance lesson with McKenna, and the woman was the devil in a pair of boy shorts and a sports bra. Several times throughout the hour, I loudly questioned our friendship, but she didn't seem to care, laughing it off each time.

"Does that mean you aren't coming back for a second lesson?" she asked, looking far too pleased with herself.

I shot her a killing scowl. "Right now I'm more concerned that you may have broken my body, so I'm not really thinking that far in advance."

She rolled her eyes at my dramatics. "Oh, you'll be fine. Just go home and soak in a hot bath. Or, maybe you can ask a certain next door neighbor to massage away all your aches and pains."

"You've been waiting all afternoon for me to set you up like that, haven't you?"

She spun on the floor to face me full-on, tucking her criss-crossed legs in close to her body. "You know it. And now that it's out there, it's time to spill. What's going on between you guys? I want to know everything."

Honestly, I was surprised it had taken her this long to bring it up. It had been two days since the cookout. Two days since Micah and I had angry sex against my bedroom wall. Two days since he went all over-protective-dude on poor little Raleigh. And two days since we rejoined the party and he spent the rest of the time touching me in some way, whether it was holding my hand, casually draping his arm around my waist, or grabbing my hips in order to pull me against him whenever he felt like it.

As it turned out, Micah didn't shy away from public displays, and it surprised me—pleasantly—to discover he was such a tactile person.

But as the evening wore on, I began to notice an unusual amount of attention coming our way. At first I attributed it to the fact that we'd entered my house only a few steps away from being enemies, then came out a while later as a couple. I assumed it wouldn't take long for the interest to wear off and everyone to adjust, but the more he touched me, the more fascinating we seemed to become.

"What's the deal with everyone being so interested in what's going on with Micah and me? Is it a small town thing or something? I don't get it."

"More like it's a Micah Langford thing."

My head canted to the side in confusion. "What does that mean?"

"Oh, it's nothing bad," she said quickly. "In fact, it's actually pretty great. We're just not used to seeing Micah being so touchy-feely is all."

"So, he's kind of private?"

"Not really. I mean, when he's interested in a woman he

has no problem showing it, but that hardly ever lasts longer than a night. Micah's not really known around here for being the relationship type. He's had too much fun being single, if you know what I mean."

I could tell by her tone that she was only teasing, but there was no stopping that sinking sensation in the pit of my stomach. It was like swallowing a brick. "So, what you're saying is he's a player."

Her eyes lit with understanding as she looked at me. Giving a slow shake of her head, she replied, "No. I wouldn't say a player. He just liked the bachelor lifestyle. But, Hayden, no one has ever seen him with a woman how he was with you Saturday. Not in all the years he's lived here. Micah Langford doesn't hold hands. I watched him with you. It was like he couldn't touch you enough. Any time you started to drift out of his reach, he was quick to pull you back."

"That doesn't necessarily mean anything. It could've been the after-effect of really amazing sex," I insisted.

She made a face that screamed *girl please*. "An after-effect that lasted six hours?"

"It was *really* amazing sex."

"Then maybe that's part of what makes you the exception for him, instead of the rule."

"What if I'm not ready to be anyone's exception?" I asked on a whisper. Most women in my shoes would've been giddy with excitement at having landed a man like Micah. But after everything that happened with Alex, I had a built-in defense mechanism that wouldn't let me spiral too far into hope like that. I had to remain realistic.

"Mac, my marriage only *just* ended. A few months ago, I

was with the man I thought I was going to spend the rest of my life with. I spent years thinking Alex was the love of my life. I'm barely over the shockwaves of my whole life crashing down around my feet, then bam! I meet this guy, like a minute after my world implodes, and the connection to him is so intense it scares the living hell out of me. What will people think if I jump headfirst into something else that fast?"

"Who gives a shit what anyone else thinks?" she exclaimed passionately. "Babe, I hate to break it to you, but your friends back in the city were a bunch of stuck-up assholes, and from what you've told me, your snobby-ass family isn't much better. The people who truly care about you just want you to be happy, however that comes about. Let those dickheads from your previous life stand in their glass houses throwing stones. You be happy and leave them to their miserable existences. Karma comes around for people like that in her own time. Trust me."

The knot of tension that had begun to form in my shoulders slowly started to loosen. But I wasn't quite ready to throw in the towel just yet. "It's not only me I have to take into consideration, Mac. I've got a little girl who has to live with the consequences of every decision I make."

Her head jerked back and her brows furrowed incredulously. "You act as if you've made one bad decision after another. You haven't done anything wrong, Hay. Your marriage ended because of *him*, not you. Stop shouldering the blame for that. You're a fantastic mother. And as far as I can see, you can do no wrong in that little girl's eyes. She sees your strength and resilience, and she's wild and crazy and

jumps head first into every single day because she knows
without a shadow of a doubt, that her mom'll be right there
to catch her if needed."

Leaning forward, she placed her hand on top of mine and
gave it a squeeze. "I know you got knocked down in a really
big way, but that doesn't mean you have to stay down. And if
you're waiting for the 'right time' to put yourself out there,
I'm telling you now, there's no such thing. So if Micah makes
you feel good, I say go for it."

Flipping my hand over, I wrapped my fingers around
hers and held tight. "You're really smart. You know that?"

She shrugged, the apples of her cheeks growing pink at
my compliment. "I've been where you are. I'd been knocked
down so much I did like you and pushed a good man away
when all he was trying to do was help me get back up again."

My heart clenched at the thought of this magnificent
woman hurting in any way. "So what did you do?"

"Well, it took me a while, but I finally pulled my head out
of my ass and saw what was standing right in front of me."
She smiled so big and bright it lit up her entire face. "Then I
dragged him down the aisle and made that shit official so he
could never get away."

At that, I threw my head back on a deep laugh. I'd seen
her with Bruce on multiple occasions now, and every single
time, he looked at his wife like she was the very thing that
gave him a reason to get out of bed each day and keep breathing. She didn't need to drag him anywhere. He probably
charged down that aisle himself, body-checking anything
that stood in his way.

"You know, I didn't know what it meant to have *real* girlfriends until I met you guys," I informed her once my laughter had tapered off. "I'm so glad I met you, Mac."

She fell into me, wrapping her arms and my shoulders and giving me a big hug. "Feeling's mutual, babe."

"But I'm still not sure I'm willing to attempt a second pole lesson."

NINETEEN

HAYDEN

I pulled into the driveway and came to a stop, tipping my head to the side in confusion. For some reason, Micah's truck was backed into my drive instead of parked in his.

It was the Thursday after the cookout, and with Micah working odd hours because of a case he was on and me having Ivy and working at the shop, it had been two days since we'd seen each other, and before that, it had only been in passing. There were a lot of texts, and some pretty hot late-night phone calls, but the relief I'd gotten the weekend before was starting to wear off. Tension had returned to my limbs, and the more time that passed without us physically connecting, the more agitated I became.

Killing the ignition, I climbed out of my car and started toward the front door. "I'm home," I called as I stepped inside. I hung my purse on one of the hooks on the wall by the front door and unwound the thin scarf from around my neck before doing the same with it.

I expected Ivy to come barreling out from wherever she

was to give me one of her signature big, body-rocking hug, but I got nothing. "Hello? Where is everybody?"

Sylvia's head popped out of the kitchen. "Hey, lovely. Good day?"

I'd run the shop by myself because Ivy's daycare was closed for the day, so my aunt had offered to stay home to watch her for me, claiming I needed to get used to running things without her there. I knew my aunt, and she had no intention of stepping away from Divine Flora, at least not fully. She was too active, and a full retirement would have driven her insane, but it was her attempt at giving me something of my own, and I appreciated the gesture enough not to call her out on it.

"It was good," I answered as I entered the kitchen. "Busy, but good. People are starting to decorate for fall, so we sold out of all the themed arrangements."

Sylvia was standing at the stove, browning meat in a skillet, as she said, "That's great, dearie. Now's about the time to make the shift fully into the new season, anyway."

"Smells good in here," I said, peering over her shoulder "What are you making?"

"Tacos. They'll be ready soon."

I looked around the kitchen, listening for the sounds of my rambunctious girl getting into something, but except for the sizzle of the meat, all was quiet. "Where's Ivy? And why's Micah's truck in the driveway?"

At my question, Sylvia peeked back at me, her eyes dancing excitedly. "Take a look in the backyard."

I turned my head to catch a glimpse out the back window, and what I saw made my feet started moving instantly.

Hugging my cardigan tighter to me, I exited through the back door and started down the garden path to the big stretch of yard behind it.

Ivy was out there, skipping and spinning around a massive pile of lumber like a little forest sprite. From the corner of my eye, I caught movement and turned to see Micah coming through the side gate carrying a stack of two-by-fours on his wide shoulder. My lungs nearly deflated at the sight of his thick biceps and roped forearms straining under the weight of the lumber.

"What--what's going on?" I asked once I was finally able to breathe properly.

"Mommy!" Ivy stopped dancing and came running up to me, plowing into my legs. "Look at all of dis!" she practically yelled with excitement as she faced the pile and threw her arms wide.

"I see it, love bug. But what *is* it?"

Micah tossed the boards onto the pile and shifted direction, heading straight for me as he pulled a pair of worn work gloves from his hands and stuffed them into the back pocket of his jeans. It was the simplest of actions, but for some reason, I found the whole thing so rugged and manly a flood of arousal dampened my panties.

"Hey, Red," he said casually as he reached out and hooked me around my waist. He pulled me into him, chest to chest, and planted a hard, quick kiss on my lips with such ease it was like he'd made this move every day for years. "You have a good day?"

"Y-yeah," I answered dazedly. "Um, what's going on?"

"Mike's buildin' me a treehouse!"

My head whipped back around to Micah—who was still

holding me against him. "You're building—that's not —*huh?*"

"A treehouse," he repeated. "She asked me last weekend, but I didn't have a chance to get to the home improvement store until today."

"Did she use *The Look* again?" I asked, ready to turn and lecture my daughter when Micah spoke again. And what he said left me speechless.

"No, she didn't con me this time. She just asked. I remembered that my little sister and I had a treehouse growin' up, and we loved that thing. Used to spend hours in there. I wanted to give Monster a little bit of that."

"You—" I gaped at him, blinking slowly. "She just *asked*?"

"Yeah."

"And you said yes? Just like that."

"Well, not *just* like that." He tilted his head down and gave my girl a very serious, very stern look. "And she had to make me a promise. Right, kid?"

She nodded enthusiastically. "Yuh-huh. I had to promise to never, *ever* kiss another boy for my whole life!"

I let out a giggle before getting serious. "Wow, Micah. This is just . . . This is really incredible.

His arm squeezed, giving me a little shake as those leafy green eyes began to smile. "It's not a big deal."

On that, he was very wrong. This *was* a big deal. Maybe not to him, but to Ivy and me it was everything. This *and* how he acted last weekend when he turned all Papa Bear. That he didn't seem to notice, that he wasn't just doing something for my girl in order to win brownie points, was a massive blow to any defense mechanisms I'd put in place.

The warmth overtaking me melted the rigidity in my muscles, and I slowly sank deeper into him. I lifted my hands and placed them on his chest, lowering my voice to a whisper as I said, "Thank you, honey. This is incredible."

His expression changed, his features growing tender as his gaze heated. "I see you like that," he rumbled softly.

"Very much."

"Good. Then gimme a kiss so I can get back to work."

Lifting up on my toes, I did just that. Mindful that my daughter was still standing right there, I didn't take it too far, but I wasn't exactly in a hurry to end it either.

Finally, I pulled away, giving him a smile I hoped reflected my appreciation.

He leaned in for one last peck before letting me go and moving toward Ivy, giving her hair a ruffle. "Come on, Monster. Let's get started."

My baby girl let out an enthusiastic whoop as she ran to keep up with Micah's long strides, and I headed back inside the house.

Silvia was standing at the counter in front of the window when I reentered the kitchen. She looked up from the cutting board where she was dicing tomatoes, her sharp-witted gaze pinning me in place, and I knew I was about to be hit with her wisdom.

"There are men in this world too ignorant to appreciate when they're holdin' somethin' beautiful in the palm of their hands, so instead of takin' care of it so it blooms to its full potential, they neglect it, letting it wilt to nothing. Then there are men who know exactly what they've got, and they use all the breath in their body cultivating and caring for it so each day it's more beautiful than the one before, even if they don't realize they're doin' it. Alex was an ignorant ass. But that man out there, he knows what he's holding in his hands, my precious girl. Don't let fear hold you back from getting what you deserve."

Moving across the kitchen, I came up behind my aunt and placed my hands on her shoulders before bending to press a kiss against the papery skin of her cheek. "I love you, Sylvia. You know that?"

She reached up and gave one of my hands a pat. "Of course I know. And I love you too. Now go start fryin' up some shells so we can eat."

On a laugh, I let her go and moved to the stove. Then I started frying up shells just like she'd ordered.

———

It was hours later . . . after a dinner with the four of us where, between Micah and Ivy, I'd laughed until the muscles in my stomach ached . . . after Micah called it a night with a scorching kiss that left me starving for more and went back to his house . . . after Sylvia had gone back to the carriage house and Ivy had fallen fast asleep in her bed.

I hadn't been able to turn my brain off to find sleep for myself. Instead of tossing and turning, I'd slipped a long cardigan on over my nightgown, put on a pair of thick, fuzzy socks, and with one of the soft, fluffy afghans Sylvia had knitted years ago draped over my shoulders, I headed out to the back garden.

Silva had put a loveseat out here years ago that I'd always favored, the cushions were faded from sun and age, but they were so fluffy you felt like you were sitting on a cloud. I headed right for it, curling up and laying my head back to stare up at the sky. The moon was full and bright, and millions of stars speckling the inky black. It was the kind of sight that took a person's breath away. Sheer beauty, and it was available to me, right here in my own backyard.

I wasn't sure how long I'd been out there when the crunch of footsteps let me know I was no longer alone. Tilting my head, I was able to make out Micah's tall, solid frame from the bulb illuminating the back porch as he headed my way. The short gate let out a creak as he opened it and stepped into the yard.

"Hey," I said softly, not wanting my voice to pierce the peaceful silence. "What are you doing out here?"

"Could ask you the same." He wound his way easily through the paths like he'd walked them so many times they were committed to memory. "It's the middle of the night. What're you doin' out here in the cold all by yourself?"

"Couldn't sleep," I answered as he sat down on the loveseat beside me. He reached across the cushions and plucked me up like I weighed next to nothing, pulling me over to him so we were snuggled together. I adjusted the blanket so it covered both of us as he settled us in and wrapped me up in his arms. "What's your reason?"

"Sleep comes and goes for me. Always has. Got up to take a piss and saw my woman sitting all alone in the dark through my window."

I let out a little snort before giggling and burrowing against him. "Your woman, huh?" There was a tiny voice in the back of my head, warning me that I shouldn't like that, but I ignored her. Sylvia and McKenna were right. I deserved some happiness.

"Yep. Got a problem with that?"

I scrunched my lips to the side, pretending like I was giving that some serious thought before replying, "Nope. I'm actually really okay with it."

That seemed to surprise him. He tilted his face down to mine, the thick slashes of his brows lifting on his forehead. "Yeah?"

"Mmmhmm."

He didn't look convinced. "So you're not gonna keep arguing with me about bein' in a relationship?" he asked skeptically. "I'm not gonna have to kiss you or fuck you into agreement?"

I tipped my face up, smirking seductively as I gave him a wink and replied, "Oh, you'll still have to kiss me and fuck me plenty. Just not to get me to agree that we're in a relationship."

His hands roamed under the blanket, the pads of his fingers finding my ribs and digging in to tickle me. I jerked against him, begging him to stop as tears of laughter started spilling from my eyes.

I collapsed against him, out of breath and still giggling when he finally stopped and curled me back into his warm body. "So why the change of heart?"

"Well, first, how upset would Ivy be if she found out I dumped her best friend in the whole world?"

"Valid point," he said, humor dripping from his words. "She'd take it hard. We're basically each other's favorite people."

Man, that was nice to hear.

I stopped teasing and shrugged, trying to play it cool as I gave him the real answer. "I like you," I answered simply.

"And I'm discovering there's a whole lot to like. But mostly, it's because I like being with you. I like how you make me feel and who I am when I'm with you. And that's important to me; I haven't felt that in a really long time."

His words were laced with concern and genuine curiosity as he asked, "You didn't like yourself when you were with him?"

I inhaled deeply. "It was more like I didn't actually know myself when I was with him. I became someone else when we were together. It started off so small that I barely noticed it was happening. He'd make a comment about my hair or an outfit I was wearing, and I wouldn't think anything of changing it. Before I knew it, I was a completely different woman. Everything I did or said centered around making him happy, but I'd packaged it so I could convince myself and everyone else it wasn't just for him, it was for *us*, for our life and our family.

"I lost who I was, but then I had Ivy, and I started to gain some of the old Hayden back. That woman who'd been fierce and opinionated. I think motherhood does that to a woman. In order to protect my daughter, I needed a bit of that old fire, and Alex didn't like that. Our life no longer centered around him. I didn't do what he wanted at the drop of a hat, without question, so we started to fight more and more. I thought it was a hurdle, and that we'd eventually get past it." I let out a sigh and shrugged against his chest. "I was wrong."

His arm tightened around me as he grunted, "Fuckin' idiot."

Lifting my head off his shoulder, I looked up at him with my brows drawn down. "Huh?"

"Him, Red. He's a fuckin' idiot. That fierceness you

mentioned . . . Christ, it's one of the sexiest things about you, baby." One corner of his mouth hooked up as he added, "Even when you're bein' a stubborn pain in my ass. That first night we met, I liked that you spoke your mind. And after, I liked that you didn't take any of my shit when we fought, that you threw attitude, giving back as good as you got. All of that's what drew me to you in the first place, and I wouldn't trade that for anything."

Warmth hit my chest again, spidering out until it entered my bloodstream and coursed through my body. "Really?"

"Absolutely. Any man worth a shit is gonna want a woman who sticks up for herself and knows her own mind." He leaned in closer, brushing the tip of his nose against mine as he lowered his voice. "And any man worth a shit knows, he gets his hands on fire like that, you don't let it go. You make it grow until it burns wild and out of control, scorching everything in its path."

I released a shaky breath, my eyes darting down to Micah's lips, desperate to taste them. "That sounds dangerous."

"Only way to live. You soak what you can out of life and burn wild, baby. Anything less is only half a life, and what's the point of that?"

Pressing harder against him, I lifted my face just a bit closer, whispering, "So you're gonna hold on and let me burn?"

"Not a chance, Red," he said emphatically. "I intend to get caught in your flames."

Then he kissed me, igniting a fire deep in my belly I wasn't sure would ever go out.

TWENTY

HAYDEN

My stomach sank as soon as I spotted that red Mercedes turning onto our street.

"There he is! Look, Mommy!"

"I see, love bug." I smiled, careful not to show how sad I was that my girl was going to be gone for another weekend. I was looking forward to some quality time with Micah over the next couple of days, but what I'd told Sylvia a couple weeks back still rang true. Handing Ivy off for a weekend wasn't ever going to get easier.

He pulled up to the curb, and sure enough the bitch formerly known as my best friend was sitting right beside him, her large sunglasses doing nothing to hide the glower she was directing at me through the window, like *I'd* done something to *her*.

Alex climbed out of the car and rounded the hood, scooping Ivy up as soon as he reached her. As much as I couldn't stand the sight of him, I'd always count my blessings that he was a good dad to our daughter. Even though our marriage failed, she still had us both, and that was all that mattered to me.

"Hey, monkey. It's so good to see you. I've missed you."

"I missed you too, Daddy!" She hugged his neck tight before pulling back quickly. "Can we gets ice cream for dessert again?"

He looked down at her and let out a small laugh. "We'll see, honey. Did you have a good week?"

Yuh-huh! I gots to play with my friends at daycare and go in with Mommy to the flower shop. Oh, and I gots a new treehouse!"

Alex looked a bit baffled as he turned to me. "You built her a treehouse?"

Ivy got there before I could answer. "My best friend Mike made it. And he gave me six dollars for the swear jar, but Mommy made me give it back," she added with a mild pout.

"Mike? Who's Mike?"

"Mike is—" I began, but before I could get anything else out, Ivy began to squirm, demanding her father put her down, and shouted, "There's Mike!"

Micah's truck came growling around Alex's car and turned into his driveway. Instead of pulling all the way in, he stopped close to the street and climbed out. He was still dressed for work in a pair of gray slacks and a sage green button-down that did *incredible* things for his eyes. His badge was still hooked to his belt, adding an element of authority to his already drop-dead gorgeous appearance. Taking in all that was him just then, it was a wonder I didn't spontaneously orgasm.

"Hey, Monster," he greeted as she ran up to him. She

launched herself into the air, and he caught her with ease, spinning her in a circle that made her squeal before settling her on his hip and closing the rest of the distance between us. Watching that, I nearly swooned into a puddle right there on the walkway.

Before I had a chance to do that, he moved right into me. Looping his free arm around my waist, he pulled me into his chest and bent his neck, pressing a lingering, claiming kiss to my lips. When he pulled back, he still didn't bother acknowledging Alex's presence as he asked, "You have a good day, baby?"

"Uh." It took practically nothing for this sexy man to leave me tongue-tied. "Y-yeah. It was good."

"And what about you, Monster? Good day?"

"Yep!" Ivy told him.

Alex cleared his throat then, demanding attention. He looked at me incredulously. "This is Mike?"

"Micah, actually. Only Ivy calls me Mike." *Oh damn.* I curled my lips between my teeth and had to lower my head to hide my laughter. "And you are?"

"Alex," my ex grated out. "Ivy's *dad*." His gaze bounced between the two of us a few times before finally settling on me, his tone almost accusatory as he asked, "So how long has *this* been going on?"

Once again, I was cut off before I could answer. "I'd say since that weekend in Richmond a little over a month ago." Micah's eyes came to me then, the green glinting with amusement. "Right, Red?"

Had it really been just over a month since I met this man? It felt like so much longer. "Uh huh," I replied, unable to form a full sentence for fear of bursting into laughter.

Alex's mouth gaped open. "I didn't—I wasn't . . ." Tugging at the collar of his shirt, he cleared his throat awkwardly. "I, uh, wasn't aware you were seeing anyone."

I wiped the humor from my face and looked back to him. "Yeah, well . . . now you are. And you guys probably need to get on the road, huh? Ivy hasn't had dinner yet."

Micah turned his attention to my daughter. "All right, Monster. Time to go. Put one there." He pointed at his cheek and Ivy gave it a smacking kiss before he put her down. I crouched down, dislodging Micah's hold so I could give my baby girl a hug and kiss. "Love you, honey. Be good, and I'll see you in a couple days." As soon as I rose back up, Micah reclaimed me.

"Bye!" She waved enthusiastically as she skipped to the car and yanked the back door open.

"Hayden," Alex said, pulling my attention from my daughter. "Can I have a quick word?" He cut his eyes to Micah for a split second. "Alone?"

"Not a chance," my new man answered on my behalf, and the only reason I didn't throw attitude was because he'd said exactly what I'd already planned on saying.

My ex bristled, and in that moment I couldn't help but compare the two men standing there. It was no surprise that Alex came up short by miles. "I wasn't speaking to you, thank you very much. I was talking to my wife."

"No," Micah gritted out instantly, "you were talkin' to *my woman*."

"She knows what I mean."

I heard the whir of the automatic window seconds before Krista's voice sounded. "Alex, sweetie? What's taking so long?"

Things were deteriorating fast, and while I wasn't thrilled Ivy would be leaving with them, I wanted Alex and Krista as far away from my home as possible. "Alex, it's time for you to go."

"Alex, come on," Krista said in a whiny, nasally voice. "I'm hungry."

He clenched his jaw while pulling a sharp breath in through his nose. "Just a second," he said before looking back to me. "I'm going, but you and I need to talk. I'll bring Ivy back a little early on Sunday so you and I have some time to sit down together." At that, I felt Micah's entire body spring so tight I thought he might snap.

"*Alex!*" Krista snapped, but he acted like he couldn't hear her.

"If you want to bring her back early, that's totally fine with me, but unless it directly involves Ivy, you and I have nothing to talk about. And if whatever you have to say *does* directly affect our daughter, you can tell me over the phone or through email."

"Hady Cakes—"

"What did I tell you about calling me that?"

His whole frame rocked back. He was so used to me being the one to jump through hoops to make him happy that he was taken aback by my tone.

"Get in your car and go," Micah rumbled under his voice. "You make me say it again, you aren't gonna like what happens."

"Are you threatening me?"

"Clue in, asshole. You're standin' on my woman's property in my town, and I'm the one wearin' a badge. How do you think this is gonna play out for you?"

I was officially done with this whole thing. Stepping out of Micah's grasp, I moved to the back door of the car and pulled it open, leaning in to buckle Ivy into her booster. "Have the best weekend ever, love bug."

"'Kay, Mommy. Love you."

"And I love you." I gave her one last kiss before closing the door and moving away. I didn't bother giving Alex another look as I started up the cobblestones toward my house. Micah's footfalls sounded on the path as he followed after me. A few seconds later, I heard a car door open and slam shut. Alex's car was gone by the time I walked into my living room and stared out the front window.

Micah came through the front door after me, closing it behind him. I could see him from the corner of my eye as he stopped no more than five feet away and crossed his arms over his chest. "That the bitch he threw you over for?"

"Yep," I muttered, still looking out at my quiet, tree-lined street.

"Shit's gone south between the two of them."

"I suspect your right. Fortunately for me, that's not my problem."

"Hate to be the one to break this to you, baby, but it's about to become your problem."

On that cryptic statement, I finally shifted my focus from the window to him. "What do you mean?"

He moved closer but still didn't touch me. Instead, he stuffed his hands in the pockets of his slacks, and I got the feeling it was in an effort to keep from reaching for me. "Shit's gone bad between them *because* she's a bitch. Told you I'm good at reading people, and I know women like that. She's a chameleon. She's good at changin' herself in order to attract men. But as soon as she's got her claws sunk into the one she wants, the real her comes out. He's seein' that side now, and he isn't liking it. But more, he's regretting the hell out of his stupid-as-fuck decision to walk away from his wife and kid. So, like it or not, it's about to become your problem, 'cause I'm guessin' Sunday is when he plans to make his play."

The skin between my brows creased with a deep frown. "Why are you telling me all this?"

"Because I need to know right now if there's even the smallest part of you that would be willing to give him a second chance."

Realization dawned in that moment. "Ah. I see," I murmured.

"See what?"

"Why you aren't touching me right now. You're holding yourself back because you're worried I might want my ex back."

There was a part of me that was still expecting some smartass, arrogant response, but he didn't give me that. "I don't think it's too much of a leap to have that concern, considering your mood sank the moment you walked away from him."

I let out a heavy sigh and turned fully away from the window, closing the last few feet between us and placing my palms on his chest. "Honey, my mood sank because I had to say goodbye to my girl. This is the first time you've experienced it, but this is how I get every time he picks her up for one of his weekends. I'm not a big fan of handing her over."

His expression remained hard, his eyes swimming with uncertainty. "You sure that's all?"

"The saying 'hindsight is twenty-twenty' exists for a reason, Micah. Sometimes it's hard for a person to see how bad their situation is when they're deep in the middle of it. I'm not saying finding out my husband was fucking another woman while we still shared a bed didn't hurt, because that shit would hurt anybody. But I *can* say with absolute certainty that I see how unfulfilling that relationship was, and there isn't a single part of me, big or small, that would give that man another chance. I don't love him anymore."

His hands finally came out of his pockets and rested on my hips.

I arched a brow, deciding the mood needed to be lightened a bit, and teased, "So . . . you really like me, huh?"

His fingers pressed in hard enough to make marks on my skin as he bent to trace the column of my neck with his tongue. I let out a stuttered sigh and dropped my head back to give him better access. "Baby, you have no idea."

I pressed closer, feeling the hard, defined ridge of his steel erection through his pants. "Then I suggest you take me to bed and show me."

The last word barely passed my lips before he bent low and tossed me over his shoulder like he'd carried those two-by-fours the other day. Then he bolted up the stairs like he was in an Olympic race.

TWENTY-ONE
HAYDEN

The sound that rattled from his chest and up his throat sent a new wave of arousal through me and pooled between my thighs. Lifting my eyes, I looked up, over his taut abdominals and rapidly rising chest, to see the cords strained and protruding as he clenched his jaw. His eyes were like green fire, pinned on me as I swirled my tongue around the fat crown of his cock.

I'd seen Micah in the throes of ecstasy, but I'd never had such an outstanding view of what he looked like when he was on the brink. It drove me wild. I felt myself getting close, and other than the hand fisting my hair, he wasn't even touching me.

Pulling a deep breath in through my nose, I relaxed my throat and took him deep. As much as I wanted to, I'd never be able to take his full length, but I was determined to get as much of him in my mouth as I could. The head of his cock bumped the back of my throat, and I swallowed on instinct, wrenching another animalistic sound from him.

"Jesus, *fuck*!" he clipped, the fist in my hair tightening reflexively. "Goddamn, my wild woman."

I started sucking faster, bringing my fist up to meet my lips on each downward glide. I was drunk on his taste, on the sounds he was making, on the fact that it was *me* bringing this man to the edge of sanity. I felt myself getting closer to my release as I brought him toward his own.

"Christ, Hayden, baby. I'm about to blow." His words were a warning to let me know I needed to move, but I wanted all of it. I was determined to watch him from my place, curled up between his bent legs.

I hollowed my cheeks, prepared to take him all the way past the finish line when I was suddenly pulled off his cock and flying through the air. I landed on the mattress with an *ooph*.

"I wasn't finished," I snapped as he came to hover over me.

"You were finished," he panted, sitting back on his haunches and pulling me up so my ass was resting on his strong thighs. In this position, I was completely open and exposed to him.

"No I wasn't. I wanted to watch you—oh *shit*!" My protest ended on a cry when he buried himself to the hilt.

He looked down at me with a self-satisfied smirk. "Yeah, baby, that's what I thought."

"Shut up and fuck me," I gritted, stretching my arms over my head to wrap my fingers around the headboard.

He let out a grunted curse and drove into me again and again. His muscles strained and beads of sweat formed along his hairline as he fucked me at a pace that was almost a punishment. And *God* I loved it. "Why the hell does the fact you're arguing while I'm fuckin' you turn me on so much?"

I smiled and stretched my limbs like a cat so he could see *everything* while I circled my hips to match each of his thrusts. "Because you know I'll burn for you," I answered in a low, husky voice.

He gripped my hips so hard I thought he might leave behind bruises, but I didn't care. I *wanted* to be able to see his mark on me long after we finished. Just the thought of that made my pussy ripple greedily.

"Fuck yeah," he gritted between clenched teeth. "You gonna burn for me now, baby?"

My head fell deeper into the pillows and my eyes slammed shut as the pressure built in my core to an almost frightening level. "*Micah,*" I whimpered, feeling goosebumps pebble across my skin.

"That's it. Almost there, my wild woman." His hands moved, one going up to pull at my straining nipples while the other traveled south to my clit. "Give it to me, Hayden. Let me hear you scream while you flood my cock."

And I did just that. Without having to worry about anyone hearing us, I let my orgasm overtake me until my throat burned from screaming his name. He kept at me until there was absolutely nothing left, my bones were liquid, and my vision spotty. Only then did he give me his weight, pumping into me so hard the headboard slammed into the wall over and over.

"Fuck, Hayden," he ground out. "So good. *Every goddamn time.*" I wasn't sure how it was even possible, but I felt another one building inside me as his length swelled.

My eyes went wide. "Oh God, *Micah.*"

"With me, baby. Come with me, now—*Uhn!*" He slammed deep and planted himself there on a wild groan. The first spurt of his release set me off, and I came again on a long, low moan. We rode it out together, clutching each other tight as we came together.

Just as he'd done the last time, he kept us physically connected once we were finished, shifting us in my bed so we were lying face to face on our sides.

I lay there with my eyes closed, feeling like I was floating on a cloud as he traced my hairline with the tips of his fingers before slowly and gently dragging them through my hair.

I managed to peel my eyelids open so I could look up at him, and saw he was watching his hand with fascination. It was as if watching my hair fall through his fingers was mesmerizing. His expression was so soft and unguarded it nearly stole my breath.

"I need to clean up," I whispered a few minutes later. I hated the thought of losing him like this, but I knew I wouldn't be able to sleep with him leaking out of me.

He moved, but not to let me go so I could get up. Instead, he rolled, throwing his legs over the edge and climbed out of the bed. I watched, with my knees curled closer to my chest, as he padded across the floor to the bathroom. I heard the sink turn on and off before he returned, carrying a damp washcloth in his hand.

He put his knee onto the mattress and leaned over me, placing his palm on my thigh and gently applying pressure until I lifted it. My heart swelled, the emotions that were bombarding me almost too much to contain. It was just as Sylvia had said. Without even realizing he was doing it, he was nourishing that beauty he held in the palm of his hands.

I sucked in a short gasp when he gently brushed the cloth over my folds. He stopped instantly, his eyes darting up to my face. "Was I too rough?"

I smiled at the concern chiseled into his handsome face. "No, honey. I'm just a little sensitive is all. But in a *really* good way."

The worry melted away, replaced with a triumphant smile as he finished cleaning himself from my skin. He tossed the rag across the room, and I was way too blissed-out to give him shit for not putting it in the hamper. Instead, I stretched my limbs, grinning at the dull aches and throbs in my body from Micah's ministrations.

My stomach chose that moment to let out a little growl. We'd been so desperate to tear into each other that I'd forgotten all about eating dinner, and my body was letting me know it now needed to be taken care of in a different way.

Rolling across the mattress, I climbed out of the bed and grabbed my panties from off the floor, stepping into them and pulling them up my legs before snatching up Micah's discarded shirt.

"For the love of God, why are you putting *on* clothes?" he grunted, looking like a mopey teenager as he stared at me from the bed.

"Because I'm starving," I told him as I did a few of the buttons up and untucked my hair from the collar. "You're welcome to stay in here and pout, but I need sustenance."

I let out a little squeak and jumped back on a giggle as he lunged for me, attempting to grab my arm and pull me back.

"Uh-uh. Food. Then play."

With that, I darted out of the room on a peal of laughter as he ran after me.

―――――

Micah

I wasn't sure what woke me, but when I blinked my eyes open, Hayden's brightly decorated room was bathed in darkness, only the faint white glow of the moon filtered through the window.

Movement at my side pulled my attention to Hayden's sleeping form. She'd been curled against me the entire night, her long, silky hair fanned out across my skin. I'd never considered myself a cuddler, but as she rolled to her other side in her sleep, the space she'd just occupied and the skin she'd been pressed against suddenly felt cold.

I wanted her back against me, but before I went about seeing to that, I felt a need that couldn't be ignored. Carefully sliding out of the bed, I quietly padded out of the room and down the stairs. I checked the locks on all the doors and windows and shut off the few remaining lights still on throughout the house. Standing at the living room window, I stared out at the street, my eyes scanning as if I were looking for some kind of hidden danger lurking in the shadows that I needed to protect the woman upstairs from.

It was a sensation I'd never experienced before. I was protective of my family and the people I loved, sure. But I'd never had someone in my life who made every protective instinct I had thrash inside of me with the need to get out. She was completely safe, tucked away upstairs, fast asleep. Even though there was no threat, I still stood there, the muscles beneath my skin twitching with anticipation like a guard dog prepared to strike out at anything that could possibly cause her the slightest hint of harm. For the first time in my life, I had someone I'd fight to the death and bleed myself dry to protect.

Once I felt the house was completely secure, I moved back up the stairs. Hayden's soft floral scent invaded my senses as soon as I entered the room, loosening the ball of tension I hadn't realized had formed in my chest.

Sliding back beneath the sheets, I reached for her, wrapping my arms around her belly so I could pull her into me, pressing my chest to her back. Burying my face in all her incredible hair, I breathed her in deeper and felt myself settle.

She let out a little hum as she nuzzled deeper into me, sleepily mumbling, "Where'd you go?"

"Just checkin' to make sure everything was locked up. Go back to sleep, baby."

"'Kay," she murmured. Seconds later, she was out again. And as I lay there, holding her tight, I felt pressure building in my chest unlike anything I'd ever experienced.

This had to have been what the guys at work were talking about when they said I'd meet a woman who'd knock me on my ass one day, because as I pulled her even closer, I couldn't shake the sense that wrapped in my arms was the most important thing in my life.

TWENTY-TWO
HAYDEN

My phone started to ring again. Letting out a sigh, I pulled it from my purse and checked the screen, seeing the same name I'd seen twice already in the past twenty minutes.

Silencing the call, I flipped it over face down on the table and picked up my coffee, taking a long sip.

McKenna looked at me from across the table we were sitting at inside Muffin Top and lifted her brows quizzically. "You need to take that? That thing's been blowing up since you got here."

"Just ignore it." Right on cue, the cell chimed with an incoming text.

We'd met at Muffin Top not only because the coffee was exceptional, but because Dani would come over to chat with us whenever there was a lull. It was supposed to have been my own personal time, where I got to hang with a couple of my new friends, shooting the breeze and talking about nothing in particular, but every time that stupid phone rang, my shoulders bunched up, knotting with tension.

"Whoever that is, they're pretty damn persistent," Dani stated.

Propping my elbows on the table, I let out a little groan and massaged my temples. "It's Alex."

When I'd refused to talk to him the day he brought Ivy home, he'd taken to calling and texting nonstop. It was a major annoyance for me, but it was *really* starting to piss Micah off.

"Maybe it's important?" McKenna queried. "What if it's about Ivy?"

"It isn't," I replied flatly. "This has been going on since he brought Ivy home three days ago."

Dani crossed her forearms and leaned closer to rest them on the table, lowering her voice so people couldn't eavesdrop. "What's going on?"

I told them all about what had gone down during his pickup the Friday before. From Micah showing up and staking his claim, to Alex's insistence that we needed to talk.

"Oh damn." McKenna dropped back into her chair with wide eyes. "I bet seeing Micah Langford all territorial like that was all *kinds* of hot."

I sighed dreamily, thinking back to how sexy Micah had been.

"Stay on track," Dani demanded, pulling me from the lusty fog that filled my head every time I thought about Micah. "So, what happened on Sunday?"

"Nothing. Like I'd already told him, we had nothing to say to each other, so I refused to have a little sit down with him when he dropped her off. But I noticed Ivy was in a mood when she got home. She was mopey and quiet all evening, and when I finally got her to talk to me about it, she told me he and Krista fought pretty much the whole time she was with them, and that Krista had been mean to her."

"God, what a bitch," McKenna seethed.

"Pretty much. I'd been ignoring his calls until I found that out, so when he called the next time, I answered and ripped into him about letting that woman be mean to our daughter."

"What did he say?" Dani asked.

"Basically that he was leaving Krista and wanted me back. That he'd made a huge mistake divorcing me, and he wanted Ivy and me to 'come home.'"

The sweet, smiling coffee shop owner slammed her palm down on the table, making us jump. "What a fucking dick!"

"Obviously, I told him he could go straight to hell, but he's got it in his head that if he keeps reminding me about all the good times we had, I'll change my mind and come back to him. That's what the texts are about."

I flipped my phone over and swiped the screen, going to the text chain that contained one long-ass message after another. I slid it to them and let them read about our weekend at Virginia Beach for the Fourth of July, the Christmas we spent in a secluded cabin together in the mountains, and all the other memories that didn't mean a thing to me anymore.

They both leaned over my phone, their attention rapt as McKenna scrolled so they could keep reading.

Dani's curious gaze returned to me once she finished. "So, none of these are getting to you? Like, you don't feel yourself softening at all?"

I jabbed my finger at the phone. "That family trip to Disney World he mentioned? I didn't know it at the time, but his affair with Krista was already in full swing by then. I can only assume that at least a few of the 'business calls' he'd taken every evening, locking himself in our room for at least an hour so I wouldn't interrupt, were her."

McKenna cleared her throat in an attempt to mask her laugh. "I know this isn't supposed to be funny, but come on! The fact that this guy's *that* stupid is pretty damn hilarious."

The thought of finding Alex's lame attempts funny hadn't crossed my mind until that very moment, but now that my friend had pointed it out, it *was* pretty hilarious.

"Oh my God," I choked out through a giggle. "You're right!"

We all fell into a peal of laughter that lasted until I had tears in my eyes. "All right, so enough about that jerk-off," Dani said after pulling in a deep breath. "Tell us about you and Micah. Everyone's still buzzing about the fact the town's biggest playboy finally found a woman he can't get enough of."

I got that same sinking feeling in my stomach I felt when McKenna had brought up Micah's bachelor ways. As much as I tried to tell myself I was being ridiculous, that things between Micah and me were fantastic, since that little bug had been placed in my ear, I occasionally caught myself playing the *what if* game. What if he cheats? What if he ends up realizing he doesn't want to be in a relationship? What if I have too much baggage?

I tried to keep my mind from journeying down that dark path, but sometimes I couldn't help it. We hadn't been together very long, but the intensity between us made it feel like I'd known him forever, and each day I woke up to find he'd taken another piece of me.

I was falling for him faster than I'd ever fallen before, and to think I could be taking that dive all by myself was terrifying.

"We're good," I replied, making sure to inject cheer into my tone. "Everything's good. It's still early, you know? We're just taking one day at a time." And maybe if I kept saying that enough, my heart would stop jumping ten steps ahead.

"I'm so happy it's you," Dani said on a sigh. "I mean, he's always shot me down any time I mentioned setting him up, and, God"—she rolled her eyes dramatically—"the women he'd pick up at the bars. It was *ridiculous*. We were all worried when he finally *did* set his sights on someone for good, she'd be someone none of us could stand. But you're you, and we *love* you."

The compliment buried in there didn't quite penetrate, so the smile I gave her felt stiff and brittle.

She kept going, oblivious to the turmoil roiling around inside of me. "Leo says now all that's left is for him to pay up on the bet."

"Bet?" I asked, my ears perking up. "What bet?"

She tried waving it off like it was nothing. "Oh, it's just this stupid thing. Trick and Hayes were giving him grief, saying sooner or later he'd fall on his ass for a woman. Micah was so confident it was never gonna happen, he said he'd split his paycheck between them if that day ever came."

A cold chill pricked at my neck, and the sip of coffee I'd just taken turned to cement in my stomach. If he was refusing to pay up, that couldn't mean good things for the future of our relationship.

Before I had a chance to twist that into something nasty and painful in my head, my phone went off. I glanced down at the screen and let out a sigh of relief that it wasn't Alex's name I saw, and quickly engaged the call. "Hey Sylvia, what's up?"

"Hey, darlin' girl. Just wanted to check and make sure you weren't already on your way back to the shop."

There was something about her tone that made my brow furrow. She sounded on edge. "Well, no, not yet. But if you need me now, I can head that way—"

"No, no!" she blurted quickly. "No, don't do that. As a matter of fact, maybe just take the rest of the day off."

"Sylvia, what's going on? Are you all right?" That question caught my friends' attention, and they stopped the whispered conversation they'd been having to listen more intently to me.

"I'm fine. Just dealin' with a little issue here at the shop. But don't you worry, the police should be here soon enough."

My back went straight. "The *police*?"

Before she could get another word out, I heard a familiar voice shouting in the background. "Is that her? You tell her to get down here right this instant!"

"Oh my God," I breathed. "Is that—?"

"For the love of Christ, Krista? Will you just shut the hell up?" a masculine voice growled through the line.

"Are you *kidding* me?" I snapped.

Aunt Sylvia let out a defeated sigh. "Believe me, lovely. I wish I were."

"I'll be right there."

Disconnecting the call, I dropped the phone back into my purse and shot to my feet.

"What's going on?" McKenna asked as she and Dani followed suit.

"Alex and Krista are at the shop," I seethed. Their mouths dropped open, their eyes bulging in shock. "I have to go. I need to get there before the cops do so I have a chance to tear them both a new asshole."

"We're going with," Dani called, scrambling to follow after me.

"Hell yeah we are," McKenna agreed. "No way I'm missing this."

I made it the few blocks from Muffin Top to Divine Flora in record time, having power-walked at an Olympic speed. I spotted Alex's Mercedes right away. There was also a police cruiser sitting outside the shop by the time we hit the parking lot, and next to it, surprisingly, was Micah's truck.

I could hear the raised voices before I yanked the door open, and what I saw when I stepped inside would have been laughable if I wasn't so pissed off.

Sylvia stood behind one of the counters with Sonya and Raul. The three of them were bent at the waist, elbows to the counter with their chins in their hands, watching the scene in front of them like they would watch a cage fight. With rapt fascination. All they were missing was a bucket of popcorn.

Front and center were Krista and Alex, engaged in a shouting match as a uniformed officer stood between them, arms out to keep them separated. Micah and Leo stood off to the side, with much the same demeanor as my aunt and our employees, only I could sense an undercurrent of anger radiating from Micah.

"What the hell is going on?" I cried just as Dani and McKenna came stumbling in behind me.

"*You!*" Krista shouted, pointing an accusatory finger my way.

My chin jerked back in bewilderment. "Me?"

"Why can't you just *stay gone*?"

McKenna leaned in and stage-whispered in my ear. "Is that your ex-best friend?"

"Yep."

"He traded way down, babe."

Krista heard that and slapped her hands down on her hips. "And who the hell are you?"

"I'm her *new* best friend," McKenna offered snottily.

"Yeah? Well no one was talking to you, so stay the hell out of it." She turned her venomous gaze back to me. "You need to leave Alex alone. You two are over! Just accept that and move on already. This is just pathetic."

"Krista," Alex growled in warning, but we both ignored him.

I tried to hold back my laugh, which resulted in me letting out a loud snort. "Are you serious? Krista, sweetheart, you may want to get a few things straight with your man before you drive forty-five minutes out of the way to confront someone," I said condescendingly. "You're just embarrassing yourself, because it's obvious you don't know what the hell you're talking about."

"I'm not her man," Alex blurted before she could get a word out. He started toward me but was stopped when Micah moved fast, cutting off his path.

"That's close enough."

My ex's face grew red, his features twisting up with anger. "You need to stay out of my way. This is between me and my wife."

"Your *wife*?" Krista shrieked.

"For the love of God, I am *not* your wife!" I cried in frustration.

Meanwhile, Micah moved closer. It was only one step, but it was more than enough to scare the hell out of any regular person. "Gave you one warnin' already, pal," he snarled. "That's all you're gonna get. You call her your wife one more time, you'll be eating all your meals through a straw."

"You can't threaten me!" he blustered, looking to the uniformed officer. "Did you hear that? This man just threatened me."

I didn't recognize the man, but I knew instantly that I liked him when he scrunched his face in confusion. "Huh? Sorry, didn't hear that."

"This is outrageous! I'll be calling your superiors—"

"Alex!" I shouted, cutting him off while sidestepping Micah so I could get this whole thing over with. "Just say why you're here and leave. This is my place of business, not the set of a goddamn soap opera."

"Hady Cakes, I want you back," he blurted. "I made a huge mistake, honey. I didn't appreciate what I had when I had it—"

"Well no shit," Aunt Sylvia muttered loudly.

"I still love you," he continued. "I never stopped. You have to believe me. I know we can get back to where we once were. Remember all the good times?"

"You mean like that trip to Disney you texted me about?"

He smiled wide, his gaze filling with hope as he took a step closer. "Yeah. Exactly! Remember how great that was?"

"Actually, we were just talking about that, weren't we, ladies?" I glanced back at Dani and McKenna. "You know, I'm curious about something. Did knowing your wife and daughter were just on the other side of the door make it difficult to get off when you were having phone sex with your slut? Is that why your "*business calls*" took so long?" I scrunched my face into a mock look of pity. "Did you have a bit of stage fright?"

I heard a snort and looked over just in time to see Leo and the other officer duck their heads, but not before I saw the grin on each of their faces.

Alex's eyes got huge as all the color leached from his face. "I didn't—that wasn't—"

"You'd already been fucking her for three months by the time we took that trip, dumbass. I guess you forgot that when you were texting me that little trip down memory lane."

"Damn," the officer muttered, shaking his head in disapproval. "That's a whole new level of stupid."

"No one asked you!" Alex rasped quickly before jerking back around to me.

"You need to take your fiancée and leave," I said firmly. "Get out of my shop and my town."

"Hayden, please. You have to listen to me—"

"No I don't. You made your choice. The wife and the child you already had weren't good enough, so you went out and got replacements. That's on you."

"She was never pregnant!" he shouted.

The weight of those words slammed into me so hard I stumbled back a step. If it hadn't been for Micah taking my arms and pressing his chest against my back, I probably would have gone down.

Everything shifted in that moment. The air, the ground beneath my feet, that goddamn organ inside my chest.

"What?" I whispered, finding it hard to breathe all of a sudden.

"She was never pregnant," he repeated, his voice tortured. "I didn't know. I thought—I . . . I only just found out there was no baby."

Krista at least had the good grace to look contrite as I slowly turned my attention to her. "You're unbelievable," I started quietly. Then my voice boomed. "God! You fucking *bitch*! You knew!"

"Hayden, baby—" Micah started, but all I could see was red.

"How many times did we cry together? How many times, Krista?" I shook my head in disgust. "I called you in tears after every miscarriage, after every failed fertility treatment!"

"Oh shit," I heard grunted, but was too lost in what I'd just discovered to pay attention to anyone else in that room.

"You poured me wine and held me while I broke down. You were the only person I had to talk to. You knew how it broke me every single time I lost a child before finally having Ivy. I lived through that pain for *years*. And you used a fake pregnancy to *steal my husband*? How fucking low can you get?"

"That's absolutely disgusting," Dani spat, staring daggers at Krista.

Her chest heaved as her gaze darted around at everyone in the shop, taking in each of their disgusted expressions before snapping, "You had everything! You had the perfect house and the perfect husband and the perfect life! You had it all, and you didn't even care! I didn't have *anything*. I was all alone!"

Micah's voice rumbled from behind me. "Because you're a miserable cunt."

My head whipped around, and I looked up at him in shock as Krista snarled, "You can't talk to me that way."

"I can talk to you whatever fuckin' way I want. Had you pegged the moment I saw you. You're a nasty bitch who wants what everyone around you has, but you're too damn lazy to work for it. You think, 'cause you got a decent face and probably starve yourself to stay thin, that shit's just supposed to fall in your lap. Then, when it doesn't, you blame everyone else. You were alone before because any man with half a brain in his head can see your bullshit from a mile away."

He tilted his chin in Alex's direction, adding, "You wised up for a second, got your hooks in a fuckin' idiot who was stupid enough to think shiny and new was better than what he was lucky enough to already have. But you couldn't keep the act up forever, and the minute he caught a glimpse of the soul-sucking leech you really are, he bolted."

Like the Krista I remembered was prone to do when something wasn't going her way, she covered her face with her hands and burst into tears—or at least pretended to—waiting for someone in the shop to come running to her rescue.

Turning my head, I pressed my face into Micah's side to stifle my giggle, but it was no use. The giggle turned into a snort, which turned into full blown laughter that lasted a solid minute.

When I finally got a hold of myself and tilted my head back to look up at him, he was already grinning down at me.

"You good, Red?"

I returned his smile, feeling his warm green eyes like a physical caress. "Yeah, sorry, honey. This whole thing is just so ridiculous."

"Are you fucking kidding me," Alex barked, ruining the moment. "Hayden, you and I really need to talk. If we could just go somewhere—"

Turning to look at him, I pinned him in place with a flat expression. "No. We aren't going anywhere to talk, because there's nothing to talk about. I'm not in love with you anymore, Alex. Stop calling. Stop texting. I honestly don't give a single shit what happens between you and Krista, but whatever the outcome, it won't change things between us. We're done."

He threw a hand Micah's way. "This is because of him—"

"You're absolutely right. It *is* because of him. It's because he lets me be me. He's never once tried to change who I am. It's also because I like who I am when I'm with him. He's never made me feel like I'm less than anything if I don't do something he wants. And it's because he's constantly showing me in little ways that he knows he's lucky to have me, and he doesn't take that for granted. Even at our best, I never got any of that from you."

He looked completely ravaged by the time I finished talking, but I didn't have it in me to care.

"For Ivy's sake, I'd like it if you and I could get along, but that's not my call to make. If you can't give me that, I'll be disappointed, but make no mistake, it won't change how I feel. You're just the man I share a daughter with, Alex. That's all."

"You—" He cleared his throat when his voice broke and started again on a pained whisper. "You're the love of my life."

I shook my head, looking at my ex-husband with pity. "For your sake, I hope to God that's not true. Because if that's how you treat the love of your life, you're going to be leading a very lonely existence."

Sensing I was done in more ways than one, Micah spoke next. "The two of you have three seconds to get in your cars and get out of my town, or I'll arrest you both for trespassing and harrassement."

Krista proved to be dumber than she looked by attempting to argue. "You can't do that! We aren't—"

The look he gave her could have turned lava to ice. "One," he growled.

She caught on after that and scurried out of Divine Flora.

Alex was slower to go, stopping beside me and staring in my eyes for a few seconds. Apparently, whatever he saw in them backed up everything I'd just said, because his shoulders sunk in defeat, and he left without another word.

With that over, I looked at the uniformed officer and said, "I'm Hayden, by the way. I know we only just met, but I swear, there's usually not this much drama swirling around me."

His lips trembled. "Fred Duncan. Nice to meet you."

"Seeing as you work with Micah, I wish we'd met under better circumstance, but I'll try to make up for it the second time."

His smile was genuine as he said, "I'll look forward to it."

Then, with a tilt of his chin at Leo and Micah, he headed for the door.

"Whoowee!" Sylvia called out, standing tall and slapping the countertop. "Talk about drama. I don't know about you guys, but I could use a drink after that. I'll go grab the bottle of gin I keep stashed in the back office."

Just like that, my aunt managed to break through the tension and make everyone smile.

TWENTY-THREE

MICAH

My cell vibrated on the bedside table, yanking me out of a fitful sleep. I hadn't had a good night's sleep more than a handful of times in the past month, even with Hayden curled up beside me most nights.

After the showdown at her flower shop, things with our relationship seemed to move at lightning speed. But it hadn't seemed rushed. It felt natural to sit Ivy down and tell her that her mommy and her Mike were in a relationship, even if she didn't fully comprehend the meaning of that.

It felt natural to start spending most of my nights in Hayden's bed. And in the past month, I'd discovered that slow, quiet sex was just as phenomenal as when we fucked hard and rough. Hell, even the few quickies we had to squeeze in every now and then were out of this world.

None of that freaked me out. In fact, with shit hitting nuclear with the Callo investigation, the only time I'd really been able to breathe over the past few weeks was when I was with Hayden and Ivy.

Knowing who was at fault and not being able to do a

goddamn thing about it was slowly starting to drive me out of my mind.

Ballistics on the bullet that killed Evan Webb had come back as a match to the bullets recovered from Darrin Callo's murder, but without the murder weapon, there was no way to link it back to Cormack.

However, the worst thing about this whole nightmare happened just two days ago when Sidney Callo had come into the department asking questions about her husband's murder. She still looked like a shell of her former self months later, and the fact we had nothing to give her to put her mind at ease burned a hole in my chest.

Pulling my arms from around Hayden's soft, warm body, I sat up and threw my legs over the side of the bed as I grabbed my phone and read the text that had just come in. *Alpha Omega. 20 mins.*

Goddamn it.

Moving across the room, I grabbed the clothes I'd discarded earlier and started pulling them back on.

I was lacing my left boot when the bedside lamp flipped on, casting a golden glow through the room.

I twisted my head as Hayden pushed up onto one hand, using the other to push her wild mass of wavy hair out of her sleepy face.

"Micah?" she mumbled, her voice thick with sleep. "What're you doin'?"

"Nothin', baby," I replied quietly. "Go back to sleep."

She became more alert as she took me in. "Are you leaving?"

I moved back to the bed and bent over her, tucking her

hair behind her ear. "It's a work thing. I'll be back as soon as I can, yeah?"

Worry creased her pretty face. "Is everything okay?"

"Yeah, Red. It's all good. Promise. Just go back to sleep." I leaned in and pressed my lips against hers. "I'll be back before you know it."

With that, I stood and headed out.

I circled a three block radius around Alpha Omega, keeping an eye out for any other cars driving through town at two in the morning. When I felt the coast was clear, I parked my truck in an alley a block away and stuck to the shadows as I jogged the rest of the way to Lincoln's offices.

The back door was unlocked by the time I got there, so I pushed through and immediately started for the conference room. Linc was already there, along with Leo, Dalton, and the rest of the team assigned to this case. But the person I was most surprised to see was Charlie. She sat near the head of the table, her arms crossed defiantly over her chest as she scowled at the room at large. The ponytail on top of her head was askew, flopping off toward one side, and she had pillow creases on her right cheek. It was obvious from her rumpled appearance, she'd been sleeping before this meeting was called.

"What are you doin' here?" I asked as I took a seat next to Leo.

She cut me a scathing glare. "Ask your guard dog. I was dead asleep—having the best dream in which I was smothering him to death with a pillow—when he dragged me out of bed, tossed me in his truck, and drove me here."

I turned to Dalton and cocked a brow in question. He shrugged like it was nothing. "My job's to stay on her and keep her safe. Can't do either of those things if I'm here and she's at home in bed."

That sounded reasonable enough to me, so I shifted my attention to Linc. "Why're we here?"

"I have some good news and some bad news. Got word less than an hour ago. You'll be gettin' a call later this mornin' that the gun you've been lookin' for in the Callo and Webb shootings has been recovered."

That didn't put me at ease in the slightest.

"And the bad news?" Leo pressed.

"The gun was found in the home of one Sergeant Wayne Gilmore of the Hidalgo County Sheriff's Department." The second name Charlie had given us weeks back. "His body was found hanging from a rafter in the garage, and there was a note on the kitchen table in which he confessed to the killings. They also uncovered close to a quarter million in cash, as well as enough meth and heroine to supply a third of the goddamn town."

"God*damn it*," I boomed, driving the side of my fist into the table top.

Charlie looked around the table, her eyes wide, the normal hardness replaced by panic. "So what does this mean?"

Leo answered, ranking his hands through his hair agitatedly. "It means, unless the medical examiner rules it otherwise, we're gonna be expected to close the case."

"But you can't!" she cried. "It wasn't him. Gilmore was an asshole and a dirty cop, but he was just a soldier. For this to end, you have to cut the head off the snake."

"Doesn't matter," I grunted. "A case like this, everything bundled together with a tidy bow like that . . ." I shook my head in defeat. "Our captain's gonna push for this to be the end of it."

"But you can at least wait for the medical examiner's report, right? I mean, you can't close a case until the cause of death is listed," she stated with no small amount of hope in her voice.

I focused my attention on her, gentling my tone and expression as I said, "That's not gonna take long, sweetheart."

"Well then *make* it take long!" she cried, slapping her hands down on the table and whipping her head around to Lincoln. "Put one of your guys on him," she insisted frantically. "That scary-looking computer dude. Have him press the guy to drag his feet a little longer."

Silence enveloped the room for several seconds before Lincoln's guy Trent broke it. "Actually, that's not the worst idea. If anyone can coerce that guy into waiting, it's Xander. He'd scare the piss outta just about anybody."

Lincoln spoke in response. "I'll have a word with him."

We called an end to the meeting shortly after, and I rose to my feet slower than the rest of the guys, my gaze pinned on Charlie. I caught her by the arm before she could clear the door, turning her around so I could see her face, most specifically, her worry-filled eyes. "You good?"

"No," she croaked, giving her head a shake. "This has to end, Micah. I need this to end."

I pulled her into a hug, feeling her body tremble against mine. This was taking its toll on everyone here, but I was starting to think this girl, a girl who'd already dealt with more shit than any one person should, was reaching her breaking point. "I know, darlin'." I gave her a squeeze, hoping like hell it offered at least a small bit of comfort. "We're gonna get this guy. We'll get him and shut this shit down once and for all, and you'll never have to worry about it again. You have my word."

Dalton came up to us, and I shifted Charlie in my arms, twisting her around so he could take over comforting her. I knew, as soon as she burrowed in instead of pulling away, that she was at the end of her rope.

We needed to end this. Because Sidney Callo deserved justice for her husband. And because Charlie Belmont deserved to *finally* have a good life.

Twenty-Four

Hayden

I felt like I'd spent the week walking on eggshells. I knew with the kind of job Micah had, his hours could be erratic, and some cases might weigh heavily on his mind, but as the month ticked by, it felt like he was living in a constant state of stress.

The first red flag had gone up when his phone started going off constantly. If he was with me when it did, he'd either ignore it or take it into another room, always saying it was a work thing. The second happened when I began to ask him what was going on. All he'd tell me was that it had to do with a case, but that he couldn't tell me any more about it.

My mind had gone back to when he and Dani had both warned me to stay away from Greg Cormack. Micah had gone so far as to tell me the man was dangerous, but no matter how many times I'd asked him to explain, his response was always the same. "I can't tell you right now, Red. But I swear I will as soon as I can."

As much as it pained me, I pushed that all to the back of my mind, telling myself it was just residual uncertainty left over from my relationship with Alex, and that I was putting past experiences on Micah when he didn't deserve it. After all, when we were together, he was still as affectionate and demonstrative as always. There hadn't been a day that passed where we hadn't had sex at least once. It was as if he couldn't get enough of me. And at night, he'd hold me so close it felt like he was trying to become a part of me.

The biggest, most glaringly obvious flag came two nights ago, after he'd left in the middle of the night, claiming another work thing. I'd tried waiting up for him, determined to get answers no matter what, but the more time that passed, the harder it was to keep my eyes open, and eventually I fell into a fitful sleep.

I'd woken when he climbed back into bed over an hour later. When he'd rolled me into him and held me close, I caught a faint smell of perfume on his skin—the sweet, scent I'd never worn before, like chocolate and caramel and vanilla. I leaned toward subtle floral body washes and lotions, and what I was smelling on his skin was more gourmand. Definitely not my style.

He'd fallen asleep quickly, while I'd lain there awake, fighting back tears. I'd spent the next two days trying to rationalize what I'd discovered, desperate to make all the pieces fit together to form a puzzle of my liking, because the truth of it was, I was in love with him, and the fear of finding out the truth made me choke up each and every time I attempted to confront him.

I'd gone as far as calling Dani to ask what she knew, but when she answered I chickened out and pretended I'd called just to shoot the breeze.

When I woke up this morning to him rolling me over

onto my back so he could kiss me long and slow before he left for work, my heart cracked, a jagged, ugly tear that stretched right down the center. I realized I had reverted back to my old ways, burying my head in the sand and pretending everything wasn't slowly circling the drain instead of being the woman Micah had claimed to like so damn much. And I couldn't let it go on for another day.

I'd planned to confront him when he got off work, but things went a little sideways when he called earlier, sounding more animated than he had in weeks.

"Look, Red, I know I've been shit at this whole boyfriend gig lately, and I hate that. Work has been a mess, but I made a reservation for dinner at The Groves tonight. Just you and me. I want to take you out on a proper date, baby."

That call was a blow to my resolve, but I'd given myself about a million pep-talks since then, reminding myself I was worth more.

When I'd gotten off the phone and asked Sylvia what The Groves was, her eyes had nearly bugged out of her head. Apparently, it was the best steakhouse in the area and far beyond. Super expensive and super swank. She'd practically been giddy as she all but shoved me out of Divine Flora, insisting I take the extra time to really "gussy up" for my special night.

Now Ivy was on her belly in my bed, her chin propped in her hands, her bent legs swinging back and forth as she watched me get ready for my date with Micah.

"So, what do you think?" I asked as I turned in a slow circle so my baby girl could get the full effect. The dress I'd chosen was a black off-the-shoulder minidress with a fun white floral pattern. It hugged my curves and the hem hit right around mid-thigh, exposing a good length of leg. I wore a pair of four-inch peep-toe pumps that had thick ribbons that twisted around each ankle and tied in a bow at the back. My hair was down in its natural wave, and my makeup was done a bit smokier than normal.

"Mommy, you look so pretty," she breathed out dramatically. "Like a princess!"

"Yoo-hoo." Sylvia's voice carried up the stairs.

"Up here," I called back as Ivy jumped off the bed, her four-year-old attention span already bored with what we were doing.

My great-aunt appeared in the doorway a minute later. "Well look at you, simply beautiful, my darlin' girl."

I ran my hands down the front of my dress, brushing out the imaginary wrinkles. "You think so? Is this okay for a restaurant like The Groves?"

She clasped her hands together and brought them up to her chest. "It's absolutely perfect. You're gonna stun that boy speechless, dearie."

I turned back toward the mirror to give myself a last once-over and tried to ignore the sinking sensation in the pit of my stomach every time I thought about Micah.

"You know, you put on a good show, but you haven't been foolin' me," Sylvia stated, moving toward the bed. She sat at the foot, crossing one leg over the other, and stared me down in that shrewd, all-knowing way of hers. "I'm not sure what's botherin' you, and now's not the time to get into the meat of it since your gentleman will be here any minute, but I want you to know one thing: No matter how bad things seem, you can always take comfort in knowing that there's somethin' good just around the corner, all you have to do is be patient. And I am always, *always* here for you. Anything you need, sweets. Any time, any place. You have me always and forever."

I moved to Sylvia, sitting down beside her and resting my head on her shoulder as she clasped my hand in hers. "How is it you're always able to make things better, no matter what?"

"It's just one of the few perks of being a million years old. I've already lived through all the nasty dips and dark days life can throw at a person, so you have the luxury of my hindsight whenever you're struggling."

"I love you," I said quietly. "And I'm so happy Ivy and I have you."

The doorbell rang, and I heard Ivy's feet pattering down the hall from her room as she squeaked, "It's him! Mommy, he's here!" like she hadn't seen Micah in ages.

I moved to the dresser and grabbed the black clutch I bought to go with my dress while pulling in a fortifying breath. "Well, I guess I'm as ready as I'll ever be."

"Knock his socks off."

I exited my room and started down the stairs. Every bit of air expelled from my lungs the moment I saw Micah standing on the other side of the door. He was dressed similarly to how he dressed for work, in a button-down and slacks, but he was also sporting a matching deep, charcoal gray jacket. His button-down was a sexy maroon color that looked amazing against his skin, the material fitted just enough to hint at the delicious rippled muscles beneath.

"Damn," he grunted, his gaze sweeping from my feet to my hair.

"That's a dollar!" Ivy proclaimed proudly. Over the past

month, I'd given up trying to convince both of them that Micah didn't have to contribute to the swear jar, and he'd given up all pretenses that he didn't spoil my daughter to an almost embarrassing extent. Ivy didn't even have to use *The Look* to get him to do her bidding. He was all too proud to do it on his own. Micah pulled out his wallet without fuss and passed my girl a dollar bill, his attention pinned on me the whole time. His rich, husky voice came out extra rumbly as he said, "Jesus, Red. You look incredible."

My belly swooped and my cheeks heated. "Thanks. You don't look so bad yourself." That was an understatement if there ever was one. I wanted so badly to say *screw the date* and lick him all over. "You ready to go?"

"Just a second." He stepped past the threshold into the entryway and grabbed me by my hips, pulling me flush against him. His mouth came down on mine in a slow, savoring kiss, and when his tongue peeked out, giving my own a gentle sweep, I sighed and melted into him. "There," he announced once he pulled back a second later. "Now I'm ready to go."

I bent to give Ivy a kiss on the cheek, reminding her to be good, before moving to Sylvia and doing the same—including the reminder to be good.

Micah gave them the same attention, even hefting my girl up so he could squeeze her tight and press his lips to her forehead. And just like every time I saw them interact, a part of me swooned. After that, we were off.

I intentionally kept the conversation light on the way to the restaurant, deciding it would be better if I paced myself. When we pulled up in front of the rustic yet elegant cabin tucked back into the trees of the foothills, I pulled in a surprised breath.

I stared out my window as Micah came to a stop at the valet stand and put the truck in park. "Wow, this place is beautiful."

"Wait until you try the food. It's gonna blow your mind, baby."

He hopped out and rounded the hood, taking my arm from the valet who'd opened my door and helped me out. With me tucked snuggly into his side, we headed inside. If I thought The Groves was beautiful from the outside, the inside took my breath away.

I took it all in as the hostess led us to our table beside a diamond-paned window with a stunning view of the trees outside draped with white fairy lights.

Once we were seated, our menus placed in front of us, I turned my attention from the window to the man sitting across from me. "Thank you for bringing me here."

Those grassy green eyes hit me as a smile pulled at his lips. "Thank you for tolerating me these past few weeks. I know things have been a little chaotic lately."

The waitress stopped at our table to take our drink orders, offering me a brief moment to find my courage.

He'd just given me the perfect lead-in, and I wasn't going to be fool enough to ignore it. "Speaking of that, how are things going at work?"

He lifted the menu and flipped it open as he casually replied, "Let's not talk about my job tonight."

I tried a different tactic, hoping it would soften him up. "It's just that you don't really talk to me about your cases or anything. I know whatever you're working on right now is giving you trouble. I want to make sure you know you can always talk to me if you need to. I can't imagine the pressures of being a police officer. I'm sure, sometimes, you just need to be able to vent."

He glanced up from his menu, giving me a quick, non-committal grin. "Thanks, but I'm good. There's not much to talk about."

One of my eyebrows shot up. "Really?" I asked, unable to hide the skepticism in my voice. "So it's just a normal, everyday thing to take off in the middle of the night after getting a call?"

That finally got his full attention. He closed the menu and lifted his bemused gaze to me, his brows dipping low over his eyes in a frown. "What's goin' on, here, Hayden? Is something wrong?"

I opened my mouth to respond, but before I could get a word out, his phone started ringing from inside his jacket pocket. He pulled it out and gave the screen a cursory glance, his jaw ticking as he pressed down on the side button to silence it.

"You don't need to get that?"

"It's nothing," he grunted, looking unhappy all of a sudden.

"You sure?"

"Positive," he clipped just as the waitress returned with our drinks. Micah lifted his beer to his lips and drank half of it in a matter of seconds.

"Uh . . . are you ready to order?" the befuddled waitress asked. It was obvious she felt the tension stewing between us and was unsure how to handle it.

We quickly placed our orders, and even though the

restaurant was beautiful, the ambience romantic, and I was in love with the man I was with, I knew the night was shot, and all I wanted was to go home. He wasn't going to talk to me. He had no intention of opening up, and I couldn't accept anything less.

"All right," Micah started gruffly once we were alone again. "I don't know what's goin' on, but it's obvious there's something on your mind, so why don't you just tell me what it is."

Once again, his phone interrupted us when it pinged with an incoming message.

"I just wish you'd talk to me," I admitted when it became clear he had no intention of reading the text that had come through. "I know you've been under a lot of pressure lately, and I know you've been stressed. I don't understand why you won't share that with me."

"Hayden, it's not—son of a bitch," he finished on a grunt when the phone went off for a third time. "I'm sorry, baby, I really need to take this. It's a work thing. I promise I'll make it quick."

Before I could form a response, he stood and started across the room, leaving me sitting in the middle of a romantic restaurant all by myself.

I sipped my wine as I waited . . . and waited. I'd gotten through half the glass by the time the waitress returned with our entrees. Setting my filet down in front of me, she gave me a look of pity, and I gave her a small, tight smile in return before she walked off.

The delicious smells wafted up from my plate, causing my stomach to let out a low grumble. "Screw this," I whispered to myself as I tossed my napkin onto the table and pushed my chair back. In the ten minutes I'd sat at that table all alone, I'd gone from worried to pissed, and I had every intension of letting my so-called date know.

I ignored the looks I was getting from the other patrons as I stormed across the restaurant and down the short hall I'd seen Micah take earlier. Around the corner were the restrooms, and just beyond that, a small alcove where I heard Micah's voice coming from. I was geared up to tear him a new one as I got closer. Then I heard his hushed voice and skidded to a stop at what he said.

"Look, Charlie, I know this is difficult, but it won't be too much longer, I swear." He paused as the person on the other end of the call spoke. "I know, sweetheart, and I'm sorry. You already know, if I had my way, this whole thing would be over. I'm tryin' my best. I just need you to bear with me for a little while longer, darlin'. Okay?"

My stomach bottomed out as I took slow, measured steps backward. When I knew he wouldn't hear the click of my heels, I spun around and hightailed it out of there.

I made it back to our table on shaky legs and sucked down the rest of my wine, nearly choking on the lump that had formed in my throat. I sat there, working to keep my breathing calm and measured so I wouldn't burst into tears, and as I waited for Micah to get off his call with another woman, I heard the distant bang of that other shoe dropping.

TWENTY-FIVE
MICAH

B etween the phone call from Charlie, threatening everything from killing Dalton in his sleep to taking matters with Cormack into her own hands, and having Hayden change into a completely different person, I felt like my head was going to explode.

I knew something had been off even before she started in with all the questions, but by the time I managed to talk Charlie down and get back to the table it had gotten so much worse. She tried playing it off, claiming she'd come down with a bad headache and wasn't feeling like herself, but I knew that wasn't it.

The tense, stilted conversation we had at dinner had turned to complete silence on the drive back, and my muscles were locked so tight from the anxiety gripping my chest, it was a wonder I didn't splinter apart.

I turned the truck into my driveway and killed the engine, trying to think of what to say.

She refused to make eye contact as she rounded the hood and started toward her house, her voice small as she said, "I think it's probably best if you stay at your place tonight. I'm really not feeling well. I need to sleep."

She didn't need sleep, she needed to avoid me, and I'd be damned if I let that happen.

"Hayden." I reached out and grabbed her arm as she attempted to pass by, turning her to face me and pulling her close. I gently pressed my fingers beneath her chin, tilting her head back so I could meet those gorgeous blue eyes. "I know something's off. Talk to me. We can figure this out."

She looked so sad, and seeing that felt like someone filled my chest with gasoline and threw in a lit match. "That's funny," she started on a whisper. "Now you want me to talk to you when I've been trying for weeks to get you to talk to me."

"Baby."

Then she asked a question that turned my blood to ice. "Who's Charlie?"

———

Hayden

His fingers clenched, grasping my arm tighter. It almost felt like he was worried I was about to slip away, and he couldn't let that happen.

"What?"

"Who's Charlie?" I repeated louder.

"Where did you hear that name?"

"I got tired of sitting at that table all by myself, and after about ten minutes, I started to get pissed. I went to find you and heard you talking on the phone."

His expression turned to stone at my answer. "You were eavesdropping on my phone call?"

I shook my head, feeling my lungs grow tighter as I got more agitated. "No. I went to confront my boyfriend about abandoning me and just so happened to hear him telling another woman if he had his way, this whole thing would be over and that he's trying his best and to please just bear with him for a little while longer."

The hardness melted from his features almost as fast as it had appeared, twisting into something that looked an awful lot like panic. "Hayden, what you heard . . . it's not what you think, I swear. I know it sounded bad, but I'd never do that to you. You have to believe that."

God, I wanted to. So damn bad I ached. "Then tell me who Charlie is. Is she the reason you came into my bed the other night smelling like perfume?"

He clenched his teeth so hard the muscle in his jaw began to tick. "It wasn't like that. I just gave her a hug, that's all. I promise, Red."

"If you want me to believe you, tell me who she is, because right now, things are looking all kinds of bad."

"I can't tell you who she is. All I can tell you right now is that there's nothing romantic between us. You have my word. She's like a sister to me."

That wasn't good enough. I believed he wasn't cheating. I felt the truth of that down to my bones, but the secrets were still weighing on me like cement blocks, making it hard to take a full breath. "Does she have something to do with this case you're working on that you won't tell me about?"

Please tell me. Please tell me.

Releasing me from his grip, he took a step away, his arms hanging down at his sides, his fists clenching so tight his knuckles bleached of color.

Please tell me. Please tell me.

"Hayden, I can't talk to you about that. Please trust that I know what's best when it comes to this." he croaked, his voice sounding as agonized as I felt. "I'm just trying to protect you, baby."

"Micah, I don't need you to protect me," I insisted, my tone pleading as I moved closer to him and placed my hands on his chest. "I need you to tell me what's happening. I need you to not keep secrets from me. I need you to let me all the way in because this half in, half out you're holding me at sucks. I'm so sick of being kept in the dark. Please just give me *something*."

"I can't," he rasped. "I'll tell you everything once I know it's safe, I swear, Hayden. I just can't tell you now."

"*Why*?" I asked in a pained whisper. "Why can't you tell me anything? I know Dani knows *something* at least. Why can she know but I can't?"

"I'm just trying to protect you."

"That's not an answer!" I cried in frustration. "That's an avoidance tactic. Stop dancing around my question and answer me. Why can Dani know what's going on, but I can't?"

"Because she's engaged to Leo!" he barked, throwing his hands up and raking his fingers through his hair. "They're getting married and we're just—"

He stopped himself from finishing that sentence, his eyes going wide like he only just realized how bad what he'd said sounded. But it was too late. I didn't need him to finish his sentence in order to feel gutted by it.

"And we're just fucking," I finished for him, my words coming out hollow.

"That came out wrong," he grated. "I didn't mean it like that."

"I'm not really sure how many other ways there are to take that," I said snidely. "I mean, it's pretty clear. Leo and Dani are getting married, so he trusts her with the big, important things like that. She's in the inner circle and I'm merely the woman you're currently banging."

"That's not the fuckin' case, and you know it," he growled.

"Do I?" I let out an incredulous laugh. "So then you've paid up on that bet you made with Trick and Hayes, then? The one where they said you'd eventually meet a woman who'd mean something to you?"

His torso rocked back in shock. "What—How did you know about that?"

God, this hurt. I wasn't sure how it was possible, but this hurt even worse than when I caught Alex and Krista in that bistro together. "You've said it yourself, Micah, it's a small town. So, if we aren't just fucking, you paid up, right?" His hesitation was answer enough. "I see," I whispered, nodding in sadness. I twisted, prepared to walk away when he cut into my path, taking me by my arms.

"We're more than that, and you know it, Hayden. You feel it. I haven't paid up on the bet because it's more than just meeting a woman I care about. They were talkin' marriage—"

He was just making this worse. I pulled from his hold

and moved three steps back. "Oh, okay. I think I'm following. So, you *do* care about me, but you don't see a future with me."

He took another step toward me but stopped when I moved back. "It's not like that! I've never felt like this with any woman I've been with. I'm out of my element here, Hayden. I'm just tryin' to keep you safe."

"I don't need you to keep me safe!" I shouted, throwing my arms wide. "I don't need a protector, Micah. I need a *partner*. God, this *sucks*," I lamented on a hollow laugh, "because while you've been keeping your secrets, holding yourself halfway out of this relationship this whole time, I've been falling in love with you."

His eyes went wide, flashing with something I was too lost in pain to try and identify. "Hayden—" he choked out, but I wasn't finished.

"You don't trust me."

"That isn't—" I held my hand up, warding him off when he started for me again.

"I'm such a fucking idiot. I fell for you; meanwhile, you don't trust me enough to give me *anything*."

"That's bullshit," he argued angrily. "I've given you more than any woman has ever gotten from me."

"Then I guess that makes me selfish, because I want more. I want it all."

After laying it all out like that, I stood there silently, my heart in my throat as I waited to see what he'd say. Like an idiot, I waited and I hoped.

And he gave me nothing.

"I think it's best if we call it a night right here," I told him, feeling the cracks start to form in my heart and spiderweb wider and wider.

"No," he declared vehemently. "We aren't doin' that. We can work through this. But you can't shut me out. You have to talk to me."

A humorless scoff bubbled up my throat. "You see the irony in what you just said, right?"

"Red, don't—"

"Micah, I need to think, okay? I need some time to myself to figure out what I want, and I need you to give me that."

His nostrils flared, and for a second I thought he resembled a pissed-off bull about to charge.

"This isn't over," he finally clipped seconds later. "You need some space, I'll give it to you, but this . . . *us*, it isn't over. You can't tell me you're in love with me then end it. I'll give you some time, but we *will* talk this out."

I didn't bother saying anything to that, mainly because I didn't have a clue *what* to say. So as much as it killed me, I turned on my heel and started toward the property line that separated his house from mine. In the time I'd been there, that expanse had never felt so wide.

And as I walked away, I made sure not to look back, knowing if I did, I'd cave.

TWENTY-SIX
MICAH

I t had been a week since Hayden announced she needed space. That was seven days in which I didn't get to see her or touch her whenever the hell I wanted. Seven nights in which I'd slept in my cold, hard bed all alone. Seven miserable fucking days where I didn't hear her voice.

It became blindingly obvious how much I needed her when my mood worsened with each passing day. There was no light to shine on the dark, no good to break up the bad. There was nothing to look forward to after unbearably long hours spent beating my head against a brick wall.

I'd been such a miserable bastard that everyone at work was giving me an extremely wide berth.

Stomping through the bullpen, I headed for my desk without making eye contact with a single person.

Yanking my chair out, I plopped down and reached out, hitting the button on my computer to boot it up. Nothing happened. "Son of a bitch," I groused, mashing the button down again. When the screen remained black, I let loose a low growl and smacked the shit out of it.

"All right, that's it," Leo declared, tossing down the file he'd been looking over in an attempt to ignore me. "This shit's gone on long enough. For Christ's sake, just go talk to her already."

"She said she needs space," I grunted, keeping my gaze on the computer screen as it *finally* blinked to life.

"That's what she said, but what she meant was she needed you to tell her the fuckin' truth. So tell her already, for Christ's sake."

I looked around to make sure we didn't have the attention of anyone else before leaning forward and lowering my voice. "I don't wanna tell her because I don't want that shit touchin' her. She thinks I don't trust her, but that's bullshit. I'm tryin' to protect her, for fuck's sake. Why can't she see that?"

"You ever stop to consider that maybe she needs you to talk about what's happening because she needs to be there *for you*?"

My body locked up tight, because until that very moment, I *hadn't* stopped to consider that.

"Look, brother, I get wanting to protect your woman, believe me. If I could shield Dani from everything bad out there, I'd bend over backward to make that happen. But life doesn't work that way. And even if I could, she wouldn't let me. She knows I need to lean on her just as much as she needs to lean on me.

"I had a woman who didn't ask questions because she didn't want my job to bleed into her nice, cushy life so I swallowed down all the shit I saw on a daily basis, keeping it to myself until I felt it eating away at my insides. From the beginning, Dani's made sure I had her to talk to so I could get all that ugliness out instead of letting it fester. She gives me that so I know, when I come home, I got nothin' but good waiting for me. When you find a good woman, man, she *wants* to be that for you. You want to protect her, but what you gotta realize is she wants to do the same damn thing for you."

Leaning back in my chair, I exhaled most of the air in my lungs and reached to grab the back of my neck as I hissed, "*Shit.*"

Leo smirked like an asshole. "See it's finally startin' to sink in. That's okay, man. It's not like you're used to bein' in a real relationship. You're on a bit of a learning curve."

I flipped him off and turned back to my computer, pretending to study whatever had just popped up on the screen. But the truth was, I couldn't concentrate to save my life, because I was too busy trying to think of a way to win Hayden back.

———

Hayden

Sylvia had tried dragging me out of the bed earlier this morning to do yoga with her in the garden, but with Ivy at her dad's for the weekend, I'd taken advantage of the rare quiet time to sink deeper into my pity party. I stayed in bed until after ten, burrowed deep into my pillows with the blankets pulled up over my head.

The only reason I'd dragged my mopey ass out and into the shower was because my stomach started to protest it's lack of food, and I'd been too depressed all week to go grocery shopping, so there wasn't a damn thing to eat in the house.

I'd put no effort into my appearance whatsoever, yanking on a pair of ratty yoga pants and a loose tee with an unidentifiable stain on the shoulder that I only wore while I was cleaning the house or gardening. I didn't bother brushing my hair before throwing it up in a sloppy knot on the top of my head.

I drove to Muffin Top on autopilot, desperate for coffee and something sweet and full of calories.

When I got to the shop and saw who all was there, I nearly turned and bailed, but the smells of sugar and coffee kept me from running like a coward.

Dani was behind the counter, chatting with Tempie, Rory, and Nona, who were standing across from her. All four of them turned to me when the bell over the door rang, and the instant they spotted me, the conversation stopped. Their mouths fell open, and their eyes went wide.

"My God," Rory stage whispered. "It's worse than I thought."

I ignored that and kept heading for the counter. "Hey guys. How are you?"

"Apparently, better than you, doll," Nona replied, her features awash with concern as she looked me over. "Are you okay?"

"Yeah, totally," I lied. Looking to Dani, I asked, "Can I get a white mocha with extra whipped cream? And add caramel drizzle on top. I'll also have a bear claw, a piece of coffee cake, and two bags of donut holes. If they're fresh."

Tempie moved closer to me, placing her hand on my arms. "Honey, what are you doing?"

I looked to my friend, my expression as blank as my voice as I replied, "What's it look like? I'm eating my feelings."

"No." She shook her head. "You're eating diabetes. This isn't healthy, babe. How about we all sit down and you talk to us instead of eating and drinking your way to a massive coronary?"

"Fine," I relented on a pitiful sigh, letting her take me by the shoulders and lead me toward a table. "But I still want that coffee."

"Of course."

"*And* the donut holes."

"Why don't we see how the chat goes?"

She guided me into one of the chairs, then she, Nona, and Rory took the other seats, all of them watching me closely, like they were afraid I was going to fall apart at any moment. They weren't wrong.

"So, how are you really doing?" Rory asked, a weak smile on her face.

I waved my hands up and down. "How's it look like I'm doing? I'm a freaking disaster. Even *Alex* looked at me with pity when he picked Ivy up yesterday. And Sylvia's forced me to work in the back of the shop all week because she said I'd scare off the customers."

Nona bobbed her head from side to side, her lips stretched into a grimace. "Well, you do kind of have this Bride of Frankenstein meets Carrie after the pig's blood vibe going right now."

Dani placed a coffee in front of me before pulling up an

empty chair. I picked it up and slugged some back. There was no caramel, but it was still damn good, so I let it slide.

"What's the point of basic hygiene when you've got no man to smell good for?" I lamented.

"Oh, wow. Okay." Tempie twisted in her seat to face me full on. "I didn't realize we'd fallen this far down the rabbit hole already. We should have intervened sooner."

"There's nothing any of you could have done." I sighed forlornly and chugged more coffee. "Micah and I are done. That's all there is to it."

"But"—Dani's expression turned quizzical—"he said he was just giving you some space. That you guys were on a break."

I snorted loudly. "Who are we, Ross and Rachel? This isn't an episode of *Friends*. A break means *break up*."

"Uh, honey, I don't think he sees it that way," Nona said gently.

I didn't want it to, but at that comment, hope took root and sprouted in my chest. "Why do you say that?"

"Well, yesterday he paid up on this crazy bet he made with Trick and Hayes forever ago."

My back went straight and my belly began doing somersaults. "What?"

"Yeah," Tempie added, explaining further since she didn't know I was aware of the bet already. "They bet him that one day a woman would come into his life who would make him start thinking about marriage and kids and that sort of thing. He was so sure that day would never come, he said he'd split his paycheck between them if it happened. And, well . . . yesterday, he split his paycheck between them."

"Wait, so . . ." I couldn't bring myself to say the words,

afraid that putting them out into the universe would jinx something.

Dani went there instead, smiling bigger than I'd ever seen her smile before. "*So . . .* I think it's safe to say the man loves you and is all in. Maybe you should rethink this break or breakup or whatever it is?"

I shot out of my seat so fast the chair screeched across the floor. "I have to go."

"What about the donut holes?" Rory called after me, humor coating her words.

I threw my hand up and waved. "No time! I'll come back for them tomorrow!" Then I ran out of the coffee shop to my car, desperate to get to Micah.

———

The tires let out a little squeal as I slammed on my brakes and threw my car into park. I tried to calm myself as I shoved the door open and climbed out, breathing deep and taking my time as I walked across my yard to his.

I wasn't even sure he was home, but I had to try.

I inhaled slowly, counting to three before letting it out and lifting my hand to knock on his front door.

I waited, anxious and nervous, as I heard the sound of the lock sliding. The door opened and Micah stood before me in nothing but a pair of light gray sweats that hung deliciously off his tapered hips.

"Hayden?" His voice pulled me from my perusal of his sinful chest and abs. "Is everything okay?"

"No, actually," I answered, my chest heaving. "It's not."

His brows arched down in worry as he stepped to the side. "Do you want to come in?"

Instead of answering his question, I asked one of my own. "Did you pay that bet to Trick and Hayes because I knew about it, or because you really lost?"

"How'd you hear—" He shook his head, already realizing the answer to that before he even finished the sentence. "Never mind. Small town."

"Just answer the question. Did you really lose or did you pay them for my benefit?"

He studied me for a beat before nodding. "I lost, Red. And I've never been so glad to lose a bet in my fuckin' life."

My breath stuttered and my eyes began to burn. "So, you see the prospect of a future with me?"

"Baby," he said tenderly, "come inside and let's talk about this, yeah?"

"Answer the question first," I whispered. "Do you see the prospect of a future with me, Micah?"

He huffed out an exhale and reached up to scratch the back of his neck. "If, by prospect of a future, you mean do I have every intention of putting my ring on your finger and makin' you mine for life, then yeah, I see that for us, Red. And I can't fuckin' wait."

A choked sob burst from my throat a moment before I lunged for him. He caught me easily, lifting me off my feet so I had to wrap my legs around his waist and loop my arms around his shoulders as we kissed so hard and so fiercely, you'd have thought we'd been separated for years.

I vaguely registered his front door slamming before I felt him lower me onto the sofa.

"I planned on comin' to see you tonight," he said against

my lips between kisses. "I was done giving you space. I was gonna tell you everything, Red, 'cause I couldn't go another day without this."

He hovered over me, resting his hips between my spread legs as we fed from each other's mouths. "I love you, Hayden. Besides my family, I've never said those words to another person until now. But I do. I'm so fuckin' in love with you it hurts."

I felt a single tear break free and slip down into my hair as I whispered, "I love you too."

"No more secrets, you have my word. From here on you, you get everything."

I was so giddy I felt like I could have floated away had Micah's weight not kept be grounded.

"Good." I dragged my fingers through his hair, scraping my nails along his scalp as I told him, "I'm so happy about that, honey. But I need you to do something first."

He pulled back and stared down at me, those green eyes shining bright with love. "Yeah? And what's that?"

"Take me to bed."

My man didn't have to be told twice.

TWENTY-SEVEN

HAYDEN

The sound of Micah's heartbeat echoed in my ear, a comforting, steady beat that would have lulled me to sleep if my brain wasn't so busy trying to wrap itself around everything he'd just confided in me.

He'd carried me to his room hours ago, and we'd spent the entire day making up for losing a week together. We had sex and napped and woke up to do it all over again. At some point that afternoon, he'd called and ordered pizza from Momma Gianna's, which we'd eaten in bed before going at it once again like horny teenagers.

The sun had long since set and he'd spent the past half hour telling me *everything*. He told me all about the case he and Leo had been living for months. He told me about Greg Cormack's involvement, and chills formed across my skin when I found out what a monster the man was.

He finally explained who Charlie was, going in depth about the young woman's life and the absolute hell she'd had to live through, not only with her current circumstances, but in her past as well. I had to fight back the desire to cry for this woman I didn't even know as he told me all about her. By the time he finished, it was easy to see how he'd come to think of her as a kind of little sister and felt such a strong need to protect her.

My heart broke for him and Leo for how they'd struggled to bring justice to one of their fellow officers. It broke for Charlie Belmont, for Sidney Callo and her daughters. But at the same time, my veins were filling with rage that this asshole was walking around free as a bird while good people were suffering.

I dragged my fingers across his chest, distractedly tracing random patterns through the small smattering of short hair as I replayed his words in my head.

"Red? You good?" I tilted my chin so I could look up at his strong, chiseled face, the moonlight bouncing off the sharp plains and edges, making him look like a Greek god. One arm was braced behind his head while the other wrapped around me, holding me in place so tightly I couldn't move. Not that I had any intention to. "Was that too much?"

I stopped drawing on his chest and draped my arm around his stomach, burrowing in and squeezing him tight. "No," I replied adamantly. "When it comes to you and your life, Micah, I'll always be able to handle it. I just hate that you've been dealing with all of this on your own. You need an outlet. You need to get this out so it doesn't suffocate you."

"You were that for me, baby. You and Ivy and Sylvia were my outlet. But it was pointed out to me recently that maybe I wasn't utilizing that to the degree I needed to. I wanted to keep all this shit from spilling into your life and tainting it."

I pushed up, bringing both hands to his chest and resting my chin on the backs of them so I could look right into his eyes. "That's the thing about relationships, honey. When you love someone, they become part of your life. Your job is part of who you are, Micah. I don't want you keeping things from me because you want to protect me from it. If you do that, I don't get all of you, and I want *all* of you."

His arm around me squeezed tighter. "I know that now."

"Good. Because I'm a whole lot tougher than people think."

His voice was low and husky as he replied, "Believe me, Red, I know how tough you are. It's one of the many reasons I fell in love with you."

"All right. Then it's settled. If you need to let something out, I can take it, so I want you to give it to me. No more secrets."

He lifted his head off the pillows and bent his neck so he could reach my lips. "Deal. No more secrets."

With that, the heavy stuff was done, and Micah let me know he was ready to move on to something much more fun by rolling me to my back and sliding his thick, hard cock into me slowly. He made love to me the same way, taking his time and savoring every second of it.

Once we finished, he cleaned me up and we tucked in for the night. Curled in Micah's arms, I slept harder and deeper than I had in a week.

———

Micah

. . .

Walking into the bullpen Monday, my mood was considerably changed from the week prior. I felt so damn good it was a wonder I wasn't whistling a damn tune.

Ivy had come home from her dad's the night before, and the moment she walked into the house and saw me kicked back on the couch, she'd let out a shriek loud enough to pierce my eardrums.

"*You're back!*" she'd screamed before throwing herself at me and wrapping her tiny arms around me as tightly as she could. As soon as mine closed around her little body, the last piece of my heart that had been missing for the past week clicked back into place, and just like that, I was whole again.

"I'm back, Monster," I'd told her, pulling in her soft scent. It reminded me of sugar and fabric softener. It was warmth and comfort, and I hadn't realized how badly I missed it until that moment. "And I promise I'll never disappear on you again."

She'd been so excited it had been a nightmare trying to get her to go to sleep later that night. I'd had to read her favorite book twice, then make up a story about a little diva rocker princess who loved glitter and playing in the dirt before she finally passed out.

"I'm guessin' by the grin on your face your weekend was a vast improvement from the week before."

I sat at my desk and kicked my feet up, looking across at Leo. "And you'd be right."

He was still smiling, but I could tell by the look in his eyes he was dead serious as he asked, "You love this chick?"

I gave it to him straight. "Yep. Never expected it to happen. Before her, I never even wanted it. But yeah, I'm fuckin' crazy about her, and I couldn't be more fine with that."

"Good. Happy for you, brother. Hayden's a good one."

He didn't have to tell me. I was all too aware of how incredible she was. "Thanks, man. She actually mentioned last night havin' you and Dani and your brood over for dinner, asked me to talk to you to set something up."

At that, my partner busted out laughing. "Man, look at you, all domesticated and shit. This is a trip."

I cut him a look, tossing a paperclip at his head that he managed to dodge. "All right, asshole. So can I tell her you're in, or what?"

"Yeah, brother," he said on a chuckle. "Count us in."

I couldn't even be annoyed he was giving me shit, because I knew that Hayden would be over the moon that Leo had said yes, and making her happy was the only thing that mattered to me.

We got to work after that, the morning moving at a normal pace. I'd gotten comfortable enough to think that maybe I'd get through the day without any nasty surprises cropping up when everything suddenly turned to shit.

My cell rang and Dalton's name flashed across the screen. "Hey man, how's it goin'?"

"Tell me she's with you."

A chill worked its way down my spine. "What are you talking about? Who?"

"Charlotte," he clipped, the man sounding more frantic than I'd ever heard him. "Is she with you? Have you heard from her at all?"

My gaze shot across the desks to Leo's and I jerked my

chin to the stairs that would take us out of the bullpen and to the back exit of the building.

He grabbed his keys and we were on our feet, moving out as I answered, "No. She isn't and I haven't. Talk to me. What the hell is goin' on?"

A string of curses blasted through the line. "She gave me the fuckin' slip," he fumed.

"Goddamn it," I clipped, picking up the pace through the parking lot. "How the hell did that happen?"

"Said she wasn't feelin' good. That she got her period and needed to take a hot bath. I didn't wanna bother her, so I let her be. When too long had passed, I knocked on the door. She didn't answer, so I kicked it down. She'd bolted out the fuckin' window."

Leo beeped the locks once we reached his truck. I yanked the passenger door open and leapt in as he started it.

"All right. We're headin' to Alpha Omega now. The other guys know yet?"

"Those calls already went out. Linc's there now. So's Xander. I'm en route, and Trent's out trackin'."

"Good. We'll see you in a few."

Leo drove out of the station's parking lot like a bat out of hell, and I sent up a silent prayer that, wherever the hell she was, Charlie was safe.

———

The AO offices were running with controlled chaos. The tension filling the air was thick enough to choke a horse, but we powered through.

For doing something so incredibly fucking stupid,

Charlie had been smart about it. She'd left her main cell at the house, only taking the burner I'd given her to stay in contact. I called the number over and over, praying that one of these times it would connect, but it was currently powered off so there was no way to trace it.

Xander was going through security cam footage of the stores and shops near her house to see if we could get a lock on the direction she'd gone, but so far, we were running blind.

Leo's voice spoke over the din of the conference room. "We have a problem. I called into the station to see who was supposed to be on shift this mornin', and Cormack no-showed.

"*Fuck*," I snapped, whipping around to Xander. "Get a trace on his phone, fast as you can."

"On it."

"It's him," Leo grated, coming up beside me. "You know it's him, man."

My heart was in my throat, panic gripped my chest like a vise, because my partner was right. Wherever the fuck Charlie was, Cormack had her. "We're gonna get her back."

"If that motherfucker so much as touches her—" Dalton snarled.

I reached out and clasped him at the back of his neck, giving him a jostle. With each minute that passed, the man became more of a loose cannon, to the point I was afraid Linc and his guys were gonna have to lock him down so he wouldn't fuck up finding her.

"She's gonna be fine," I assured him. "That girl's got steel in her spine, man. You know that. We're gonna find her, and she's gonna be okay."

"Got a trace," Xander called out, rattling off the address where Cormack's phone was pinging.

Linc pointed at him, ordering, "Get that address to West and Trent, tell them to move their asses. Red lights and stop signs are only suggestions today."

I lifted my phone, prepared to dial Charlie's burner again when the screen came to life, flashing the letter *C*.

"Thank fuck," I rasped. I looked to Xander to see he was prepared to start a trace as soon as I answered. I engaged the call, putting it on speaker. "What the fuck were you thinkin'?" I boomed through the line. "Where are you?"

My question was met with silence.

"Charlie?"

"Guess again," a man spoke. "But I got your girl's phone."

At the sound of Cormack's voice coming from Charlie's phone, red began bleeding into my vision. "Motherfucker, if you hurt her—"

"Gotta say, Langford, it surprised the hell out of me you were able to flip her. Out of all the assholes working for me, I always thought she was the toughest. Never thought she'd be the one to flip. Then she started up with that PI prick, and I knew something had to be going on there."

"Cormack, you let her go now, you can still walk away from this," I tried to reason as desperation clawed at my throat.

"Oh, I plan to walk away from this. Unfortunately, your girl here isn't gonna be so lucky. Hope you didn't get too close to your CI, my man, 'cause she's not gonna live long enough to see another day."

The call disconnected after that, and when I looked to

Xander, he shook his head, telling me there hadn't been enough time to get a lock on his location.

The only chance we had of finding Charlie, and it was gone.

I'd just broken every promise I'd made to that girl. I'd failed her. And the pain that caused was enough to take me to my knees.

Twenty-Eight
Hayden

"I can't believe I let you talk me into a second lesson," I wheezed after sucking back my entire bottle of water.

McKenna looked at me like I was being ridiculous. "You did great, and look!" She pointed at where I was standing. "You're still on your feet. That's a *huge* improvement from last time."

"Yeah, well, I guess that's something."

She waggled her eyebrows as I picked up my gym bag and slung it over my shoulder. "And just think, you'll be able to put on a sexy little show for Micah in no time. Imagine the appreciation he'll dole out for that."

I let out a laugh and moved in to give her a tired, sweaty hug. "Point taken. I'll come back for another lesson."

"Good. And I'll call you this week. We'll do coffee. And hey, I'm glad you're happy again, honey."

Man, I had some of the *best* friends here in Hope Valley. "Thanks, babe. See you soon."

I headed out of the studio and down the back hall of

Whiskey Dolls. I pushed through the door to the alley where I'd parked when my cell phone started ringing.

Pulling it out of my bag, I answered and put it to my ear. "Hey, honey."

Micah's voice came out in a rush. "Red, where are you?"

"I'm just leaving McKenna's club. I should be home in about fifteen. Is everything ok—" My words died when something hard slammed into my temple. Everything went black just before I hit the asphalt.

———

I came to with a pain in my head that felt like my skull had been split clean open. Something wet clumped my lashes together when I tried to blink my lids open, making my vision muddy as it dripped into my eye.

The full realization of my surroundings didn't hit me until I tried lifting a hand to wipe it away and discovered they'd been bound together. So were my feet. And I had what felt like duct tape wrapped around my head, covering my mouth. I began to panic, thrashing around in my small, dark confines, yelling against the tape.

Whatever I was in was moving, because I was thrown around like a rag doll when it lurched to a stop.

Trunk, my brain registered. I'd been knocked out, was bound and gagged, and had been stuffed into someone's trunk.

What the fuck?

I started screaming louder from behind the tape, kicking my legs out the best I could and beating on the lid of the trunk. It flew open a second later, and the sudden burst of sunlight made it impossible to see.

I blinked rapidly to clear my vision, finally able to see who'd kidnapped me at the same time I felt his hands close around my arms. I fought even harder, trying to get away. Curling my hands into fists, I swung them wide and hard, connecting with his nose.

Greg stumbled back, cursing, "Goddamn *bitch*!" He lunged back into the trunk and punched me in the same temple he'd hit the first time. My arms and legs instantly fell limp as stars burst in front of my eyes. "You keep fighting I'll make this a lot fucking worse than it needs to be. And trust me, you don't want that."

I let out a pained groan as he hefted me out of the trunk and tossed me over his shoulder. All I could see were dead leaves and twigs scattered about beneath Greg's feet. He climbed up a set of steps and kicked a door open. He moved inside the building and dropped me to the ground unceremoniously, knocking the breath out of my lungs and making my bones scream in agony.

I whimpered when he reached for a knife he had tucked into his belt. Every inch of my body protested as I attempted to slither away.

"Stop moving," he gritted. Reaching out, he cut the bindings on my feet first, then the ones on my wrists. He unwound the tape from around my head, and I sucked in a sharp hiss when he ripped it off my skin, yanking out some hair with it.

Fear fueled my movements as I pushed to sitting and scuttled backward, trying to get away from him. My heart started beating dangerously fast when my back slammed into a wall. Glancing around, I saw we were in a cabin that looked like it hadn't seen signs of human life in well over a decade. It could have been a set out of a horror movie, and I wouldn't have been surprised.

Greg moved across the room, grabbing one of the dust-covered chairs from a small, crudely built table. He carried it closer, setting it down in the center of the room, effectively blocking off the only exit out of this hellhole, and sat down, forearms to his knees.

I couldn't stand to look at him, so I shifted my attention to the side, sucking in a sharp gasp when I saw the bruised and battered body of a woman lying on the floor near the corner.

"Oh my God," I cried, crawling across the floor and reaching for her. I sat back and rested her head on my thighs, prodding at her throat in an attempt to find a pulse, but my hands were too shaky.

"Relax," he grunted. "She's alive. For the time being."

My head shot up, tears welling in my eyes, mixing with the blood that had dripped into them from the gash on the side of my head, created when he'd knocked me out. Bile slithered up my throat, making it burn as I asked, "What did you do?"

"Nothing she didn't deserve," he hissed through gnashed teeth. "This is what happens when you rat."

Rat. Oh my God. Looking down at the woman's face, I couldn't make out a single thing thanks to all the swelling and mottled bruises everywhere. "Charlie?" I whispered, hoping this wasn't the woman Micah had told me about only a couple days ago, the woman who'd endured more than anyone's fair share of hell on earth. Her body gave a little jerk, and one of her eyelids opened just a fraction.

God, no. Desperation to get us both out of here began coursing through my veins.

My voice rattled as I told him, "You don't have to do this. You can leave right now. Get in your car and drive away. You'll be long gone by the time anyone finds us."

He raised his arms at his sides and looked around. "You aren't really in the position to be bargaining right now, beautiful." That endearment made my skin crawl. "There isn't a chance in hell of your little boyfriend finding us any time soon, and by the time he finally picks up the trail, I'll be long gone and you'll be dead."

I wanted to cry. I wanted to curl up in a ball and beg and plead, but my pride wouldn't let me. That fire that Micah loved so much forced my chin up and my eyes into a glare as I demanded, "Then why haven't you done it yet, huh? What are you waiting for?"

He looked at me curiously, his eyes taking me in slowly. "There's one thing I have to know first."

"What's that?"

"Why him?"

My head canted to the side in confusion. "What?"

"Langford. Why him? The man's fucked and thrown over more than half the women in this goddamn county. What was it that made you pick him over me?"

"It wasn't a choice. Despite what you've twisted up in your head, I was never interested in you."

"Yeah, well, it doesn't matter now." he said, sending a sick chill down my spine. "Word gets around. I didn't peg you for the kind of woman who likes it that rough." His eyes did a sweep of my body in a way that made my skin crawl. A twisted smile curled his lips, making my stomach clench. "If I'd known that from the beginning, I'd have played it very differently."

He canted his head to the side like he was studying me. "Maybe I still will. Been dying for a taste ever since you waved your ass all around that night at The Tap Room, just begging for attention." He stood and took a step toward me. I slid back, but there was nowhere to go. "Maybe I'll find out for myself how rough you like it before I put a bullet through that gorgeous face."

"Stop," I cried as he bent down and grabbed hold of my ankle. He yanked until I landed on my back then dragged me across the floor as I kicked and screamed. "Let me go! *Don't touch me!*" I fought as hard as I could as he came down to the ground, pinning my body with his weight.

"That's right, beautiful. Keep fighting."

I threw my head back and screamed at the top of my lungs as I clawed at him. He grabbed my wrists and pinned them to the ground with one hand so I bucked my hips and kicked my legs, trying to dislodge him, screaming and fighting with every single bit of strength I had as his other hand moved down between us to the waistband of my pants.

"Get off her!" I heard just before the chair Greg had been sitting in came down over his back, breaking into a million pieces.

"You cunt!" I wasn't sure when Charlie had gotten up, or how she'd found the strength, but as Greg let out a shouted curse and turned on her, I rolled away. I managed to stumble to my feet in time to see him land a powerful backhand across her face, sending her flying across the room and crashing to the floor.

I lurched forward, tripping on my unsteady legs as he reached around to the back of his jeans. I caught a glint of something shiny just before he pulled a gun from his waistband at the small of his back.

I rushed forward, but it was too late. The bang of the gun going off was deafening. "*No!*" I screamed, throwing myself at Greg's back.

He lost his balance and went down, losing purchase of the gun as his hands shot out to break his fall. Once we hit the ground, I shoved off of him as fast as I could, Army-crawling toward the weapon.

His fingers clamped around my ankle, pulling me back a foot, and I clawed at the dirty floor, kicking back with all my might. As soon as my foot connected with his face with a sickening crunch, he let out a bellow and released his hold just long enough for me to throw myself the remaining distance. There was no way I was dying here today. Not at the hands of this asshole. And I wasn't going to let Charlie, either.

My fingers wrapped around the cold, steel handle of the gun at the same time he got hold of me and flipped me to my back. I didn't hesitate to squeeze the trigger as he lunged. I fired over and over until the deafening boom turned into rapid clicks.

Shock filled his eyes and his body jerked unnaturally before he slowly fell to his knees. I rolled quickly when he started coming down, getting out of the way as he collapsed face first on the floor.

I braced on my hands and knees, sucking in ragged

breaths as blood started to pool out from beneath him, slowly crawling across the dingy floor.

I wanted to burst into tears, but that wasn't an option. Adrenaline carried me back across the room to where Charlie was.

"No, no, no, no, no," I chanted as I pressed my hands over hers on her belly. She let out an agonizing cry as I increased the pressure. Fear radiated from my chest as blood seeped through our fingers.

"Hey, look at me," I pleaded. That one good eye came to me, and I offered a wobbly smile. "You're gonna be okay, all right? I'm gonna get you out of here."

Her voice was small and thin as she asked, "You're Hayden, aren't you?"

"I am. And you're Charlie. I need you to stay with me, okay?"

She pulled in a breath that rattled unnaturally in her chest. That wasn't good. "He told me about you," she said with a small, weak grin. "You and your little girl. Talked about you a lot."

I let out a watery laugh as tears spilled from my eyes. "He told me about you too, sweetheart. So I know how tough you are. Stop talking and save your strength, okay? I'm gonna get us out of here. But I need you to hold on for me."

As much as I didn't want to leave her, I wasn't going to get us out of there if I didn't move. Scrambling back to Greg's body, I felt around in his pockets and hit pay dirt when I heard the jingle of keys.

"I got it!" I cried when I yanked the keyring from the dead man's pocket. "I have his keys, we're gonna get you in the car, and I'm gonna drive us out of here. Deal?"

"You know, I really like you for him." There was more rattling as she laughed, followed by a cough that made blood splatter past her lips. "You're feisty."

"That I am. I'm also determined. So what I need you to do is put your arms around my neck and try your best to hold on, okay? I'm getting us the fuck out of here."

———

I was sitting in one of the hard waiting room chairs, curled into a tight, shaky ball. I rocked back and forth as I thought back to that drive. What had only taken ten or so minutes had felt like an eternity, especially when the rattling sound coming from Charlie's chest had stopped.

Tears welling in my eyes and I gave my head a shake. I couldn't let myself go there. I *couldn't*. I kept repeating over and over that she was going to be okay. But I didn't know that for sure, and it was killing me. Worry over a girl I didn't even know, over a girl who'd saved my life, eclipsed everything else. I didn't even feel the pain in my own body.

I sniffled and batted away the freshest stream of tears when I heard his voice.

"Where is she? *Hayden*!"

Shooting to my feet, I bolted for the door, slipping on the tile as I ran. I jerked to a stop just outside the waiting room doorway when I saw Micah barreling down the hall. Leo was at his back, as were a few other men I recognized from Sylvia's cookout. There were also faces I hadn't seen before.

His name came out as a garbled sob. He started running as soon as he spotted me. "Christ, baby. Jesus *Christ*," he rasped as his hands skated all over my body. I couldn't blame him for the reaction, after all, I was covered in blood. "Fuck, where are you hurt? We need to get a doctor in here." He turned, prepared to shout the place down, when I finally managed to get the words out.

"It's not mine," I told him, my voice raw and thready. "It's not mine, Micah."

His eyes returned to me, and I gave him the hardest part, losing hold of my tears as I said, "It's Charlie's. She was there. He was—" I squeezed my eyes closed and gave my head a vicious shake. "She saved me. B-but h-he shot her."

His voice came out in an agonized whisper that tore me apart as he asked, "What?"

"I took his keys and got her to the car and drove her here. S-she's in surgery."

"*Jesus Christ*," he repeated, yanking me against him and holding so tight it was a struggle to breathe.

"Micah." My whisper was almost impossible to hear. Burying my nose in his chest I inhaled his scent, letting it soothe me as I admitted, "I killed him."

Then I broke down.

———

Micah

Between Dalton and Hayden both refusing to leave her bedside and demanding answers every time they came in, it was a wonder the whole nursing staff hadn't quit.

Charlie had pulled through her surgery, but she wasn't

out of the woods. She'd been in ICU for two days before she started showing enough signs of improvement and they were confident enough to bring her out of the medically induced coma.

She'd been moved to a regular room just yesterday. She'd been in and out of it since then, only coming to for a minute before the medication kicked in and she passed out again.

I stood at the window, looking out at the mountains beyond our little valley, lost in thought when a small gasp, followed by a low groan, pulled my attention back to the figure in the bed.

"Shit," Charlie hissed in pain.

I moved across the room quickly, careful to walk on quiet feet so I wouldn't wake Dalton or Hayden, who'd both been going on no sleep for more than forty-eight hours. Exhaustion finally set it, causing both of them to crash only hours ago. Dalton was stretched out on the poor excuse of a loveseat, his head and feet hanging off the ends. Hayden was in a recliner, curled into a ball with her head on her knees.

"About time you woke your lazy ass up," I said once I reached the side of the bed.

Her lips pulled into a grimace as she attempted to adjust her position. "Remind me to never get shot again. This does *not* feel good."

I helped her sit up, then braced my hip on the bedframe, crossing my arms and glaring down at her furiously. "You ever get shot again, I swear to Christ, I'll kill you myself."

Her eyes grew glassy and her chin began to wobble. "I'm sorry," she croaked as one tear broke free and trailed down her battered cheek. "I'm so—"

I placed my hand on hers and gave it a squeeze. "Stop it.

I'm just glad you're okay. That's *the only* thing that matters to me." She closed her eyes for a second and pulled in a breath to get control of herself before looking back at me. "Why'd you do it?" I finally asked, that question had been plaguing me for days. "Why'd you run, Charlie?"

"I didn't have a choice," she whispered, her voice small and weak from everything she'd endured. "He called me. He'd found out something from my past and was using it against me."

My fingers around hers clenched. "What did he have on you?"

"He—he found out about my sister."

The air expelled from my lungs as my muscles locked up. "You have a sister?"

"I haven't seen her in years. I don't even know where she is. But he found out somehow, and he threatened to track her down if I didn't find a way to meet up with him without Dalton knowing."

I shook my head, trying to comprehend what I'd just heard. "Charlie, I—"

"You can't tell anyone," she insisted. "I don't want anyone knowing. If they do, they'll go looking, and I've stayed away all this time to keep her safe. She didn't grow up the way I did. She had a good life. I don't want to screw that up for her."

God, that killed. "Darlin', don't you think she'd want to know you? You're her family."

"I'm no good," she gritted, that steel and stubbornness returning right before my very eyes.

"Charlie, you aren't—"

"Just promise me, Micah. Swear you won't tell anyone."

I hesitated, my gut twisting painfully. It was a promise I didn't want to make, but I'd do it anyway. Because it was for her. "All right, sweetheart. This stays right here."

Relief flitted across her features, and slowly, the Charlie I'd come to know and love reappeared. "I met your girl, by the way." She smiled as best she could with most of her face still swollen. "Just in case you're wondering, I totally approve."

It was my turn to pull in a calming breath. "I know what you did," I told her on a husky whisper. "She told me you saved her, and for that, I owe you *everything*."

"Micah—"

"You're absolutely incredible, and I'm so thankful I get to know you," I stressed. The quiver in her chin came back, but I wasn't done. "For the rest of my life, Charlie. You'll hold a special place in my heart no one else will ever be able to touch as long as I live. You got me?"

She sniffled and nodded her head.

"You have family here, darlin'. Whether you want us or not. You're stuck. You're the best person I know."

A tear broke free. "The feeling's mutual."

EPILOGUE
MICAH

T *hree weeks later*

To say things had been tense since my woman shot and killed that piece of shit Cormack would have been a massive understatement. When word got out it was one of our own that had killed Darrin Callo simply because the man was a good cop, it had shaken the whole department. After that nightmare of a day, things in his operation began to unravel quickly.

After it came to light that the deputy in Hidalgo had been framed for Callo's murder, a task force was put together, led by me and Leo. Two other Hope Valley officers were arrested for being a part of his drug ring, as well as a handful of cops from Grapevine and Hidalgo. That wasn't counting the people involved who *weren't* in law enforcement.

We were dismantling Cormack's operation, piece by piece, and we weren't going to stop until there was nothing left.

"Langford," I heard Hayes call. Lifting my head from the report I'd been filling out, I looked over and saw him jerk his chin toward the entrance of the bullpen.

When I shifted my focus in that direction, my whole body locked tight. Sidney Callo was climbing the last step and heading in our direction.

"Look alive," I muttered to Leo just as the young woman reached our desks.

"Detective Langford," she greeted before tilting her chin to Leo. "Detective Drake."

"Afternoon, Mrs. Callo," I returned. "What can we do for you?"

There was still a sadness in her eyes that I feared might never go away, but I guess that was to be expected. However, even with that, she looked a bit better than she had the last time we'd seen her.

She clutched her purse in front of her, her fingers gripping the straps so tight her knuckles were white. "I just . . . I don't mean to interrupt—"

"No interruption at all, ma'am," Leo insisted, pointing to the chair beside his desk. "Would you like to have a seat."

"No, I won't be here long. I just wanted to come in and tell you . . . well, thank you. Thank you for not giving up. Thank you for pushing until you got to the truth." She stopped to sniffle as her eyes grew glassy. "It won't bring him back," she rasped, "and my girls and I will still miss him, but . . . this helps. You got justice for Darrin, and that really helps. So . . . thank you."

She moved before either of us could speak, surprising me by leaning down and giving me a quick hug. She did the same to Leo, then stood tall and gave us a watery smile. "I'm grateful for you both. Now, I'll let you get back to your job."

With that, she turned and started toward the exit, and as I watched her disappear down the stairs, I felt as if a weight had just been lifted from my chest. Because I knew, with the people of this town at their back, she and her girls were going to be all right.

———

Hayden
Four months later

My body no longer experienced the same aches and pains it had when I first started taking pole lessons with McKenna, but that didn't mean I wasn't still stiff as I climbed out of my car and started up the front walk.

After weeks of poking and prodding, I'd finally convinced Charlie to come with me today—or more to the point, I threatened to drag her out of her house by her hair if she didn't agree, and I had to say, it rankled a bit that she turned out to be a complete natural while I was still flopping around like a toddler who was trying to walk and eat an ice cream cone at the same time.

It had been months since she nearly died trying to save me, and with every day that passed, we grew closer. She'd been hesitant at first, attempting to push me away, but I'd been persistent. She was a woman who meant something to

Micah, but what was more, she'd become a woman who meant something to *me*, then to my family.

Charlie was good to her very core, it didn't take much to see that, and I wanted to do everything I could to give her as much good as possible, so I gave her me, Micah, Ivy, and Sylvia. Once she accepted that—not that she had much of a choice since my baby girl was as persistent as me, and she'd taken an instant shine to Charlie—I gave her my friends. They'd accepted her with open arms, and she was officially part of our crew.

What I *couldn't* give her, no matter how hard I tried—and I'd tried really freaking hard—was Dalton. The man was crazy about her, but the woman had put a wall around herself that rivaled the ones of a maximum security prison, and she wasn't having any of it. Micah liked to call me stubborn, but I was nothing compared to her.

My man told me over and over to leave it alone, but I'd seen the way she watched him when she didn't think any of us were looking. There was something there, and for Charlie's sake, the rest of the girls were determined to see this through.

No matter how much she fought us on it.

"I'm home," I said as I closed the front door behind me. I hung my purse on the hook by the door and pulled off my coat and scarf, doing the same with them.

"Hello?" I called when I didn't get any kind of reply.

It was Micah's day off, which meant he'd kept Ivy home from daycare because he liked having those days, just the two of them. It had become their thing ever since he'd moved in with us three months earlier.

"Where is everybody?" I asked the silence as I moved down the hall. The kitchen was empty, but a glow from outside the window caught my attention, and when I turned to look, I lost my breath.

Moving to the back door, I pulled it open and stepped onto the porch, lifting a hand to my lips as I took in all the beauty around me.

There were fairy lights strung up everywhere, from the garden all the way to Ivy's treehouse. Glowing paper lanterns hung from all the trees. It looked like something out of a fairy tale, and standing in the middle of it all was Micah, with Ivy to his left and Sylvia at his right.

"What's going on?" I asked as I got closer. "What is all of this?"

Micah stepped from between my family and moved to me. "The first time I met you, I knew I'd found something special. There wasn't a day that came after where I didn't regret walking away from you. Then I ran into all that beauty and fire in the middle of a grocery store, and the first thing you did was throw attitude."

I sniffled and lifted my free hand to bat the tears from my cheeks. "That's because you deserved it," I said on a laugh. "You started it."

He smirked, making my belly flutter. "Red, you're stubborn, and full of attitude. You're also loving and loyal. You're wild. And when you burn, it's the most beautiful thing I've ever seen." I covered my mouth to stifle a sob as he continued. "There isn't a single thing about you I'd want to change, because I love it all. And I know down to my bones, that I'll keep loving it until I take my last breath."

He took my left hand and lifted it up. I sucked in a gasp, feeling my eyes go wide when he slipped a stunning antique ring on my finger.

"Micah," I breathed, looking into those beautiful green eyes.

"You're my safe place. Even when I'm having a bad day, you make everything better, and I want to spend every day from here on out sharing my life with you. I want us to protect each other. And I want you to be my wife."

"He already asked me!" Ivy shouted from behind him, jumping up and down exuberantly. "I said yes!"

He nodded in confirmation, one corner of his mouth kicking up in a smirk. "She did, so it's kind of already a done deal."

I threw my head back on a long, deep laugh as Micah pulled me against him and banded his arms around me. "Well, then I guess it's settled," I said on a giggle, staring up into the gorgeous face of my fiancé.

"Good, because, just so you know, Monster was prepared to use *The Look* if necessary."

"You forget, that look doesn't work on me." I arched a single brow. "You're the easy target, honey."

At that, he gave me a big, brilliant smile. "Sure the hell am. And I'm not the least bit ashamed of it."

I threw my arms around his neck and lifted up on my toes, pressing my lips against his in a slow, steamy kiss.

"You ready to spend every day for the rest of your life burnin' wild with me, Red?" he asked once I pulled back.

I felt my lips stretch so big my cheeks hurt as I gave him the God's honest truth. "I can't wait."

The End.

Thank you so much for reading.
Keep reading for a peek at Dalton and Charlotte's story
PLAYING FOR KEEPS

Sneak Peek of Playing for Keeps

Chapter 1

Charlotte

Sunlight shone through the open blinds of my window, illuminating my figure in a warm, golden glow as I stood in front of the full-length mirror and stared at my reflection.

Happiness and sunshine were a contradiction to the

emotions swirling inside of me as I took stock of the litany of scars that peppered my face and body. Wounds that had healed but left reminders behind in the form of physical imperfections. Most specifically, the pink puckered scar on my abdomen a couple inches above and to the right of my belly button. There was another that cut right through the arch of my left eyebrow that I could fortunately cover up whenever I filled my brows in, and another that slashed across my right cheekbone. Then there was the thin silvery line that angled across the bridge of my nose—a bridge that was no longer straight as an arrow thanks to having been broken.

The scars might have been months old, but if I paid them close enough attention like I was doing right then, I could still feel the burn of the skin opening up when each of the wounds had been created.

As it usually did whenever I started to really study myself, my vision began to grow fuzzy, and I found myself getting lost inside my own head.

There were some people in the world who led charmed lives. Most others were happy to live ordinary lives, filled with ups and downs, happy times and sad.

Then there are those like me.

I wasn't one of the fortunate few who led a charmed life. Hell, I wasn't even lucky enough to be one of the majority. More times than not, I'd have given anything to be blissfully ordinary.

The downs I lived through were nearly constant. Each day felt like a tumble even lower than the one before. Ugliness followed me around like a putrid black cloud everywhere I went. For every good day I experienced, there were countless bad ones that followed. For every happy moment, guaranteed sadness would follow in its wake.

It was a crushing weight I couldn't get out from under no matter how hard I tried, but I must have been a glutton for punishment because no matter how many times I got knocked down, I always forced myself back up. No matter how many bad days I experienced, I couldn't let go of that microscopic glimmer of hope that things might get better. Even though they *never* did.

Most people would have learned their lesson and given up hope for a turnaround, accepting the bad and learning to live with it, letting it taint them and turn them into something or someone else altogether. But despite my hard exterior, at my center I was still a soft, gooey optimist.

And it was that optimism that had gotten me into so much damn trouble.

In my attempt to pull myself out of the gutter, I'd blinded myself to the wolf in sheep's clothing. I'd hitched my wagon to a man I thought was a knight in shining armor. Turned out, just like every single man who'd come in and out of my life, he was a monster.

Malachi Black had the looks and the smooth charm that made me believe he was something he wasn't: namely, a good and moral person. I was far from the first woman he'd fooled, but *I* should have known better. I'd had more than my fair share of scumbags and users and criminals filter in and out of my life; I should have been able to spot the threat he was from miles away. But I'd been seduced by a set of dimples, an easy smile, and firm, hot muscles.

If only all criminals were as ugly on the outside as they were on the inside. However, that wasn't the case with

Malachi. He had the sexy looks that belonged on the cover of a magazine.

By the time I realized the man didn't have a single decent bone in his body, it was too late. I wasn't just stuck, I was trapped, held prisoner in a life I'd willingly walked into with rose-colored glasses affixed to my face.

He might have been arrested a while back and locked up for a *very* long time, but the black mark he'd left on my soul remained, and by letting him into my life, I'd let in another monster as well. One that was arguably worse because he hid his evil behind a shiny badge and a uniform.

If Malachi Black was a blight on humanity, Officer Greg Cormack had been the devil incarnate.

In a long line of mistakes, getting tied up with those two men was the one I regretted the most. The penance I tried to pay in an attempt and make things right had nearly cost me my life—literally. Yet it still didn't feel like enough. The mess I'd tangled myself in had cost one good man his life and put countless others in danger, and I wasn't sure if there was enough atonement in the world to fix the damage I'd been a party to.

I was ripped from my depressing thoughts by the ding of my cellphone. I dropped my T-shirt, covering the scar left behind from that unforgiving bullet that tore through my abdomen and moved to grab my phone off the bedside table and check the text that had just come through.

Hayden: *Just a warning, Micah said if you try to cancel on dinner tonight, he'll come over there and drag you here by your hair. Don't forget to bring wine. Love you!*

If you had told me a year ago, or hell, even six months ago, that I would be best friends with a woman like Hayden

Young, I'd have laughed in your face. Given what we'd both lived through, I was certain she'd want nothing to do with me, that I would have been a reminder of a nightmare she wanted to forget. But the strange bond that resulted from a shared trauma was something Hayden had insisted on cultivating, not running from.

Before we met, I'd been working as an informant for a detective by the name of Micah Langford. I'd wanted to help him and his partner, Leo Drake, take down Cormack and the other dirty cops and criminals he had working for him after he'd stepped in to take over Malachi Black's drug operation when Malachi had gone to prison. Hayden and Micah had been dating at the time, and to say our first meeting had been an unfortunate one would have been putting it mildly.

Hayden was one of the good people who'd gotten hurt in my tangled mess. Cormack had abducted her as a way to get back at Micah for coming after him, and I'd been shot trying to save her.

She'd been forced to kill him while I'd lain bleeding on that dirty floor in a desolate cabin in the middle of nowhere, and I worried constantly that having to do that was going to scar her in a very profound way.

I'd tried pushing both her and Micah away after everything was said and done, thinking they were better off without me around, but no matter how much I fought it, they refused to let me slip away quietly, all but forcing me into the fold of their lives. I'd gone from having no one to being an extension of their family.

I had dinner at their house once a week, saw Hayden and my ever-widening circle of friends for lunch or coffee at least twice a month, and she'd even asked me to be a bridesmaid in her wedding when Micah popped the question a couple months ago.

I shot off a quick reply, letting her know I was just about to head her way and started across my studio apartment toward the front door.

The place was the size of a matchbox but the white-washed brick walls and view of the foothills and mountains that surrounded the valley from pretty much every window made the lack of space totally worth it.

I grabbed my purse from the kitchen counter and headed out. Just as I shoved my key into the lock, the door across the hall from mine opened, and my neighbor's curler-bedecked head popped out.

Deloris Weatherby was at least eighty years old—and that was being generous—cantankerous as hell, nosey, and a bit —*a lot*—dramatic. Most of the other tenants in the building found her salty and suspicious nature annoying, but I saw a lonely old lady who was just trying to connect with people the only way she really knew how.

"Hey, Ms. Weatherby," I said with a wave of my hand.

Her eyes were cartoonishly small behind her Coke-bottle glasses as she looked right then left down the hallway. "Oh good. It's just you. I heard a door and worried it might be a burglar."

"No burglar. Just me," I assured her.

"I thought they'd finally come for my Precious Moments figurines. I have one of the biggest collections in the state, you know. It tends to make people jealous."

Oh, I did know. She'd told me about her extensive collection countless times. She'd even invited me over for lemonade once and spent two hours showing them off, giving me a very detailed history of when and where she'd gotten every tiny statue.

"Don't worry, Ms. Weatherby, your collection is safe. No burglars in sight."

"Well, that's a relief." With her knickknacks no longer under threat, she let out a relieved sigh and pulled the door open farther, revealing her brightly colored muumuu and fuzzy house slippers. "I just made a fresh pitcher of lemonade if you want to come in for a glass."

A sense of panic washed over me. Even with those crazy thick glasses, the woman was still blind as a bat, so she couldn't tell the difference between salt and sugar. It was something I'd discovered the hard way.

"I'd love to Ms. W, but I'm actually heading out. Maybe another time?"

She gave me a suspicious look. "You aren't going out carousing, are you? Young people these days. Always carousing." She pointed a gnarled, arthritic finger in my face. "That'll get you in trouble. You could pick up some good-for-nothing lowlife, and next thing you know, he's breaking into your building, stealing all the neighbors' most valuable possessions so he can pawn 'em to pay for his crank! It could happen. I just saw it on *Dateline*. All her neighbors were robbed blind! And the police never found her body," she added, almost as an afterthought.

"I'm not carousing," I promised. "Just having dinner with some friends."

One of her bushy white eyebrows hiked high on her wrinkled forehead. "At a bar?"

"At their house."

"And these friends . . . are they the criminal types?"

"One owns a flower shop and the other is a cop."

That seemed to finally placate her. "Well . . . all right then." That finger came back into my line of sight. "But if someone offers you a funny-looking cigarette, you say no. Understand? It could be *the weed*. And you make sure you watch them pour your drinks. I saw a show where a woman was on vacation and someone slipped something in her drink, and she woke up in a bathtub full of ice missing her liver."

Sweet Jesus.

I began backing away slowly toward the elevators, reminding myself to have a talk with my little old neighbor about all those crime shows she watched when I had the time. "You got it, Ms. W. Tell you what, I'll pour all my own drinks. How's that sound?"

"They could still have put something in the bottle, but I guess that'll just have to do. I'll keep a lookout. If you don't come home by morning, I'll call the police to start a manhunt."

"Sounds good. See you later, Ms. Weatherby."

After a quick stop at the store—because I had indeed forgotten the wine—I pulled up in front of Hayden and Micah's house. I made my way through the jungle of plants and flowers that made up their front yard and knocked on the front door.

It flew open a second later, and I nearly went deaf from the frequency of the high-pitched shriek. Hayden's daughter from her first marriage, Ivy, began to jump up and down in her little glittery pink biker boots. Her long curly red hair was a wild mess of tangles down her back and shoulders, and her neon pink tutu and skull leggings were covered in dirt, probably from playing in the garden in the backyard.

"Charlie! You're here!"

"Hey there, munchkin. How's it going?"

"It *was* good," she stated crestfallenly, "but then Mommy told me I couldn't have five dollars to get ice cream at school tomorrow." Her cheerful demeanor fell in an instant. Her eyes went big and began to water while her chin began to quiver. "Do you think *you* could give me five dollars?"

I gave my head a shake and tried my hardest not to laugh. "Uh-uh, girly. I know what you're playing at, and it's not gonna work."

Hayden's voice sounded from inside the house just seconds before she appeared in the entryway. "Ivy Young. What have I told you about using *The Look*."

Ivy dropped her head back and huffed dramatically. "I can only do it to Mike, 'cause he's a sucker."

Hayden beamed, proud as hell of her little girl's capability to manipulate her soon-to-be stepfather. "That's right. Now go wash up. We'll be eating soon." Ivy went skipping off, the five dollars all but forgotten.

"Look at you, raising your girl right."

"Thanks. I think so." She pulled me into a quick hug before taking the bottle of wine and waving me inside.

"That Charlie?" Micah called from the kitchen. "I heard the door. Is she here?"

We turned the corner into the kitchen and I spotted him with his hip propped casually against the counter, an open beer in his hand. He gave me a blank look.

"Yeah, I'm here."

"Well, would you look at that? She *is* alive," he stated

sarcastically. "I was starting to wonder since I haven't heard from you in *forever*."

When it came to me, Micah had a tendency to be a bit overprotective. And by *a bit* I meant it was so over the top it bordered on downright intrusive at times.

It had started when I was working with him and Leo to take down Officer Cormack and only got worse after I was hurt. No matter how many times I told him it wasn't his fault, he still blamed himself for the fact I'd been tortured and shot. As time progressed and I healed, our relationship morphed into one where he began to look at me not as a responsibility but almost as a little sister. It was kind of sweet . . . when he wasn't being a royal pain in my ass.

"I just saw you three days ago," I said with a roll of my eyes. "Don't be so dramatic."

"I'm not being dramatic," he grumbled. "All I'm saying is you could maybe call once in a while. For all I knew, you could've been lyin' dead in a ditch somewhere."

I felt my lips pull up in a smile, something I hadn't done a whole lot of in my life until recently. "That's the very definition of being dramatic, Micah."

"Whatever," he continued to pout.

I moved to him and lifted up on my toes, placing a kiss against his cheek. "I'll call more often. Promise." He was being totally ridiculous, I knew that, but if a little more effort on my part was all it took to put him at ease, I'd do it. I owed him more than I could ever say. He'd saved me in more ways than one. He proved there actually were people in this world who were trustworthy, he'd given me a family and a place where I felt like I belonged, and I'd forever be in his debt for that.

"That's all I ask." His arm came around my shoulders, and he gave me a slight squeeze before putting me in a playful headlock. "Now let's eat. All that worrying really worked up an appetite."

CLICK HERE TO KEEP READING

Discover Other Books by Jessica

WHITECAP SERIES

Crossing the Line

My Perfect Enemy

WHISKEY DOLLS SERIES

Bombshell

Knockout

Stunner

Seductress

Temptress

HOPE VALLEY SERIES:

Out of My League

Come Back Home Again

The Best of Me

Wrong Side of the Tracks

Stay With Me

Out of the Darkness

The Second Time Around

Waiting for Forever

Love to Hate You

Playing for Keeps

Fire & Ice

Opposites Attract

Almost Perfect

THE PEMBROOKE SERIES (a WILDFLOWER spinoff):

Sweet Sunshine

Coming Full Circle

A Broken Soul

CIVIL CORRUPTION SERIES

Corrupt

Defile

Consume

Ravage

GIRL TALK SERIES:

Seducing Lola

Tempting Sophia

Enticing Daphne

Charming Fiona

STANDALONE TITLES:

One Knight Stand

Chance Encounters

Nightmares from Within

DEADLY LOVE SERIES:

Destructive

Addictive

ABOUT JESSICA

Born and raised around Houston, Jessica is a self proclaimed caffeine addict, connoisseur of inexpensive wine, and the worst driver in the state of Texas. In addition to being all of these things, she's first and foremost a wife and mom.

Growing up, she shared her mom and grandmother's love of reading. But where they leaned toward murder mysteries, Jessica was obsessed with all things romance.

When she's not nose deep in her next manuscript, you can usually find her with her kindle in hand.

Connect with Jessica now
Website: www.authorjessicaprince.com
Jessica's Princesses Reader Group
Newsletter

Instagram
Facebook
Twitter
authorjessicaprince@gmail.com